My legs felt ready to buckle.

The latch popped, and there was a sustained push. It wouldn't take much, just the slightest opening would be enough to let the gene eaters out. Maggie showed up next to me. If I'd had any energy to spare, I would've yelled at her to go away. She quickly got into position, pushing with her arms, using the opposite wall to brace her feet.

I thought that I could hear the offworlders on the other side wheezing as their lungs lost their form. I thought I could hear them scratching at the walls, digging with fingernails that peeled off on the bare metal. I thought I heard a lot of things that I couldn't have possibly heard.

I thought I heard silence. I let up just a tad, just as a test, but as soon as I did, I knew I was done. I slumped over onto the floor, my lungs bursting. Maggie held firm for a few extra seconds, and then she gave in, too.

The corridor began to dim as some of the lightsticks began to peter out. I felt the weight of six more bodies being added to my name. Screw it. I wasn't going to let myself worry about those sadistic bastards. They weren't human. They were trash. Trash with wives who loved them, trash with kids . . . *Stop it.* I quashed that train of thought before it went off the tracks. They killed Adela. Screw 'em.

"Raw. Visceral. Compelling. As unforgettable as a stabbing."
—Mario Acevedo, author of *X-Rated Bloodsuckers*

Turn the page for more about Warren Hammond's KOP novels. . . .

"Warren Hammond has done something unusual and intriguing in this series, which began with *KOP* and continues with *Ex-KOP*. It's a masterful mix of SF and noir mystery, starring the usual flawed antihero Juno Mozambe, who seems to suffer constant bludgeoning while consuming vast quantities of cheap brandy in Lagarto, a slum planet where corruption is rife and life is cheap. I look forward to seeing where Hammond takes his unique series next."   —*BookLoons*

"Denver author Warren Hammond is well known for the gritty futuristic detective novel *KOP* and its sequel, *Ex-KOP*. By taking the best of classic crime noir and reinventing it on a destitute colony world, Warren has created some uniquely dark tales of murder, corruption, and redemption."   —J. A. Konrath

Praise for *KOP*

"Gritty and steamy, Hammond's *KOP* is both a throwback to the glory days of hard-boiled action thrillers and a prescient vision of the next place where technology and human frailties will intersect. Its blood-specked armor plating gradually—and impressively—reveals a genuine heart."

—K. W. Jeter, bestselling author of
Bladerunner 2: The Edge of Human

"A corrupt policeman, an overgrown jungle city that gets only five hours of sun between seventeen-hour nights, and battling crime gangs set the extremely noir scene for Hammond's solidly constructed, fast-paced SF debut. Hammond's writing is workmanlike with occasional terse highlights, offering rewards to fans of both crime novels and science fiction."

—*Publishers Weekly*

ex-kop

WARREN HAMMOND

A TOM DOHERTY ASSOCIATES BOOK
NEW YORK

EX-KOP

Edited by James Frenkel

A Tor Book
Published by Tom Doherty Associates, LLC
175 Fifth Avenue
New York, NY 10010

www.tor-forge.com

Tor® is a registered trademark of Tom Doherty Associates, LLC.

ISBN 978-0-7653-5137-1

First Edition: October 2008
First Mass Market Edition: March 2010

Printed in the United States of America

0 9 8 7 6 5 4 3 2 1

For Kathy

acknowledgments

MY sincerest thanks to Richard Curtis, Jim Frenkel, and Shawn Stugart.

one

I RELISHED the brandy as it burned down my throat. The knot in my stomach was acting especially hateful. I sucked down a few more gulps to dull the cramping in my gut. I didn't feel sufficiently soothed, yet I capped and pocketed the flask.

My knees were hurting so I readjusted, trying to find a comfortable position in the cramped closet. I bumped the door, knocking it slightly out of position. I pulled it back in, just short of closed, perfectly slivered for my camera.

I reached for my flask, but stopped when I heard footsteps in the hall. My heart began to race despite the alcohol's tranquilizing effect. I resisted the urge to hold my breath; I just kept breathing—nice and natural. I heard a key in the door. I pushed my eye up to the crack and saw the two of them enter. Mildew tickled my nose, and I had to hold my breath to keep from sneezing. Clothes fell to the floor—first a halter top, then a mini, and finally panties. She took a seat on the bed, wearing nothing but a strained smile. She moved her hands up her stomach, across her bare breasts, and up into her hair. She looked nervous; her movements came off stilted. What was supposed to look erotic wound up looking clumsy and silly. Her nervousness started to infect me. I was afraid that I'd misjudged her, that she wasn't ready for this. My pits prickled with sweat.

He came into view and stood in front of her. "Lay back," he said. "I want to look at you."

The hooker lay back, putting her hands behind her head.

"You like what you see?" She tried to sound playful, but the words came out forced and anxious.

He studied her like a monitor sizing up its prey. He didn't look *at* her; he looked *through* her, just a piece of meat. "Spread," he said with a malicious vibe.

She parted her legs for him, but kept her knees nervously angled inward, like she was about to submit to a cold-fingered gyno.

I focused on my task. I used my left hand to pull the black plastic away from the lens and immediately covered the lens back up. A short exposure was all I needed. I used my shaking right hand to turn the metal rod three times then pulled the plastic away again.

He took off his clothes, slowly, methodically, leering at her all the while. As he stripped, he flexed his sculpted offworld body. Pecs and abs rippled under baby-smooth skin. He told her to watch as he pulled out his megamember. She oohed and aahed, her voice cracking uneasily on the *ah*. I could tell she didn't like the way he was looking at her. She wasn't ready for this, dammit. He, on the other hand, was getting off on her discomfort, the two of them stiffening in very different ways.

I kept up my silent picture-snapping routine—my left hand acting as a shutter, and my shaky right advancing the film three twirls at a time. Uncover-cover-twirl-twirl-twirl. These pics were going to score some serious cash. A high-powered offworld lawyer doing a small-time hooker. I hoped he was married. It would only increase the value.

He crawled on top of her, his offworld-white skin looking pale as he thrusted within the clutches of her Lagartan-brown limbs. I uncover-cover-twirl-twirl-twirled to the rhythm of their sex.

I had spent half a day taking test shots until I got things just right—the lighting, the camera angle, the shutter speed, not at all easy with this improvised camera. The lens was salvaged from a real camera, but I had everything else special-built to my specs—no motors, no flash, no zoom, no power of any kind. Back when I was a cop, my partner and I once surveilled an off-worlder with a flycam. We thought the thing was undetectable. We had it flying in the shadows, but the bitch had some shit wired into her brain that detected the thing at fifteen meters. It was only the size of a coin for chrissakes. I wound up in the hospital with a fried hand that healed up nicely except for the fact that two decades later it started shaking like a fucking leaf—some kind of nerve damage.

We should've known better. Trying to match an offworlder's tech was a fool's game. Us Lagartans were so outclassed it was a joke. The only way to beat an offworlder was to go low tech. The arrogant SOBs were so caught up in their souped-up gizmos that they couldn't imagine how they could be hurt by anything that didn't have a power source. I kept uncover-cover-twirl-twirl-twirling.

He was pumping quickly now, and she was rocking her hips, earning her fee. His hands slid up her sides, across her chest, and settled threateningly around her throat. She tensed, her hips stopping their grinding. He began to caress her throat, slow and gentle. She responded with tentative hip undulations. I thought he was going to choke her out, but he didn't. He just kept the threat going as he pistoned harder and faster.

What the hell? His tech-enhanced skin shifted from offworld white to red—bright red. I watched as his feet shrunk down to hooves. Demonic cackles rang around the room as horns sprouted from his head. He completed the transition in seconds, topping it off with a pair of goat legs and a goatee. She was in a full panic now. *Shit! Calm down!* He was just getting his kicks, making her think he was the devil.

She sucked in panicky breaths, her chest heaving under his

thrusts. She turned her head, her eyes reaching for me. *Oh shit!* I wrapped my hands around the camera, ready to bolt. *Don't say it!* She tried to call my name but thankfully couldn't get out more than a fear-strangled grunt. He tickled her throat with black fingernails that were more claw than nail. He wrapped his hands around her throat. She was jerking her body, trying to get out from under him. He wasn't choking her; her squealing proved it. He just got off on the thought of it.

Get a fucking grip! She paid no heed to my unvoiced order, her mind probably freaked on the thought of giving birth to some demonic spawn. She scratched his shoulders and his back, but the wounds self-healed instantly. Her face was so panic-stricken red that it practically matched his hellfire skin. *Relax, relax, relax,* I told her in my head as I kept uncover-cover-twirl-twirl-twirling. *He's not really the devil. He's just another perverted offworlder. Just hang in there a little longer.*

He grunted through a final plunge and collapsed onto her. She coughed and wheezed through the tail end of her hyperventilation. She tried to wriggle out from under him.

Then I heard her scream, "Juno! Juno! Get him off me!"

SHIT! He was up in an instant, scanning the room, his face full of satanic fury. She rabbited for the door. I heard the door fly open. *Fucking hell! She calls out my name and then she ditches me.* My hands were on the camera, my shaky right out-of-control gyrating. He went for the bathroom first—lucky, very lucky. I burst out of the closet and sprinted for the hall; it was only a couple meters. . . . Lucifer spun on me; his hand went up, taking aim. Needles came firing out of his fingertips. I heard the snicks as they stuck into the wall behind me. I busted out the door, the tripod hitting the doorjamb and collapsing onto my fingers. I ignored the pain and surged for the elevator across the hall. The damn hooker was already onboard, and she had the doors closing. I paid good money to have that elevator waiting for *me*. I slammed my body between the closing doors, momentarily sticking, and then falling through, only my foot still outside. I yanked my foot painfully through doors that slapped shut an instant later. I looked back, seeing needles bounce off the glass doors as the elevator began to descend.

Before I got a chance to breathe, she was all over me, slapping and scratching, nails and hair. Staying on the floor, I used the makeshift camera and tripod to fend off the worst of her adrenaline-fueled attack. The thrill of the escape made a smile break across my face. I couldn't help it. Mistaking amusement for mockery, the whore intensified her attack. I covered my face as best I could and succumbed to the beating, my smile continuing to widen.

The elevator finally opened onto the lobby. I peeked through the hooker's blows and saw a tour group gawking at the naked woman beating on the old guy. A couple smacks later, she, too, noticed the onlookers and plastered her naked body against the elevator wall. Security was approaching— must've spotted us on the elevator's cams.

I stood up, grinning from ear to ear on a close-call high. My smile wilted when I spotted a set of needles embedded like darts in the sole of my shoe. *No, no, no!* Panic struck like lighting. My lungs seized. My stomach went to lead. I frantically checked my legs and ankles to see if any of the filament-sized needles had gotten through. I yanked off my shoes and looked inside them to see if any of the needles had penetrated through the leather—nope. I whirled around, using the mirrored elevator walls to search for the telltale sparkle of a needle. *Looks clear . . . calm down.* I checked again . . . And again . . . And one more time. Finally satisfied, I forced oxygen into my starving lungs and wiped my sleeve across my brow. Not wanting to touch the needles, I scraped my shoe over the gap between the elevator and the floor until they safely fell free. If one of those things had gotten through, it would've infected me with fast-acting plague that would've brought me a medieval death inside thirty minutes.

Security had the hooker wrapped in a blanket now, and they were hurrying her out of the lobby. I made for the back exit. Security didn't try to stop me. I paid them well.

two

My pounding heart began to stabilize as I walked out into the driving rain. The nighttime streets were empty except for geckos that scurried through puddles to avoid my footsteps. I tucked the camera under my arm and rubbed my hands together, letting the rain wash the seeping blood off my cat-scratched skin. I pulled out my flask and took a couple long swigs to deaden my fritzing nerves. I couldn't believe that whore almost got me plagued. That'd be the last time I'd use her. No loss. On this planet, hookers were as plentiful as lizards.

I checked the time. It was early. The sun couldn't have been down for long. I still had two hours before I had to meet Maggie. Enough time to get home and drop off the camera? Fuck it; I didn't want to go to that place. I couldn't stand it there since Niki had been gone. I'd just show up early to our meeting.

Couldn't take a cab. Driving was impossible with all the washed-out streets and flooded intersections. Every fall, when the rains started, I'd move my car to high ground and pay some stiff a weekly rate to guard it so it wouldn't get stripped or stolen. If you wanted to get anywhere this time of year, it had to be by boat. I headed for the river, weaving around puddles so big that they just about qualified as ponds. Water seeped through the seams in my shoes. It had been fifty-two days of rain, and there was no end in sight. The Lagartan rainy season had been known to stretch to over a hundred waterlogged days. Noah had nothing on us.

It was fall despite the winterish date. On Lagarto, there's no correlation between the seasons and the months. We crawl around the sun every 680 days, making our year almost twice as long as Earth's, yet we still use a slightly modified version of the Earth calendar so our seasons are always out of sync with the date. The best thing to do is just ignore the date. Trying to figure that shit out would give you a headache.

I crossed the street, driving my feet through weeds that grabbed at my ankles. Uprooted plants caught on my feet the way river muck would catch on a branch, and I had to stop every hundred meters to kick off the clumps. This city was always a half step from turning back to jungle, and even closer during the rains when they couldn't keep the streets clean of creeping growth. Koba was the capital of this planet, a planet almost entirely covered by ocean and desert. It was only here, in the jungles near the northern pole, that human life was easily sustained. Picture a blue and brown face with green hair, and you've got Lagarto, the lizard planet.

I reached the docks and dropped into the first manned skiff I found. The pilot handed me a sopping towel that I used to wipe my face. I tossed it on the floor, next to a practically overflowing bucket positioned under a leak. I had to yell my destination to be heard over the roar of the rain hammering the rust-eaten roof.

The pilot eased the boat out into the swollen Koba River. Stilted shanties lined the riverbank, water sheeting off rickety roofs. We skimmed through black water, putt-putting upriver to the Phra Kaew market, only a few blocks from the Koba Office of Police, my former place of employment, where I'd spent three long decades as a cop. I'd spent some of that time investigating crime, but the majority of my thirty was spent serving as the chief's right hand. I was his enforcer, his ham-

mer, the most feared SOB the force ever saw. That was before
the chief got killed, before I got bounced out of the job. . . .
Before I got old.

The boat dropped me on the Phra Kaew docks. I stuck to
the covered walkways as I ambled through the crowded warren of fruit stands, spice shops, and bakeries. I paid little attention to the locals who were out for an after-dinner stroll. I
needed to eat something, but I wasn't hungry. Since Niki's accident, I'd almost completely lost my appetite. The knots in my
stomach always made me feel full, like I'd get sick if I tried to
eat anything. I thought I could probably get something sweet
down, so I stopped at a street cart that had rounds of fried
dough stacked up like a miser's gold coins. The kid in front of
me got hers sprinkled with sugar; I got mine drizzled with
honey, just the way Niki always liked. I ate as I walked, not wor-
rying about getting my fingers sticky. Soon enough, I exited the
market and received a fresh soaking that I took advantage of by
rubbing my fingers together until the rain washed them clean. I
walked the last couple blocks to The Beat, a cop bar behind
KOP station.

A table of fresh towels sat next to the door. I dried off as best
I could and dumped the towel into a sodden hamper under the
table. I took in the smoke-filled surroundings: a group of vice
dicks took up three tables by the window; beat cops crowded
the back room, their blue unis spilling into the main; police
brass stood in a closed circle by the can. I checked out the bar,
thinking a stool at the end would be perfect—no luck. Badge
bunnies ran the length of the bar, sitting there in their hiked-
up skirts, sipping brandy with lipstick friendly straws.

People started to notice me. I could see them exchanging elbows, a few of them nodding my way. This used to be my turf.
My entrance used to shake the place up. I'd walk in, and my

enemies would make a rush for the back door, fleeing like roaches when the lights come on. No shakeup tonight. Tonight, they did their best to ignore me.

I found an open table and took a seat on a wobbly chair. Water dripped off my pant legs, pooling at my feet. The tabletop was scarred and creviced, its surface blanketed by mold. A brandy showed up. At least the waiter remembered me. I slammed down half the contents and tuned the place out. . . .

"Juno, how ya doin'?"

I brought my eyes back into focus. My visitor was hommy dick Mark Josephs—thirty years of service, and he was still the force's biggest asshole.

"Fine," I said.

He sat across from me. "What ya doin' here? I ain't seen you in forever."

"I came to meet Maggie."

"You shittin' me? What you want with that bitch?"

I took an annoyed sip of my drink instead of answering.

He sensed my irritation and reworded. "Seriously, Juno, why are you meeting her? Are you pokin' her or what?"

Again, I sipped my drink, silent.

"C'mon, Juno. Why you bein' so sensitive?"

"Don't call her a bitch," I hissed.

Josephs squinted at me, trying to read my expression. I hoped it said, *Pissed off.*

Josephs slapped the table, a huge grin on his face. "You are doin' her, aren't you? Don't try to deny it, Juno. I can see it on your face."

"I'm not doin' her, Josephs."

"Bullshit. Ha! Who'd a thought an old dog like you could land a hot young ass like hers. Shit, every guy in homicide's been achin' to stick their ice picks into the ice princess, and here you are actin' all cool." He held up his glass for a toast. "Score one for the old men."

I finished off my glass, making a point not to clink glasses. "You got it wrong, Josephs. I'm married."

"Don't try to pull that I'm-a-good-husband shit. I know Niki's been in the hospital, so you ain't gettin' none at home. You gotta get yours somewhere. Am I right?"

I could feel the blood in my cheeks. My shaking hand was clutching into a shaking fist. "Shut the fuck up, Josephs. You don't know what you're talking about."

"The hell I don't. You're a man, and a man's got to get his. So what if you bone a hot thing on the side. I don't know what you're gettin' so worked up about. There's no shame in it."

It was a mistake to come here. I was tempted to walk out.

Instead, I nodded to the waiter for another.

Josephs gestured at the door. "There's Ian," he said.

I followed Josephs' gaze to a couple who had just entered. Ian Davies, Maggie's newest partner, was toweling off. It'd probably been a year since I'd seen him. He was second-generation cop. I never liked his father. He was one of those big talkers, always talking like he was going to kick so-and-so's ass but never doing it. He retired a few years ago, but not before he found a spot for his kid. Not that it did the old man much good with his son. Word was Ian didn't even talk to his pop anymore.

Ian's face looked fuller than it used to. I'd always thought he was too scrawny to be a cop, but now it looked like he'd firmed himself up. His neck finally looked thick enough to hold up his baby face. His wet shirt was suctioned over bulky muscles that stretched around what used to be a skeletal frame. He must've started shooting 'roids. No doubt about it.

With Ian was a woman I'd never seen before. There was no way I would've forgotten her if I had. She was wearing a black open-backed dress. Its wet fabric clung to her hips and her braless breasts. Her black hair hung straight down her bare back. I watched her pull her hair over her shoulder and wring it out with a towel, tossing it back over her shoulder when she was done.

"Who's that with Ian?" I asked.

"That's Liz. She and Ian go together."

She took Ian's elbow, and they walked past our table, taking up posts near the bar. Her hair stuck to her back, water beading down into her waistline. Josephs noticed me watching her. "You want me to introduce you?"

"No," I said.

"You afraid Maggie'll walk in and see you talkin' to her?"

Holy shit, he was pissing me off. Maggie was like a daughter. "How many times do I have to fucking tell you? There's nothing between me and Maggie."

"You serious?"

"Yes, you dumb shit. What have I been saying?"

"Then why are you meeting her?"

"I don't know. She says she has a job for me."

"What's the job?"

"Didn't I just say I don't know?"

"Yeah, I guess you did. Shit, it's good to see you, Juno. There aren't many guys that've been around as long as you and me. The force has changed since you and Paul been gone. Now they got all these political types that don't know shit runnin' things."

I gave a disinterested "Uh-huh." Everybody knew the Koba Office of Police had gone to hell. Cops were calling their own shots these days. They were all working solo, taking kickbacks from drug dealers, bookmakers, slavers, gene traders—you name it. They were all out for themselves. It wasn't the bribes I objected to. Cops took bribes back when Chief Chang and I ran the force, too. Hell, we encouraged it. The difference was that when we were in charge, the bribes were for the force as a whole, not for the individual. In our day, cops were just the collection agents. The money was pooled and divvied up fair. KOP was unified, and as such, it was a political force in this city. The pimps, the dealers, the mayor, the crime lords, they all had to negotiate with us. Chief Chang was a power broker of the highest order.

And I was his enforcer. I tore a path of shattered bones through KOP's rank and file. Through fear, I brought stability. With violence, I brought order. Chief Paul Chang's control over KOP was absolute.

Our reign came to an end when KOP's then chief of detectives, Diego Banks, made a power grab. That was almost a year ago, or a year and a half going by the Earth calendar. He plotted the murder of Chief Chang and forced me into retirement. KOP was his and his alone. But the new chief had a problem keeping the dirty money flowing into cop pockets the way Paul Chang did. Paul was in tight with organized crime. Paul took a percentage of their profits in exchange for freedom from prosecution. Banks didn't have the same standing with the cartels that Chief Chang did. He couldn't negotiate anything close to the same rates. When cops realized the money wasn't flowing down from the top like it used to, they started keeping their bribes for themselves.

It didn't take long for KOP's chain of command to fracture. Entire squads went rogue. Chief Banks couldn't maintain order. Corruption and dysfunction ruled the day. And when the new mayor rode the resulting wave of public dissatisfaction into office, he sent Chief Banks packing and replaced him with Chief Karella, a political type who looked good for the cameras, but knew next to nothing about running a police force. The police empire Paul and I built was crumbling away. KOP was turning into jungle, just like the rest of this city.

As thoughts of our fallen empire dissipated, I found myself studying Ian's woman, Liz. I watched her entertain the group of men gathered around her, the whole lot of them competing for her attention.

"Maggie should be along any minute," said Josephs. "She always stays a little later than Ian, like she's tryin' to prove she's a better cop than he is."

"She is better," I stated.

Josephs made an exaggerated smirk as he mock jerked off. "Fuck that. There's no way she's a better cop than Ian."

"Who has the higher case-solved percentage?"

Josephs threw his hands in the air. "Who gives a shit about numbers? Everybody knows the brass throws her the easy cases."

"You actually believe that?"

"You know how rich she is, Juno. How else can you explain the fact that she made detective in under six months? She's got those kiss-asses wrapped around her finger. Now I hear the brass likes her for squad leader. Can you believe that?"

"She'd be better than Ian. The guy's a pussy," I said.

"Not anymore he's not." Josephs insisted. "If you told me that a couple years ago, I would've agreed. Shit, I don't know how he survived those first couple years on the street. Remember how his pop used to talk about him? He built him up like he was some tough-as-nails bruiser. Said he was the baddest guard at the Zoo. I remember thinkin' that we could use a guy like that, and then the kid shows up lookin' like the gun on his belt was goin' to tip him over. But I'm tellin' you, that wussy boy you knew is long gone. He's toughened up, turned into a real ass-kicker. I wouldn't have a second thought goin' on a drug raid with him backin' me up. That's how much I think of him. You know me, Juno, I wouldn't say that if I didn't mean it. All the young guys look up to him."

Josephs popped a pill and swallowed it dry. "I don't know why you're stickin' up for Maggie, but you gotta know where she stands. Everybody wants Ian as squad leader. Nobody respects Maggie. She's just a rich girl playin' detective. If the brass gets their way, and she ends up squad leader, nobody's gonna do a goddamn thing she says. She ain't got the balls for it."

Josephs ranted on. I could care less what he thought of Maggie. Half of it could be true, and I still wouldn't care. Maggie and I had worked together before. She'd earned my respect. She was a smart cop and a tough cop. And she was something I never was—a *clean* cop.

Like marbles finding the low point of a floor, I found that my eyes had gravitated over to Liz. Around her, I counted six guys, all puppy-eyed. Even the passed-over badge bunnies were staring at her, except they were all dagger-eyed.

"Are you gonna stare at her all night or are you gonna let me introduce you?"

I unhooked my eyes from Liz and turned them back on Josephs. "What good would that do?" I was fully aware of the fact that I'd left the door open by not just saying no.

"You have to let me introduce you, Juno. I mean, do you *see* that body of hers? You wanna know the best part?" Josephs got a sparkle in his eye as he answered his own question. "She's into cops, Juno. I'm telling you, she can't resist 'em."

"I'm not a cop anymore. Besides, I thought she was with Ian."

"Sure, she and Ian are an item, but a woman like that's not exclusive." Josephs leaned in close, like he was telling a secret. "Couple months ago, I came down here and tied one on. I mean I got ripped, wound up closin' the place. So then I walked down to the corner to wait for a cab. I was standin' in front of that seafood place; you know the one with the fishnet over the door?"

I nodded.

"So I was just standin' there waitin' for a cab to come along. I flagged one down, except it turned out that it wasn't empty. Liz got out, and we got to chattin', you know about cops and shit. Next thing I knew, she brought me upstairs. She's got a place right above the restaurant. She brought me in and poured us a couple. I was sippin' mine slow, but she was suckin' the shit down like there's no tomorrow. Before I knew it, she was all over me. She started doin' things to me, Juno. Things I never seen before. You wouldn't believe the shit she's into. I'm tellin' you, that was a night to remember—fuckin' A! You gotta meet her. You won't regret it."

I looked over at Liz as Ian suddenly stepped out from her circle of admirers. A holo appeared in front of him, Lieutenant Rusedski of homicide.

"Somethin's up," said Josephs.

My phone rang. A holographic Maggie materialized in an empty chair. "I can't make it," she said. "I have to go down to the South Docks. There's been a murder."

three

THE hommy dicks all cleared out, Liz trailing out with Ian. Must be a big case to warrant the whole squad going down to the docks. It was too bad. I'd been looking forward to seeing Maggie. We hadn't been seeing much of each other since Niki's "accident." That was what I'd tell people it was. An accident.

My glass was drained. I dropped a couple bills on the table and hit the street. My almost dry whites soaked through in seconds. City lights reflected off the smothering low-hanging clouds, adding a smidge of gray to the black sky.

I headed down the block, my feet taking it slow. It was time I went to the hospital for my nightly visit. My stomach roiled at the thought. I hated that place. Niki didn't belong there with the invalids and the cripples. I'd get her out soon, I told myself. She'd be good as new. It would be like turning back the clock.

I began planning the best way to get there from here. Knowing roads were useless during the rains, I tried to imagine a map of the city's canal system, but I couldn't think straight; instead of canals, all my mind could see was hospital corridors and plastic tubes.

A rare flyer skimmed the rooftops. On its underbelly, a neon sign flashed the tour company's name. You didn't see many tourists during rainy season. As the Koba River's water level steadily rose, the tide of offworld tourists would do the opposite. Constant rain kept all but the most hardy offworlders happily floating in space. Thinking of the boxy camera tucked under my arm, I bet there was one more offworlder who wished he'd stayed in his climate-controlled orbital home.

I found that my feet had stopped at a doorway. They'd stopped on their own, without any conscious orders from my brain. I looked up through the fishnet, to the window above the restaurant. Liz's window. Warm, yellow light beamed out into the rain. I took a minute to stare at the window, ignoring the rain that splattered my face. Then I crossed the street, stopping and turning around when I reached the other side. Now I could see the utilitarian drapes . . . a tilting lamp, but nothing else. I saw shadows shifting on the ceiling. I liked to think they were cast by her, moving through her apartment in that clingy open-backed number, but I knew that the bucketing rain was probably just fucking with my vision.

The hospital loomed in my mind, its smell, its sterility. I started walking again, but in the opposite direction.

I baby-stepped my way down the moss-slick steps to the pier, where a pair of uniforms stopped me. I reflexively reached for my badge, finding an empty shirt pocket. "I'm here to see Maggie Orzo," I said.

One of the cops recognized me. "She know you're coming, Juno?"

"Yeah. She knows."

"Where can I find her?"

"She's probably where they found the body, somewhere inside that barge over there."

At least a dozen uniforms were on the pier, most of them scanning the ground with bobbing flashlights. They wandered aimlessly around, as disorganized as flies, looking for clues, but not having the sense to form into proper grid-search lines.

I stepped up to the antique vessel. Back during the brandy

boom, it was part of a fleet of barges that ran on the river. It was hard to picture it in its heyday: its engines chugging, its deck bustling with river rats, its spider-leg robotic arms swinging pallets of fruit containers on and off deck. Those days were long gone. Now it was just one more abandoned hulk, another reminder of this world's once proud past.

I slip-slided up the algae-coated gangway and made my way sternward, across the waterlogged deck, careful to avoid tripping over cleats and lizard nests. Once inside, I shook off the excess water and climbed a set of narrow metallic stairs that led to the bridge. Electronics were scattered about the floor. Ruptured control panels sprouted entire gardens of wires that stretched out from round holes where gauges used to be. Rain sprayed through broken-out windows. I looked out, down onto the broad deck. Robotic arms stood tall around the eye-shaped deck, reaching up and out like eyelashes.

Flatfoots hovered around a doorway, peeking in on what had to be the crime scene. I tapped a couple shoulders to move them aside. Battery-powered lights sat on the floor, giving the cabin a strange bottom-up lighting pattern that my eyes took a few secs to adjust to. Just inside the cabin was a body, nothing more than a bloated gray sack of skin wearing police blues. In the middle of the cabin was a blood-spattered block of wood surrounded by a pool of watery blood. The floor was littered with small gray sacks—former lizards. One was still alive, its front half trying to walk, its back half a gray blob acting as deadweight.

Ian stomped the half-dead gecko into the decking then turned to face me. "Get out."

I disregarded the order. "Hey, Maggie."

Detective Magda Orzo tiptoed from dry spot to dry spot until she stood by my side. She was overdressed as always—a pressed blouse, pleated pants, and matching pumps—expensive duds, probably offworld manufacture. The ensemble looked snappy despite its saturated state. She spoke to me in a serious voice. "So far, it's just like the first one I told you about."

I had no clue what Maggie was talking about, but thought it best to play along. "Sure looks like it, doesn't it."

Ian confronted his partner. "What's he doing here?" He was pointing at me.

Maggie responded without pause. "I asked Juno to come. I thought we could use another opinion."

Maggie was lying. She hadn't asked me to come. She'd cancelled our appointment, and she'd never told me about the "first one" or any other one. Whatever the job was that she wanted me to do, she didn't want Ian knowing about it. To keep up Maggie's charade, I'd have to play the part of the wise old detective—which itself was a lie. After a long pause, I asked, "What have you got so far?"

Ian turned his back on us without answering.

Maggie rolled her eyes at her partner. "About two hours ago, Officer Ramos called in. He said he was walking the pier, and he saw some suspicious activity on this boat."

"What kind of suspicious activity?"

"He didn't say. He just said he was going to investigate."

I looked at the bulging body. "I assume that's Officer Ramos?"

Maggie nodded affirmative. "I figure the killer was at the tail end of the cleanup stage by the time he came investigating. Ramos must've walked in when the gene eaters were in full force."

No doubt about that, I thought as I looked at Officer Ramos's overly swollen form. He looked ready to pop. Gene eaters were some scary offworld shit, a strain of microbacteria that attacked DNA. They'd invade cells and reproduce at an absurd rate, destroying every DNA molecule they'd find and ravaging the cells in the process.

The killer had treated the entire cabin, probably with a fogger. Gene eaters were gaining popularity as a way to destroy blood evidence and any hair or skin cells that may have been left behind. We were only safe now because gene eaters were genetically wired to be sterile at the twentieth generation. Having rendered all DNA evidence ineffective, they naturally died off inside an hour. Otherwise they could wipe out a whole planet. Like I said—scary shit.

I moved to the center of the cabin, stepping over the unlucky lizards that had come looking for a free meal and wound up *becoming* the free meal. I leaned over the knee-high wood block in the middle of the floor and studied the blood pooled all around it. The blood looked runny instead of its usual syrupy consistency, a surefire sign that the gene eaters had done their job.

Maggie said, "Check out the scorch marks on top."

I examined the set of centimeter-deep blackened gouges burned into the wood. I tried to count them, but my brandy-clouded brain lost track at five. My attention shifted to a hollow scooped on one side on the otherwise cubical block, wondering what it could be for.

As if she could read my mind, Maggie answered my unvoiced question. "We think it's for the vic's chin."

A picture flashed into my mind. The vic on his or her knees, neck stretched across the block, chin resting in the hollow so the throat could lay flush on the wood. The scorch marks were obviously left by a lase-bladed weapon, most of them probably left by practice chops, the most recent left by the actual beheading.

"So am I to assume there's a decapitated body around here somewhere?"

"No. He never leaves the body behind."

"Why not leave the body to be gene eaten with everything else?"

She said she didn't know with a shake of her head.

"And the scene's always been gene eaten?"

Maggie nodded a grim yes. Grim, because the obvious conclusion was that the killer was an offworlder. Gene eaters didn't come cheap. A Lagartan would have to cough up a couple kilos worth of pesos to buy a batch. If a Lagartan was rich enough and desperate enough, I could see how he might buy a batch, but Maggie said there were others. How many, I didn't know, but it wouldn't take more than two or three batches to break most bank accounts. There was no way the killer was Lagartan. There were cheaper ways to cover up a murder. I should know.

"Any idea who the vics are?" I asked.

"Nope. Not without the bodies. We've tried to match the dates to missing persons reports, but we can't get definitive matches. There're too many missing persons."

I knew what she meant. Slavers smuggled Lagartans off-planet to work the belts at a steady rate. KOP probably received three or four missing persons reports a week, and that was just Koba. They didn't count the rest of the planet. Go out to the fringe towns where the warlords were in control, and there was no telling how many people went missing. Koba was the only city on the planet with even partially accurate record keeping.

I pointed at a trio of coin-sized bloodless circles on the floor. "How about those?"

"They're from a tripod."

"He films it?"

"That, or he has an accomplice who does the filming. No way to tell."

I felt a clap on my shoulder. "Juno."

I recognized the voice without turning around. "Abdul," I said, already grinning.

"What brings you here?"

I turned to look at my old friend. "Maggie asked me to come. She wanted to get an experienced detective's perspective."

The coroner looked at me with eyebrows arched behind his superthick glasses. Abdul knew I couldn't be serious. He was well aware of the fact that I'd spent far more of my career strong-arming than I did Sherlocking. "I see," he said noncommittally.

Abdul scanned the room, his magnified eyes swiveling through his specs. He took it all in: the blood, the block, the bloated body. "Looks familiar."

"So I hear."

"Got any wisdom for us, Juno?" It was Ian who was asking, a smug look on his face.

"I'll need some time," I responded.

"Didn't think so," he said, and he walked out, brushing into me on his way. There was a time I would have jumped his ass for even coming close to me. Maybe Josephs was right; he was no pussy anymore.

The old coroner hunched his already hunched back over the jellied body of Officer Ramos. "This could get messy," he stated.

Maggie and I took his cue and stepped out to give Abdul and his staff some space. It wasn't easy to bag a gene-eaten body—like zipping up a human-sized water balloon.

Maggie and I walked past the uniforms gathered outside the cabin, their tough talk predictably anti-offworld. They'd been rattling away the whole time, saying stupid shit like, "If I caught the guy that did this, I'd shoot him first chance I got," or "I'd douse him with his own gene eaters and see how he likes it." I knew they were ticked at losing one of their own, but put one of them face to face with the offworld killer, and they'd do one of two things: drop to their knees and beg, or run faster than they'd ever run before—just like I did a couple hours ago.

There was no such thing as a fair fight with an offworlder. Their technology was centuries ahead of ours. True, Lagarto once had the foundation for a tech-rich society but that had been squandered away generations ago. Our economy was founded on Lagartan brandy, a cash crop that funded a flurry of construction during the boom. They put up a top-notch spaceport from which brandy was boosted into space by the freighterful. The freighters docked with Lagarto's orbital station, an engineering marvel in its day. The thing was huge, the size of a city. It could service even the largest of the spaceliners that made the multiyeared hauls to the rest of the Unified Worlds.

At the boom's peak, there was a freighter going up every ten minutes. They should've known how fragile it all was, an economy based on a single product. It went to hell when a lone smuggler managed to sneak a couple saplings back to Earth and published the brandy tree's genetic code. That was all it took for Lagarto to lose its market. All twenty-seven planets had the trees adapted to their own environments and began raising their own fruit and distilling their own brandy. Lagarto went deep into the red, and in order to pay the government's debts, the pols had a fire sale. They sold off the spaceport, the Orbital, and even the rights to mine the belts, which were the only things left that this system still had going for it. The bastard pols embezzled the profits for themselves and left this planet a charity worker's bonanza. We led the Unified Worlds in every category: poverty, illiteracy, starvation, unemployment, disease, infant mortality. . . .

Maggie and I made it back outside. Ian was there, holding a

baggie with a vid inside. He was talking to a female officer who, upon seeing Maggie, said, "I found a vid, Detective."

"Where?" Maggie asked.

"It was on the pier, in the weeds. Maybe somebody dropped it."

"Have you watched it?"

"No. I brought it to Ian the moment I found it."

"Good work, Officer . . . ?"

"Kobishi." She beamed in the dark.

"Good work, Officer Kobishi."

The young officer saluted and then strode across the deck, heading for the gangway. Based on the salute and the fact that I didn't recognize her, she was a definite newbie, probably at her first ever crime scene.

Holding up the bagged vid, Ian asked, "Anybody got a vid reader?"

I shook my head.

Maggie said, "No. We'll have to ask the med-techs if we can borrow their equipment when they're done documenting the scene."

"Yeah," said Ian as he neatly folded the baggie over the vid and tucked it in his shirt pocket. "Call me when they're ready." He walked away, following the same path taken by Officer Kobishi.

Maggie and I stepped out of the high-traffic area of the deck and found a semidry spot under one of the age-frozen cranes.

"How's Niki?" she said.

"Fine," I said as a reflexive kick response.

"Will you tell her I'll be by soon? It's probably been a week since I went to see her. These barge murders have me all tied up."

I told her flat out. "You gotta duck this case."

"I can't do that. I've been working this for too long."

"How many have there been?"

"Tonight's the thirteenth. This guy's a serial."

Even more convinced, I said, "You've got to get out. The killer's an offworlder."

"So?"

"Don't play stupid, Maggie. You know what can happen if you try to arrest an offworlder."

She resisted looking at my bobbing hand. "Don't worry about that, Juno. When I find him, I'll bring a whole squad."

"So what if you do. You can bet that if he's got the money to buy gene eaters, he's got the money to buy the judge, too."

Maggie looked away out over the water, her face now in total shadow.

I knew she didn't want to hear it, but I kept up the pressure. "And what happens when the press gets a hold of this? You've been lucky so far that nobody gives a shit about a bunch of nameless victims, but that won't last much longer. There's a dead cop for chrissakes. Eventually, somebody's going to leak the fact that an offworlder has killed thirteen people including a cop. The public will throw a fit. They're already pissed about how fucked up this city's gotten over the past year. They'll demand to know what the police are doing about it, and you're going to have to stand there and say you don't know squat. How will that look on your record? Trust me, Maggie, you need to drop this case."

"I can't, Juno. Ian's gung ho on this one. When it was clear we weren't getting anywhere on it, I told him we should step aside and let some fresh eyes have a look at it, but then he got all territorial about it."

"So ask for a new partner. You don't like that prick anyway. Get yourself out and let Ian take this one."

She turned back to me, her face barely lit. "I already asked for a new partner. Lieutenant Rusedski wouldn't hear it."

"Why not?"

Maggie let out a frustrated sigh. "Rusedski wants Ian to get the squad leader post. I had no idea Ian was even interested until he put in for it right on the deadline. For weeks, I'd been after Rusedski for a letter of recommendation. He kept promising he would do it, but he never delivered. Then Ian submitted his application *with* a letter of recommendation from Rusedki. That's when it all made sense why Rusedski made Ian and me partners. You see what I mean? Rusedski wanted to put Ian through for that job all along, but he knew that the brass liked me better because of my case-solved percentage. . . ."

There was no need for her to go on. I could see what Rusedski had been doing. By partnering Maggie with Ian, they'd share all their collars. Her successes would be his successes. It was only a matter of time before their case-solved percentages converged. "Still," I said, "you don't want to be out front on this one. Just drop it. Let Ian be the one to put his ass on the line."

"I hear you, Juno, but somebody's killed thirteen people. I can't just let it go."

I shook my head. What could I do? She still believed in right and wrong. I changed the subject. "What's this job you want me to do?"

"You shouldn't have come here, Juno. I doubt Ian believed that crap about getting a second opinion. He's got to be wondering why you're really here."

"Sorry. I didn't know it had anything to do with him."

"I know. I should've told you. I thought that if we met at The Beat, it would look like we were just hanging out, and I could point out Ian's crew."

"His crew?"

"He's at the center of a clique with some guys from homicide and a few beat cops."

"And you think they're up to no good?"

"I know it. What I need is proof. I called you in because I want you to check into the Juarez case."

"Juarez? The vid station exec?"

"Yeah."

I remembered the case from the news: Vid station bigwig and wife cut up by their teenaged daughter, a hot little vix with a wicked streak. "But you solved it months ago."

"I don't think the daughter did it anymore."

"Isn't it a little late? Wasn't she executed?"

"Not yet. Her conviction was just last week. She's scheduled for the fifth of December."

I worked it out in my head. Today being the twenty-ninth, that was nine days away. It would only be six on the standard Earth calendar, but our months are each three days longer in order to make up for the fact that each of our days is two hours shorter.

"Why the change of heart?" I wanted to know.

"The day after sentencing, I got a call from a woman who said the girl didn't do it."

"Who's the woman?"

"It was anonymous."

She had to be kidding me with this. "And you believe her?"

"I know it sounds thin, but she said she knew who really did it."

I couldn't keep a sarcastic tone from slipping into my voice. "Let me guess, she knows who did it, but she can't tell you who it is."

Maggie shot an annoyed look out of the shadows. "That's right."

"Didn't you take the girl's confession?"

"No, Ian did that on his own. We don't really partner on much, Juno. We each pretty much do our own thing."

"And you think he lied about her confessing?"

"No. She confessed. It's all on vid. But he must've coerced it out of her somehow."

"If you think he framed her, why don't you just check it out yourself?"

"Because I don't want anybody finding out I'm investigating another cop."

That I understood. There was no faster way to end a career. "But if people find out I'm checking into your partner's cases, they'll still guess you're behind it."

"Guessing is different from knowing. I can always deny I had anything to do with it. As far as the brass is concerned, it'll be good enough."

"It won't be good enough for the average uniform."

"When I'm a squad leader it won't matter. They won't have a choice."

Now *that* sounded like a future chief. Maggie made no bones about the fact that she had her eyes on the KOP top spot. She was after me all the time, trying to get me to become her consigliore. She'd say, "Who better to help me take over KOP than somebody who's already done it once?"

At first, I didn't believe it was in the cards for her. Number one: she was a woman in a male-dominated police force. And number two: she had a good heart. Either handicap might be possible to overcome, but the two together seemed insurmountable. Even so, she was doing her best to disprove me. Her work was top-notch, and her family had high-placed political connections that she worked to her advantage. She was the youngest detective on record and was already trying to angle her way into a squad leader post. From there, sergeant wouldn't be far out of her reach. The only serious hurdle she'd hit in her career so far was her association with me. The traitorous Chief Banks tried to keep her pigeonholed in the records department, but she was too smart and too well-connected to stay exiled for long.

No, I wasn't a believer yet, but I was on the verge of becoming her first convert.

"Why would he coerce her confession?" I asked. "Weren't you and Ian already partners then?"

"Yes."

"So your performance records were already linked, which means he wasn't just trying to pump up his solveds. What other motive could he have?"

"That's what I want you to find out."

"Listen, Maggie, let's cut the bullshit. If you want that promotion, just say the word. I'll take care of Ian."

Maggie got in my face. "This isn't about that, Juno. It's not about what I want. It's about that girl who's going to get gassed for something she didn't do. How can you think I'd put a stupid promotion above that?"

"What do you expect me to think? The way I see it, Ian's going to steal that promotion out from under you, and you know you deserve it more than he does. I can't help but think that's why you're so ready to believe some woman you don't even know before your partner. Who knows who that woman was who called you? She could be the girl's aunt or something. That's hardly enough reason to believe Ian coerced that confession."

I was glad Maggie's face was mostly in shadow. It cut down the glare she was sending my way.

"Maybe you just want it to be true," I said. "That way you can throw some dirt on Ian and take him out of the running.

Listen, if you want that squad leader job so bad, let's skip the goose chasing and take Ian out of it ourselves."

Maggie came at me all righteous. "I don't work that way, and you know it. I wouldn't be going through this trouble if I didn't think there was a chance that the girl didn't do it. A good chance."

"How can you be so sure?"

Maggie leaned in close, forcing me to tilt back in order to keep my brandy breath under wraps. "I never really believed she could've done this," she said. "I interviewed her the morning she found her parents' bodies. I'm telling you, she was genuinely upset. I didn't think there was any way she was faking until Ian found the murder weapon with her prints on it. And then when Ian got her to confess, I went ahead and signed off on it even though I never really believed it. I should've trusted my gut. I mean, think about it. What kind of girl kills her parents? She'd have to be delusional. Don't get me wrong, she's your typical troubled teenager, but she's not crazy. There's just no way she could kill her parents, Juno. Do you see what I'm saying? I know she didn't do it. I just know it."

I tried to reconcile Maggie's image of the Juarez girl with the one on the news. Where Maggie saw an innocent child, everybody else saw a manipulative little bitch. Maggie was way off on this one. "She confessed, Maggie. Leave it at that."

"I know she confessed, but I'm telling you, Ian must've forced it out of her."

I ran my hands over my face to keep from screaming at her. Sometimes she could be such a fucking Pollyanna. She was acting like it was some universal truth that children don't kill their parents. She had no idea that I'd spent most of my childhood fantasizing about different ways to kill my father. I would've done it, too, if a bad batch of shine hadn't beaten me to it. The

SOB died in my mother's arms of methanol poisoning. Far better than he deserved. Even now, after all these years, I could feel
my pulse quicken at the thought of my mother with black eyes.

Maggie let out a long exhale. "At least go talk to her, Juno.
Get a read on her, then tell me if I'm crazy."

Frustrated, I said, "Dammit, Maggie, why can't you just accept that she did it?"

"Teenaged girls don't just go off and kill their parents, Juno."

"The hell they don't!" Niki wasn't much older when she
went and did exactly that. I took a deep breath. "Did you ever
stop to think that maybe her parents were abusive?"

"Don't you think she would've told us if they were? Why are
you being so stubborn about this?"

I wanted to go home and drink myself to sleep. "I can't help
you." I started for the gangway.

Maggie stopped me, her hand clutching my arm. "Why not?"

"I just can't."

Niki and the Juarez girl began to melt together in my mind,
their stories intermingling. Emotions began to cycle through
me rapid-fire—guilt, shame, anger, regret.

"I'll pay you," she said.

Her words barely registered. In my mind, I'd flashed back
decades. The sight of Niki's freshly slaughtered parents dominated my senses. I couldn't take this case. I couldn't handle it
right now. It cut way too close to home.

Maggie said, "Did you hear me? I'll triple whatever the rags
are paying you."

I put my flask away. I didn't remember getting it out. Then I
said, "You'll pay triple?"

I slipped as I stepped off the gangway. My camera went tumbling along with the tripod. I barely avoided the same for myself
by grabbing hold of the rail. A circled group of hommy boys

turned toward my commotion and quickly dismissed me, but one of them came over—Josephs. "Looks like you need a hand, Juno. Let me show you out." He grabbed my elbow, tight.

I jerked my elbow free and snatched my camera out of a puddle. "I know the way."

"What's your problem, Juno? I'm just trying to help you out."

"I don't need any help."

He took hold of my elbow again and put his mug in my face. "Neither do *we*."

"What's that supposed to mean?"

Josephs paused before answering. "I'm givin' you a courtesy, old boy. I don't know why that rich bitch of yours thinks you can help solve this case, but you're not a cop anymore, and you don't belong in our business."

"I don't take orders from you, asshole."

"Listen to me, Juno. We go back a long ways, so I'm tryin' to be civilized. We know we got a serial on our hands, and we're gonna find him. Last thing we need is for you to start dickin' around in this case, okay?"

"Save the tough-guy routine, Josephs. I turned Maggie down."

His hand let go of my elbow and moved up to pat my shoulder—back to best pals. "Why didn't you just say so? Shit, Juno, you never change. Give you a choice between walkin' around a fire and walkin' through it, you walk through it every time."

I reinforced the lie. "Killer's obviously an offworlder." Holding my shaky right hand up, I said, "I've been burned once already by those bastards. No way I'm going back for seconds. I'm too old for that shit."

"You still got sense, Juno. I gotta hand it to you, you still got sense."

Taking a closer look at the group of hommy boys, I saw they had somebody closed inside their circle. "Who's that?"

"A camera guy from the Libre. We caught him snoopin'
around, tryin' to get some footage. Ian's givin' him the biz."

"Was he on the barge?"

"No. He never made it that far. They caught him as soon as
he jumped down to the pier. What a dumb shit, thinkin' he
could get through. You see all the cops around here?"

The cameraman was getting pinballed now. They were
shoving him around the circle, bouncing him left, right . . . and
now he was down. He looked like he was crying, but I couldn't
tell for sure because of the rain.

Josephs laughed. "Look at that fat fuck. How much you
wanna bet he's pissed himself?"

"Yeah."

"Seriously, Juno, you wanna put some money on it?"

"How can you tell? It's fucking raining. His pants are
soaked."

"You can feel it. Piss is warmer than rainwater."

"I'll pass."

"One thing's for sure," he said. "This case won't be in the news
anytime soon."

For Maggie's sake, I hoped he was right.

At this point, the camerman had gone fetal. Ian nabbed the
poor sap's cam from the ground and popped it open. He slid the
vid free and walked over to the pier's edge and then whipped
the thing out into the darkness, making sure that what little
footage the cameraman might have shot would never air. He
came back into the circle and beanballed the guy with his own
camera.

I heard Maggie's voice calling from the ship's deck up above.
"Ian! They're done! We can watch the vid now!" Maggie
must've been going out of her mind waiting to watch the vid Officer Kobishi had found, thinking that the whole beheading

could be captured on it. No way, I thought. Luck like that didn't exist on this planet.

Ian threw one more kick into the camerman's gut and then came strutting for the gangway, pulling the vid from his pocket as he passed Josephs and me. Josephs was right. Ian was no pussy anymore.

four

MY eyes opened. The clock told me it was morning, but it sure as hell didn't feel like it. I rolled out of bed and navigated through the house with the lights off even though the dawn was still in its dim stages. My hungover head throbbed with every heartbeat, and my stomach was rumbling. I found the medicine chest and pulled the door wide: vodka, gin, whiskey, and brandy. I thought about the call I needed to make and decided to make it a double dose.

When I placed the call, the entire room was instantaneously bathed in the unnatural glow of Niki's holo. I squinted at her image as my eyes adjusted to the piercing light. She looked radiant in more ways than the obvious. She was dressed in a cruel open-shouldered number that hugged all the curves and left plenty of leg for my eyes to soak up. Half her black locks were pinned up, the other half curlicued like shaved chocolate over cinnamon shoulders. Her face was lit with a smile so sharp that it stabbed straight through my heart. My Niki.

"Why didn't you . . . come last n—night?" Niki's mechanically timed voice shattered the perfect-Niki illusion. The Niki that stood before me was just a holo, a scanned image of Niki made years ago, long before her "accident." The offworld telco that stored her image could beam this faux-Niki anywhere on Lagarto.

"I was working a job," I stated as I imagined the dashing version of me that appeared in Niki's hospital room instead of my actual sleep-deprived and liquor-ravaged self.

She croaked out the words superslow. "What kind of . . ." I bit my lip as I waited for the next exhale of the respirator. ". . . of job?"

"Maggie asked me to look into a case of hers. I have to go out to the Zoo this morning so I don't miss visiting hours. After that, I'll be by, okay?"

"Don't b—bother."

"I'll be there after lunch," I said, rushing the words out of my mouth before I clicked off. I couldn't stand to listen to her anymore. Her voice always sounded like she was holding her breath as she talked. It sounded wrong, unnatural. I couldn't take the way the respirator's pumping would interrupt her midsyllable with the hideous sound of air being accordioned into her lungs. The respirator never stopped, in and out, in and out, grating my nerves, grinding them down, in and out. And then there was that tube that ran into the hole in her chest, right there in her chest, they didn't even cover it with bandages, it was just there, out in the open, you could stick your fingers through it, right into her body. . . .

My stomach burned like it was on fire. I downed another shot to douse the flames.

I needed to keep busy. I went to the front door and found the disc Maggie had slipped under the door. I carried it back into the living room and held it up for my home system to read. Everything was here, everything on the Juarez case. Maggie had been thorough. I menued over to the crime scene for starters.

My living room went bloody, and it wasn't my living room anymore. It had become a bedroom. It was furnished in the usual way—bed, end tables, dresser. It was the bed that was the focal point of the butchering. The linens were sliced into blood-drenched rags. Springs and stuffing erupted from charred gashes. The headboard and wall behind it were singed with haphazardly placed burn marks.

I stepped into the holo-bed, my legs disappearing beneath its gory surface. I took a close look at Margarita Juarez's corpse, at the dozens of slices that ran deep into her flesh. The wounds were cooked well-done and squirming with maggots. I looked up at the ceiling where there were patches of bubbled paint covered in a thin mist. The heat that ripped through those gashes was so intense that it flash-fried the flesh and kicked off enough steamed blood to melt the paint on the ceiling.

I moved through her body to the bed's edge and looked down at the body of Hector Juarez where he'd fallen onto the floor. Half his torso was under the bed, where he'd tried to crawl to safety. His legs were sliced and grilled. Bone showed through in a few places like the skewer in a leg kabob.

I moved to the foot of the bed, sliding left and right until the majority of scorch marks pointed at me. This was the spot; this was where she stood. She snuck up to this spot and flicked on her lase-whip. I was certain that the crackle of the whip would've woken them. They would've seen her face in the whip's glow. They died knowing it was their daughter who did this to them.

I menued out of the crime scene and navigated my way into the confession. The death scene disappeared, and my living room was back, but only for a second before it was replaced by a white room, so white that my living room furniture showed through the holographic white walls of the KOP interrogation room. I knew this room well. How many people had I brought into this very room, only to bring them back out bloodied and defeated?

In the middle of the room was a beat-up table. Sitting on opposite sides were Ian and the girl, Adela Juarez, soon-to-be convicted murderer. Her looks were pure Latin. No sign of the mixed blood all Lagartans carry in their veins. There was no kink to her hair, no slope to the eyes. I rotated the scene, looking at her eyes from different angles. I watched the way her eyes focused when she talked. I studied the way they wandered when she listened. She had dark eyes, made darker by the secrets she was keeping behind them. I recognized those eyes. They were Niki's eyes—not in shape, but in essence. They had that same haunted vacancy. Maggie was flat wrong. This girl did it, and she had good reason.

I consciously had to snuff thoughts of Niki before they overwhelmed me again. I selectively skipped ahead, watching the interrogation develop. Ian confronted her with his evidence: her fingerprint-covered lase-whip, her fallen-through lie of an alibi, no sign of a break-in; in fact, all the doors had been locked. Ian worked her smart and professional. He didn't fall for her schoolgirl routine when she tried out the pouty lips, the scrunched-up nose, and the baby talk. Then when she switched to the femme fatale, he didn't go for her smooth talk and subtle flirtation. She even tried out the girl next door with a pearly smile and a bouncy attitude, but Ian still stayed on task. "I know you did it," he'd say. "There's no point in lying anymore. Just tell me why you did it, Adela? Did they deserve it?"

It took me an hour to surf through the ten hours worth of vid. Ian wore her down using her own hopelessness against her. In the end she broke. She spilled how her parents were forbidding her to see her boyfriend. They couldn't do that. She was seventeen. She could see whoever she wanted. She railed on about how her parents were going to split up, how she and her mother would have to move to another house when she didn't want to move, she shouldn't have to, this was her house, the house she grew up in. They were ruining everything!

Ian wasn't buying it entirely. He worked the abuse angles. How did they punish you when you did something wrong? Have you ever seen your father get angry? How about your mother? Ian moved the conversation in a sexual direction. Did you ever see your parents kiss? Do you think your father was handsome? Adela hung to her story. She was too ashamed to admit what her father did to her. It was all right there, in her eyes, Niki's eyes. Niki never admitted it either.

Ian wrapped it up. Let her keep her secrets. No point in forcing it out of her. He had her sign the papers. No sign of coercion, just straight-up police work.

The rain had calmed to barely a drizzle. The sky was brighter than normal. Still couldn't see the sun, but I could pick out the bright spot behind the clouds. The skiff puttered out from one of Koba's innumerable canals and began motoring across the Koba River. I looked over at one of Koba's bridges stretched over the water to our port side. The bridge's walkway was clogged with merchants pushing carts loaded high with rattan rugs, fern-frond hats, monitor-bone carvings, and countless other varieties of handmade schlock, the whole lot of them heading to the Old Town Square to take advantage of the semi–rain-free weather, all of them hoping to sell an item or two to one of the few tourists on planet.

Coming around the bend, I could see the walls surrounding the Zoo. Mexican scientists were the first to settle Lagarto. They'd come all the way from Earth to study our lizard-dominated ecology. Not since dinosaurs ruled the Earth had there been a planet where reptiles were the highest form of life. They set up what was, at the time, a first-class research facility on the banks of the Koba.

They loaded the facility full of biological specimens—no telling what they could learn from alien biology. After all, Lagarto had one of the most developed ecologies of all the discovered planets. They were going to cure the incurable and unlock the secrets of Darwinian evolution. The scientists dissected every species. They extracted oils from every organ. They injected earth-bacteria, instigated cancers, spliced genes, and created laboratories so full of reptilian mutants as to make Dr. Moreau proud. And in the end, what did they learn? *Nada*.

I took a hit off my flask, thinking not all was for naught. When they ran out of tequila, they started experimenting with the local fruit. . . .

Scientists flocked to farming when the brandy boom hit. There were fortunes to be made. The research funding dwindled year after year, and then when it was finally axed altogether, the handful of die-hard scientists who were still doing research at the facility opened up all the cages as a sign of protest. Thousands of species of bug and lizard infested the buildings. That's when us Lagartans took to calling it the Zoo.

It sat abandoned for many years, until well after the economic collapse, when crime had begun reaching epidemic levels. The government needed more prison space and rather than build a new prison, they converted the research facility into a jail. People liked the idea of throwing criminals in the Zoo—poisonous lizards and nasty bugs crawling all over.

I slapped a five-hundred on the skiff's pilot, hopped onto the dock, and climbed the long staircase leading up the riverbank. The Zoo lay before me, its ten-meter walls topped with broken glass set in cement with the jagged edges up. On the corners stood tall towers crowned with glassed-in booths for the zookeepers. I remembered that Ian used to work here. After he'd failed the KOP physical on his first try, his father set him up as a guard until the next go-round. He did a year, maybe two, as a zookeeper before finally coming over to KOP.

I walked through the front gate. I stayed inside the yellow

lines painted on the asphalt as I stepped across the no-man's land between the outer walls and the facility itself. Just outside the yellow lines, I could see the evenly spaced laser heads embedded in the ground, ready to fry anything bigger than a fly that crossed their path. There were plenty of rotting lizard parts littering the trail, some of them still smoking. I strode through the entrance. A zookeeper sat at the desk. "What you want?" he asked.

"I'm here for visitation. Adela Juarez."

The guard gestured at the scanner. I stepped through as another guard checked his monitor and saw that I was unarmed. He made me wait a minute while the system looked up my DNA. My identity established, he signaled me through. I walked through a series of gates, finally entering the prison proper.

When I reached the warden's office, nobody bothered to greet me. I knocked and entered, immediately catching an earful from the block super about how I didn't have the authority to enter that office. The food stains on the front of his shirt and the piece of what could be fish stuck in his beard told me he was more upset about me interrupting his early lunch than anything else. I went back into the hall and waited for a good five minutes before he came out with a wiped face and a bulging stomach that exerted maximum button stress. He called to one of the zookeepers and assigned him the job of being my personal escort.

The guard opened the gate and led me down a long corridor, past the infirmary and the library. The walls were alive with mossy growth. I couldn't see the floor through the ferns. As we waded through the overgrowth, the floor popped with activity, insects and lizards both going airborne. I brushed a beetle from my shoulder. I felt something in my hair that I swiped away with a swat.

I heard somebody screaming. His protestations echoed

through the block for a few seconds before they were drowned out by cheers. Probably rape. Maybe guard-on-inmate, maybe inmate-on-inmate. No way to tell.

We took a set of steps down a level. The stairs had been recently torched to keep them fern free. Each step we took was accompanied by a poof of ash that quickly turned my pant legs black. A right turn took us onto death row, though it wasn't really a row. It was more of a square with evenly spaced cages arranged into rows like desks in a classroom. Each cage was a simple cubical structure, the entire cage composed of latticed rebar. My escort snatched up a wooden stool and zigzagged me through the cages, the soon-to-be-dead peeking out through the openings. My escort set the stool next to a cage near the center then moved out of earshot to allow some privacy.

I took a seat on the stool, lifting my feet up onto the rungs to keep them off the infested floor. I looked through the food hole at the face of young Adela Juarez sitting on her cot. Her eyes looked like they'd aged years since her interrogation. She passed a pot through the hole. I took it from her hands and knew not to check inside. I held the almost full piss pot up for the guard who came and took it off my hands.

"Who are you?" she asked.

"My name's Juno Mozambe."

"You a lawyer?"

"No."

"Are you here to take pictures?"

"No. I don't work for the press."

"I know that. My father ran the vid station for the Libre. I'd know you if you were a reporter."

"Then why did you ask if I wanted to take pictures?"

She shrugged.

I honed in on her eyes, looking for that same dark twinkle I saw in her interrogation, that little something that said there

was a whole lot more to her than what was visible on the surface. I saw sadness, and I saw fear, but I couldn't find that same
spark that I knew so well from looking into my wife's eyes. A
couple months in this cage must've driven it out of her. Time I
got this over with. "You killed your parents."

"You gonna tell me who you are?"

"A friend sent me."

"What friend? Did Raj send you?"

From the case file, I remembered that Raj Gupta had been
tagged as the accused's boyfriend. She'd claimed she was with
him all night the night her parents died. Problem was the kid
didn't back her up. He admitted that she was at his house ear-
lier that night, and that they had sex in his bed, twice. But then
he went on to say that she left a little after midnight, which
gave her plenty of time to get home since her parents weren't
attacked until 1:52 A.M. It was an analysis of the maggots re-
trieved from the Juarezes' wounds that nailed down the time of
attack so accurately. The maggots had just reached fifth generation and from there, it was simple math: one hour and twenty-
three minutes per generation, plus a mere four minutes for
initial infestation. Lagartan flies act quick.

I could imagine the look on Adela's face when she'd found
out her boyfriend didn't alibi her. The little vix thought she had
the kid pussy-whipped. She thought he'd do anything she said to
keep getting between her legs. She must've thought she was the
hottest lay on the planet. Turned out her boyfriend was thinking, "Not so much."

"You killed your parents," I said as I brushed some flying
roach from my shoulder. "I saw what you did to them."

"You a cop?"

"You must've really hated them, the way you sliced them
up."

"I'm not saying another word until you tell me who you

are." She made a show of clamming up tight by crossing her arms across her chest and squeezing her lips together.

This might take a while. All I wanted was a simple admission so I could go back and tell Maggie that Ian arrested the right person. Then I could collect my fee. I needed that money.

We stared at each other for a few, and then she started looking around, like there were a lot more interesting things to look at than me. I needed a strategy. I could hint around about her father and see if she'd just come out with it. *My father raped me.* That was all I needed to hear. She hadn't admitted it to Ian, but that was before she'd been sentenced to death. She'd had some time to think about it since then. I'd tried the same hinting around with Niki. There were times over the years, especially during her down periods, where I thought she'd be better off if she admitted what her father did to her. I'd drop little hints, give her little openings to bring it up. I thought it might make a difference if she could unbury the secret. It never worked. She locked that history down so long ago that I wasn't even sure she still had a key.

And now Niki was in that hospital, paralyzed, breathing through a fucking tube. . . .

All the sudden, I found myself going at Adela full bore. "How'd it feel to slice up your own mother?" I had no control. The words shot out like daggers. "I wish I could've seen it. You swingin' that whip around, lashin' out at her. Can you imagine what it was like for her? I bet you can. One minute she's sleepin' and the next she's got this whip comin' at her. She puts up her hands to protect herself and a second later her hands are gone, whipped right the fuck off."

Her eyes began to water. She fought to keep her trembling lips pressed together.

I got on a roll, the venom spraying from my mouth. "And your father, I bet you were going for his crotch, weren't you?

You wanted to whip his cock off so he couldn't hurt you anymore. But he rolled over, didn't he? That must've made you
sooo angry. . . ."

"Who are you?" It came out as a whisper.

I had my face pressed up against the bars. "Oh, but you
taught him, didn't you? He'll never touch you again, will he?"

"Why are you doing this to me?" Tears were streaming now.

"He used to come in the middle of the night, right? He'd
wait until your mother fell asleep before he came to visit his little
princess. He'd tell you that there was a special way for a daughter to show how much she loved her father. He'd press himself
up against you, wouldn't he? I bet his cheek felt scratchy when
it rubbed against yours."

"Stop it," she said as she swiped away the tears.

"Why won't you admit it? People think you're a spoiled little
brat. They think you killed your parents because they wouldn't
let you see your boyfriend. They think you're a petty little
bitch that never got spanked. Is that how you want people to
remember you after they gas you?"

She was crying full out now. She stuttered out a "No."

"So tell me," I ordered. "Tell me about your father. Tell me
what he did to you. People need to know that you're not who
they think you are. They need to know you were defending
yourself."

"He didn't do any . . . anything to me."

"Then why'd you kill him?"

"I didn't do it," she said between sobs. "I didn't kill him."

She was good. I almost believed her the way she said it. "I
watched you confess."

"I n-never confessed."

"I *watched* you."

Her crying reached that moaning and bubbling stage. "I'm
telling y-you, it n-never happened. I didn't c-confess, and I

didn't k-kill my parents. I loved them. Why w-won't you believe m-me?"

Visions of quick cash dissipated. Maybe I could get the guard to let me in her cell. I could grab her by her pretty little throat, *make* her admit it.

To hell with it. I was outta here. I waved for the guard.

"Wait," she whined, little-girl charm coming through strong. "Please help me. Please believe me. I didn't do it."

I was already on the move. I decided that I'd just tell Maggie that Adela divulged her father's molestation. That was why she did it. It was the truth whether Adela would admit it or not. Maggie was wrong on this one. When I watched that interrogation, I *knew* Adela was abused. I knew those eyes.

The knot in my stomach clenched at the thought of lying to Maggie, but it was for her own good. The last thing she needed was to get into a pissing match with Ian. Whether he was dirty or not, she was better off staying out of his way. I saw the way he was tossing around that cameraman. I saw the way those young cops were following his lead. Ian was dangerous. Even if it meant he beat out Maggie for that promotion, there'd be another one coming up soon. KOP was in flux, and that meant opportunities. Maggie just needed to stay focused on her caseload.

I left the Zoo, unable to shake the feeling that the real reason I was so willing to lie to Maggie was because I wanted her money. I *needed* that money.

five

My calves ached by the time I reached the bottom of the stairs that led down from the Zoo to the river. I was already sweating. The sun was out for the first time in days. The docks jutted out in front of me. It was time to go to the hospital. On cue, my stomach stepped up its flipping and flopping. Damn hospital. I hated that place. I tilted my flask back and swallowed the last couple drops. I stopped at a newsstand by the dock and bought a minibottle, slugging down the entire contents in a couple swallows.

I walked out onto the warped dock, where moored boats were scraping against the pilings. There was a man coming my way. I moved to the left to let him pass, but he kept walking down the middle of the dock, claiming it as his own. Who did this asshole think he was? I angled closer to the edge, and he aimed in the same direction. Hair bristled on the back of my neck.

I suddenly recognized him. He was one of the hommy boys; Hoshi was his name. He was coming right at me. I ducked and moved back for the middle, but the brandy impaired my agility. Hoshi had a hold of me, and he was pushing me to the edge. I tried to counter by shifting my weight but wound up losing my balance instead. I was tipping off the side. I grasped at his arm, wanting to pull myself back up, or even pull him over with me—either way. I got a hold of his sleeve, but he yanked his arm free, and I went over backward.

I landed hard on the deck of a boat, my shoulder and back screaming in pain. Hoshi hadn't jumped down yet, but there was already another one on me, his foot pinning my throat. I squirmed out from under, but he recovered quickly, this time coming down with his knee in my face. I kicked out, but my legs couldn't find leverage. They were both on me now, holding me down. I reached my hands out, grasping for anything. . . .

I stopped resisting when I felt the barrel of a lase-pistol digging into my temple.

"Good to see you, Juno."

I strained to make the face out through my tears. "Ian?"

"That's right, boy-o. And you're going to listen up, because I'm only going to say this once. You stay the fuck out of my business, you hear me?"

I nodded my head, totally conscious of the lase-pistol rubbing my skull.

"Good. And you're going to do something else. You're going to get Maggie off my ass. You're going to tell her that whatever she thinks I did, I didn't do it. You're going to tell her that I'm a good cop, a great cop. You're going to be my character witness, you get me?"

Again I nodded.

The two of them got up. I stayed down. Hoshi flashed his badge at a couple onlookers who took the hint and moved off.

Ian turned back to me, his lase-pistol leveled at my chest. "You're not so tough now, are you?"

I kept silent as I tried to rein in my galloping heart.

"Say it, boy-o."

"Say what?"

"Say you're not so tough."

He can't be serious.

Ian wagged his piece at me. "Say it."

I was about to launch into a four-letter frenzy, but then I looked at his piece and then his wild eyes. I took my time answering, making sure my voice didn't quiver. "I'm not so tough."

"Did you hear that?" Ian said to Hoshi. "He's not so tough. I gotta say, I'm a bit disappointed. My pop used to tell me about you. He respected you, said you were a real badass. Turns out my pop was full of shit."

A voice sounded from the dock. "You got him?"

"Yeah, we got him."

I couldn't see the voice's face—he was backlit by the sun—but I could make out the girth of his shadow, which was double-wide. "Okay," he said. "Unless you need anything, I'll be going back up then." He sounded like he was out of breath.

"We got it under control, boy-o. Good work."

"No problem, Ian." His eclipsing shadow moved on, but not before I ID'ed him as the block super who had chewed me out, the sloppy eater with fish in his beard.

Ian gestured with his piece, "What's wrong with your hand, boy-o?"

"Old injury."

"Bullshit. I think you're scared. Imagine that. Juno Mozambe shaking like a little girl. You're not used to being on the other end, are you? You're used to being the one that's in control, beating out all those confessions, knocking all those cops around. You were a real force. You even beat my pop down one time. You remember that? Can't say I blame you for that one. You should've done him in and saved me the guilt of cutting ties with the bastard. Yeah, you used to be a real mean bastard. But now, turn the tables, and you're just a little faggot, cryin' for mama."

"Fuck off."

"Ooh, a little sensitive now, aren't we?" Ian was hovering over me now, flaunting his weapon. I looked over at his accomplice. I calculated the odds: no way I could snatch Ian's piece and kill both of them without getting cut in half. Still, it might be worth it if I could kill Ian before I died. As if Ian could tell what I was thinking, he tucked his weapon away, out of my reach.

"Stop moving your hand; it bothers me," he said.

"I can't."

"I said stop."

"I told you. I can't."

Ian dropped on top of me, grabbing my right hand with unbelievable strength. I twisted from under his weight, my left going for his holster. I stopped cold when I felt the muzzle of a lase-pistol jabbing into my back.

"Don't fight it," Hoshi said.

Ian had a hold of my pinky now. "I told you to stop moving your hand." The pain had already electrified my brain before the sound of the snap could reach my ears.

I lost all control, screaming like mad as I thrashed and yanked, trying unsuccessfully to wrench my hand free until, two snaps later, things mercifully went black.

six

I woke up feeling something crawling on my face. I swatted the gecko away with my left. I held up my shaking right, fingers pointing every which way like some fork gone horribly wrong. Pain ricocheted up into my wrist with every sway of my quaking hand.

I couldn't see straight. I couldn't think.

It was all I could do to muster up a simple course of action.

First step: I hit the newsstand and bought up enough minibottles to make a maxibottle.

Second step: I paid a thousand pesos to a teenager with a boat—take me to the city morgue and bring me to Abdul Salaam.

Third step: I knocked back minibottle after minibottle until I couldn't feel a damn thing, not my fingers, not the stomach pain, not a damn thing.

I moved through the hospital corridors. With this hand, I looked more like a patient than a visitor. Abdul did a fine job wrapping it, not bad for a coroner. He'd splinted my four fingers into a karate chop and left my unbroken thumb free. Ian must've gotten bored when I passed out, stopping after the index finger.

Who did that punk think he was? Bracing me. *Me!* In my mind, I kept replaying the scene with different endings: sometimes spinning out from under his grasp and snatching his lase-pistol; or other times I'd just tackle him and bash his head into the decking until he went limp; or better yet, I'd pull a lase-blade out of my belt and watch the look on his face as it sizzled into his chest. Then, just when I'd really start getting into my fantasized victories, the shame of being nothing but a drunken old has-been would bring my broken-fingered reality front and center, which would just end up making me all the angrier.

Rage seeped into my gait, my footsteps becoming footstomps as I turned onto the long-term-care ward. I saw the nurses wheeling their carts, the patients shuffling in their open-assed gowns and thought that if just one of them so much as looked at me . . .

Let it go. You got your money. That was all that mattered for now. I didn't need any more trouble with Ian. Niki had to be my top priority.

From Abdul's office, I'd called Maggie as soon as I'd sobered enough to speak without slurring and told her that the girl fessed up. I told her that the girl was getting dicked by her father, and she decided to de-dickify him. End of story. Maggie sounded short of 100 percent convinced, but her whole premise that the girl was innocent was flimsy from the get-go. I persuaded her to get off Ian's case, despite the fact that, in reality, I knew Ian was involved. How, I didn't know, but I had four broken fingers telling me so.

Maggie had wanted to get together and buy me a drink, but I'd declined. If she found out about Ian's little finger-snapping fiesta, she'd go all out investigating him. Then how long would it be before Ian and his posse showed up at my door ready to break the rest of my bones in order to find out what I'd told her? It was better this way, safer for both of us.

I'd chatted with Maggie a while longer, letting her vent about police politics, with me listening, wishing I was still a cop. Right before I hung up, I recited my account number despite the protestations of the knot in my stomach. I needed that money. Maybe when this was over, and Niki was fully rebuilt, Maggie and I could partner up again and find out what Ian was up to. Together, we could bust that asshole.

Not since I was a kid had I had to worry about money. As the chief's right hand, I'd pocketed a shitload. If it was illegal, we took our cut: opium-den dinero, hooker fuck-bucks, bookie vig, chop-shop swag, gene-smuggler scratch . . . My palms were so greased I couldn't have held onto sandpaper.

Niki and I lived high, spending recklessly to no consequence. There was always more coming in than going out. But when I was forced to resign by the bastards who murdered the chief, the trend lines went from black to red. Not being a cop anymore, I had to start earning my dough or give up the life. I found good work hiding in closets, peering through windows, exposing scandals when I could and creating scandals when there were none to expose. It wasn't glamorous, but the scandal rags paid well. It was a long way down from running KOP, but it kept me in the game. Barely.

Then came Niki's "accident." I spent most everything I had on the offworld tech it took to reconstruct her, and I still had a fresh-grown spine to pay for. The money I got from Maggie would get me over the top on the next spine payment, but I still had four more to make. Offworld medical didn't come cheap, and they didn't accept local currency. For every hospital bill, I had to exchange bagfuls of pesos, getting mere handfuls of offworld dollars in return. Still, I knew that if I could pull down another half dozen nice paydays, I'd be able to cover. Last resort, I could sell the house to make the final.

The docs said Niki's new spine was coming along on schedule. I was commissioning the work on the Orbital—there was no tech like that on Lagarto. I could connect up at any time and look at it in its tank, a glass cylinder filled with brown gel,

Niki Mozambe written on the lid. It didn't look like much yet, just the worm in a tequila bottle, but it'd be having a major growth spurt soon.

I entered Niki's room. The lights were off. A wall of monitors gave the room an electronic radiance. I didn't turn on the lights. I knew Niki liked it dark, no matter what time of day.

"What happened . . . to your h—hand?" Niki said between pumps of the respirator.

I bent over and kissed her on the lips, getting a lukewarm response. "Remember I told you I was going to do a job for Maggie. It got a little ugly, but it's done now. And it paid well. You'll be up and about in no time."

"Save your . . . money."

"We're not going to go through this again, are we?"

The way she was jutting her jaw told me we were. "I don't w—want this," she said.

"Yes you do. You're just out of sorts right now, trapped in this room all the time."

"It's more th—than that, J—Juno."

I took a deep breath. Today, her paused speech annoyed me even more than normal. "I know it's hard, Niki. But it'll be over as soon as we get your new spine in. You'll feel better when you can walk again."

"Why don't you f—fucking get it, Juno? You can fix my body . . . all you want, but I'll still be b—broken."

"Stop talking like that," I said, fidgeting in my seat. "This hospital is just getting to you, that's all." I stood and flicked the lights on. "What do you expect being in the dark all the time?"

She rolled her eyes, those same fiery eyes that drew me in so many years ago with their flaming mystery. She stared at me, her eyes burning into me, making me feel small. I wondered just when it was that those eyes turned on me. They used to warm my soul, but now they seared and scalded instead. I

looked away from her to get out of the heat, thinking five
more minutes, then I could go, my daily duty fulfilled.

Another minute of the respirator's incessant hissing and
wheezing passed before she spoke again. "It's not this . . . room
that makes . . . me feel trapped. . . . And it's not . . . this limp useless b—body, either. . . . It's being . . . trapped inside of *me* . . .
that I c—can't stand."

The photos were coming out grainy—all the better. Gave them
that undercover feel. I clothespinned the first one, no easy task
single-handed, but I managed. I was used to doing most things
with my left.

I kept working, moving prints from tray to tray, holding my
right hand clear to keep the wrappings dry. It was such a tedious process, developing pictures from actual film. Hard to
believe this was once the way it worked. Lucky for me, there
were still a few hobbyists out there who liked to do things the
hard way, the predigital way. If I hadn't been able to find film, I
never would've successfully built a camera low-tech enough to
be undetectable by an offworlder.

I hung what looked like the best of the batch, the devil poking and choking that whore. That had to rate some good coin.
Even if the offworlder was nobody important, it would score
strong on shock value.

I felt a headache coming on—always happened when I spent
too much time in the red light. Knowing it would be a while
before I could turn the other lights on, I decided it was time for
a little break. I took a hit off my flask and cleared a place to sit,
tossing a stack of pic rejects on the floor. I'd have to watch my
sloppiness when Niki came home in a few months. It was finding pics like these that sent her tailspinning in the first place.

It had been one of my highest payouts. There was a local
pol who I'd heard had a thing for young poon, the younger the

better. I tailed him for less than a day before I spotted him picking up an underaged hooker on one of Koba's many Kiddie Korners. I followed them to an empty lot and snapped a few shots through the window of his car.

I'd been careless and left the pics out when I left the house. Niki found them and went off on a pain-pill binge, popping herself vegetative. I found her halfway to dead with one of the pics crumpled in her hand. It wasn't until after a screaming-fast ride to the hospital and a thorough stomach pumping that I smoothed the pic back out and saw why it sent her free-falling. I cursed myself for not noticing the resemblance the pol had to Niki's daughter-raper father.

When they released her, I spent an entire month at home to be by her side. I thought she was doing better, getting over the shock of seeing that picture and the memories it brought back. She was getting to be her old self again. I thought it was safe to start working again. I was a shitty nursemaid anyway.

I'd started with small jobs, the kind of thing that would only take a couple hours a day. I couldn't be positive that she was stable so I dropped a biomon into her hair when she was sleeping. The thing was top of the line. It crawled down to her scalp and burrowed under the skin. It didn't have much capability, but it was practically microscopic, next to impossible to detect. I could call into it anytime and get a report on her movements and vitals.

That was how I knew she'd jumped off a bridge. That was how I'd been able to get to her so fast, fast enough that the docs were able to revive her—she'd only been dead for fifteen minutes.

They were able to rejuve her brain, but practically everything else had to go—both legs, the rib cage, a half dozen organs, and a hip joint. I could've saved a bundle if I'd bought all used parts. Used parts were common enough. Lagarto's poor

would often have their organs harvested in order to pay for
their funerals, not that there'd be much left of the body to bury
after harvesting. There were plenty of organs around, just not
many people who could afford to pay for the transplant surgery.

But I didn't want to take any chances with used parts. Not
with Niki. Niki wasn't going to get a hophead's liver or a glue-
sniffer's lungs. No fucking way. This was *Niki* we were talking
about. This was the Niki who could look into my eyes and see
more than a broken-down thug. This was the Niki who had
been by my side for all these years as I waded through the river
of shit that was my life, right there with me, step after foul step.
And she'd never pinched her nose. Not once.

I'd made it clear to the docs that she'd get nothing but top-
notch parts. They grew everything fresh from Niki's own DNA.
Piece by piece, they rebuilt her. The only thing she still needed
was the spine to pull it all together. Then they could pull the air
tubes and seal up her chest. That done, a couple months of re-
hab and she'd be fully healed.

The phone rang. I picked up—voice only. I didn't want a
holo in my red-lit bathroom ruining my prints. "Yeah."

"Guess who, boy-o?"

My nerves rattled when I recognized Ian's voice. My vision
went redder than the darkroom. "What the fuck do you want?"

"You got my message, didn't you?"

I looked at the cast on my hand. "Loud and clear."

"Good. Meet me at Roby's. Midnight."

seven

———

THE nightlife on Bangkok Street was in full swing. Being midnight, it was late enough that everybody had a good buzz going, but still early enough that you didn't have to step over puddles of vomit. I weaved through the crowd out front of one of the clubs that was taking advantage of the rainless night by putting a bathtub full of shine on the street with a handwritten sign advertising a bottomless cup. For a thousand pesos, you get a tin cup branded with the club logo that you can use to self-serve a scoop of the white mash. Once you've sucked out the last of the alcohol, you dump the mash and go back in.

I moved down the block, stepping over the little piles of mash, my gut on fire. I wasn't sure why Ian wanted to meet with me, but I felt compelled to comply. There was something in his voice, something in the way he asked if I'd gotten the message that told me I had to. I pushed my rage to the back of my mind. I put a lid on my boiling stomach. I needed to be thinking straight.

At Roby's, I was stopped by the bouncer. He was done up in gladiator garb—boots, skirt, and one of those helmets with the upside-down brush on top. At the mention of Ian's name, he ushered me inside where fiendish music dug into my ears with its reverbed drone. I struggled to see; my eyes were slow to adjust to the near-black lighting. The place was small, no more than twenty tables. Over the floor, pantyless dominatrices rode swings that hung from the ceiling. On the stage, three

Roman centurions with strap-ons play-whipped a bare-breasted woman tied to a stake.

The tables were occupied with offworld clientele, all of them showing off their artificially enhanced perfection. The men had milky skin stretched over weight-lifter bods. Their faces all had piercing eyes and laid-back smiles that were underscored by strong jawlines. And the women, they all showed off their no-end-in-sight legs, which were topped by hourglass waists and a pair of melon tits. A couple tables of offworlders were morphed out into some seriously freaky shit. I saw a snake-headed medusa, a dude with a bat's head, a lobotomy-scarred zombie . . .

"Quite a show." The words barely registered over the music.

I turned toward the voice. It was Liz, Ian's squeeze. Gone was the cool elegant woman my eyes were glued to at The Beat, and in her place was a kinky librarian. Her eyes were framed by horn-rims, and her hair was pulled up into a bun held together with a pair of slender spikes. She was out front with her cleavage, her breasts overflowing a studded black leather bra only partially obscured by a half-unbuttoned white blouse. She took me by the good hand and led me past the bar and into the side room, her hips swiveling beneath a conservative plaid-print skirt that had been cut to show some not-so-conservative thigh.

"Ian will be along soon," she said as she gestured me toward a table made to look like a medieval rack surrounded by bar stools. I took a seat at the end with the gears. She slid onto the stool next to mine and waved for drinks. "I'm Liz." I could hear her clearly now, the music reduced to nothing more than the pounding beat.

I peeled my eyes off Liz and scanned the windowless room. The lighting was brighter in here. The walls were castle gray with black lines painted on to make it look like it was built from stone blocks. The ceiling was black with a pair of moss-covered chandeliers assembled out of what was supposed to look like human bones. Around the perimeter, upended skull sconces sprouted electric candles with flame-shaped bulbs. I counted four cops at a corner table. I spotted Hoshi, Ian's finger-cracking accomplice, who toasted me from across the room, his date sitting in a mock electric chair at the head of the table.

"Ian told me about you," said Liz as the drinks arrived in goblets.

I raised an eyebrow.

"He said you used to be a cop."

I nodded.

She picked up one of the rack's four iron cuffs and slipped her hand through it like a bracelet. "He said you were close to Chief Chang."

"That's right." From the goblet, I took a sip of brandy and was irked by the metallic taste from this cheap Henry-the-Eighth shit.

She pulled her hand free from the shackle, rattling the chain it was attached to. "Is it true that you used to be the chief's enforcer?"

I answered with a question of my own. "Why does Ian want to talk to me?"

"He didn't say. He just said that I should keep you company until he gets here."

"How long have you known him?"

"A long time," she said with a playful smile. "I heard you once beat a man to death."

It was more than once. Again, I changed the subject. "Who's that guy?"

Liz followed my eyes to an offworlder sitting with a young cleavage-popping local. They were seated at an operating room table with a holographic autopsy-scarred corpse on top.

"That's Horst. Why do you ask?"

"He's been staring at you."

"How do you know he's not staring at *you*?"

It wasn't so much what she said that made me smile. It was more the way she looked with that big girly grin, totally at odds with her naughty librarian getup. "Who is he?" I repeated.

"Just a businessman who likes to hang out in clubs like these."

The offworlder's body was so perfect that he looked plastic, like he was some mannequin come to life. He was definitely watching me now, our eyes meeting uncomfortably. He held up his goblet in a long-distance toast. I toasted back, taking another sip of brandy that tasted like it came from a can. I set my goblet down on the rack, wondering if they'd used real blood to stain its surface.

The offworlder came walking over with his powder white skin and his inky black hair. He was wearing pressed black pants with a billowy white shirt and a black cape that left him looking two fangs from a vampire. He gave the back of Liz's hand a little peck and slipped into the chair next to hers. He held his hand out for a shake, and I brandished my shaking splinted right.

"My," he said as he took his hand back, "looks like you had a bit of an accident."

"Something like that," I responded.

"I'm Horst Jeffers," he said with a barely noticeable offworld accent.

"Juno Mozambe."

"It's nice to meet you, Mr. Mozambe. I hope I'm not intruding. I just saw you and Liz talking, and I thought I'd introduce myself. So tell me, what is it that you do, Mr. Mozambe?"

"I'm between gigs." An uncomfortable silence followed as he waited for me to elaborate. I didn't. Instead, I turned the question back on him. "How about you?"

"I'm a businessman," he responded, matching my ambiguity with some ambiguity of his own.

"What kind of business?"

"I'm in tourism."

He was still being vague, but I let it drop.

He turned to Liz and eyed her up and down. "You've really outdone yourself, sweetie. I just love this getup."

She accepted the complement with a coy smile.

Sweetie? I thought she was Ian's sweetie. I asked, "How do you and Liz know each other?"

"We run in the same circles, she and I. Over the years, we've gotten to know each other. Quite well, I might add." He put his arm around her shoulder and squeezed. Liz pecked his cheek in response.

I remembered what Josephs had told me about her: a woman like that's not exclusive.

I took a sip of my brandy and must've made a face because he said, "Tastes awful, doesn't it?"

"Like shit."

"Don't you love this place?"

I took a look around the room. "Not bad, I guess."

"No, not Roby's," he said. "I mean Lagarto."

"It's home."

"Have you ever been offworld, Mr. Mozambe?"

"No."

"So few of you Lagartans have. Have you ever wanted to?"

"No."

He turned to Liz. "Now there's a man who knows what he has. You could learn a thing or two from him."

Liz rolled her eyes at him.

Horst laughed an easy, flawless laugh. "She's been after me to take her up with me."

Liz turned to me. "I'd like to see what life is like in the stars. What's so wrong with that?"

"You're not missing anything," he said to her. To me, he said, "She won't listen. I'm amazed how many of you Lagartans sit down here feeling sorry for yourselves, thinking life is so great up there, but I'm telling you, I'd rather be here. If it weren't for my business calling me up a few months a year, I'd live here full-time."

"And just what is it that you love so much about Lagarto?"

"Lagarto is *real*. You don't know what it's like to live inside a metal tube your whole life, where water comes from a faucet instead of a river, and food comes in plastic packages. Life up there is overrated. It's all so artificial. Do you understand me, Mr. Mozambe?"

I nodded politely as my brain tried to reconcile the fact that these words were coming out of this mannequin-man.

"There's no weather up there," he continued, "none of this fantastic rain. It's always the same temperature, and the air tastes the same every day. It's a sterile existence in space, a miserable, sterile existence."

Liz chimed in with a challenging attitude. "If it's so bad up there, then why haven't you all moved down to the surface?"

He put his hand over Liz's. "Because people are fools, my dear. They're so used to their disinfectants and their antibacterials that they can't get over the thought of breathing unfiltered air. They think that if they come down here they'll get sick on the water, or catch a nasty case of the rot. Some of these people haven't seen an insect in their lives, and you can tell them all you want about the marvels of bug spray, but they won't listen to you. It's only the adventurous spirits that make the journey. To me, you haven't lived until you've taken a dip in the Koba. You don't know what life is about until you eat meat from a monitor lizard that you killed yourself. And the people? I love your people." He kissed Liz's cheek. "They have so much character. They live with the faces their parents gave them, with all their glorious imperfections. They get wrinkled when they get old, and they wear their scars proudly instead of having them erased. Your women carry their babies to term instead of gestating them in tanks. You see how impersonal a practice that is? How can a mother truly appreciate her child unless she's gone through the pain of childbirth?"

I said to Liz, "When did you say Ian was getting here?"

Horst looked offended. He wasn't used to being interrupted, but I didn't care. I was sick of hearing his bullshit. All that crap about us having "character," and here he was pawing all over Liz, a drop-dead beauty. If he loved our "glorious imperfections" so much, then why wasn't he cozying up to some cross-eyed, acne-scarred, big-nosed, frizzy-haired, flat-chested gimp?

"Ah, I didn't realize you were waiting for Mr. Davies," he said. "I'm sure he'll be along any minute, Mr. Mozambe. Sorry for rattling on the way I have. I'll leave you be." With that, he stood up and went back to his autopsy table and sat next to his cooing cooze.

Liz had a slight grin on her face.

"Why are you smiling?"

"He's not used to being put in his place like that."

"You like seeing him put in his place?"

"Sometimes."

"What does he do?" I asked.

"He already told you. He's a businessman."

"Do you and he . . . ?"

"We used to. He was a lot of fun. But I ended it before it got serious."

"You sure he got the message? It looked like he was trying to tell me something, the way he was getting so close to you."

"He gets a little jealous from time to time."

She ran her hand across the rack's surface and began fiddling with the shackle again. I found my eyes moving from one rack to another. She caught me in the act and smiled naughtily, fully back into her kinky librarian persona. I felt a good kind of stirring in my stomach that made its way down into my pants. For the first time in forever, I felt intoxicated on something other than booze.

The sight of Ian strolling in slapped me sober. He stopped to peck Liz on the forehead and dropped onto a stool to my right. Finding myself caught between a man and his flirtatious girlfriend, I rejected the guilt that wanted to creep in—this fucker broke my fingers.

"Good to see you, boy-o."

I answered with silence.

Ian gave Liz a leave-us-alone nod.

"Nice meeting you," she said to me as she stood. She moved off to the doorway and leaned against its frame, peering out onto the main floor.

I took my eyes off her and squared them on Ian. His hair was slicked straight back from a high forehead perched on top of wild eyes. *What happened to this guy?* It was like he was a different person. I couldn't see any sign of the meek momma's boy I'd known in the past.

I asked, "What do you want?"

"You like to get right to the point, don't you, boy-o. Can't say I blame you. You must be on the edge of your seat wondering what it is I want from you. Here's the thing, Juno. I wasn't thinking things through when we got together this morning. It's not everyday I get a chance to lay some muscle on a legendary badass, you see what I'm saying? I couldn't help but get all caught up in the fun of it." He winked at me. He actually *winked*, the fucker.

As the waitress passed, Ian waved for a drink. "Truth is, I got carried away, and I missed an opportunity to get a step ahead of my partner. You have to understand that I don't react well to people getting in my business, you see what I'm saying? I just wanted that bitch partner of mine to butt the fuck out. She thinks she's so smart, trying to sell me that bullshit about calling you in on the barge murders. Like I'm gonna believe she thinks a washed-out heavy is going to solve that case. No offense, boy-o, but get real. Half of hommy's been working that case for months and hasn't got shit. And all the sudden, I'm supposed to believe that what we need is supersleuth Juno Mozambe."

Ian looked at me, waiting for me to agree, expecting me to say something like, "Yeah, that's right, Ian. I *am* a dumb shit. I don't know what Maggie was doing feeding you a line like that."

After a few seconds of silence, he said, "Let's get right to it, boy-o. Here's how thing are going to work between us. First you're going to tell me why Maggie's getting all suspicious. Then you're going to walk out that door and you're going to find a way to get close to her. That bitch is fucking paranoid. She's always off doing her own thing and not telling anybody what she's up to. I don't know why, but she trusts you, and we're going to use that. You're going to make up some reason to get close, be her confidant. Then you're going to give me daily reports on what she's doing. I'm talking *detailed* reports, you hear me? I want the kind of shit that says she woke up at five twenty-five; she took a piss at five twenty-six, and she stuffed in a fresh rag at five twenty-seven. Are we straight?"

"How much you paying?"

"What?" he said, incredulous.

What was it with this guy? He broke a couple bones and thought I would be his errand boy? Fuck that. My loyalty was with Maggie, complete and absolute. But I needed money in a bad way, and I wasn't about to pass up an opportunity to score some cash. I could take his money and feed him a bunch of bullshit on Maggie. "I said, 'How much?' "

Ian burst out laughing and slapped the table, shackles bouncing with a clank. "You are one cold bastard, boy-o. No wonder the old chief liked you so much."

I grinned to cover my bafflement. Why the hell was he acting so surprised?

"I can't believe you," he said. "I really can't. I don't stun easy, and I'm sitting here stunned outright. I mean, I pinched that air hose until she went fucking purple, and here's her husband saying, 'How much?' " He slapped the table again, shaking his head in disbelief.

I could hardly breathe. I took a shaky sip of my drink, barely keeping that fake grin going. Did he just say what I thought he said? He pinched her air hose shut? Niki's air hose? With a sickening flash, it suddenly made sense. How he must have threatened her to get at me. How he thought I would spy on Maggie to keep Niki alive. I practically choked on my brandy, feeling like it was *my* air hose that he had pinched shut.

He'd asked me on the phone if I'd gotten his message. And I'd said yes. I thought he was talking about the broken fingers he gave me. But that wasn't it at all. He was talking about the message Niki was supposed to give me after he'd cut off her air supply.

Why didn't she tell me?

Ian waved for more drinks. "You must have ice water in those veins of yours, boy-o. Don't you care what happens to her?"

The world was spinning. My face felt like it was on fire. Feeling the pressure to say something, I thought fast, "You know how much that hospital costs? Shit, you'd be doing me a fucking favor." Let him think she's not important to me. Let him think he can't get to me by going through her. That was the best way to keep her out of this.

He nodded his head slow as he thought it through. "I have to be honest with you, boy-o. It never occurred to me that you'd want to be rid of her. Why don't you just do it yourself?"

I shrugged.

"You don't have the heart for it, do you?"

I conjured up a guilty-as-charged face.

"I'll tell you what. I'll pay you your regular rate, and if you do good work, as a bonus, I'll pinch that hose till she flatlines. How's that sound?"

I couldn't speak. But knowing she was safe for now, I nodded my head up and down.

eight

I SPRINTED for the river, my lungs forcing me to slow after just a block. FUCK! I took long loping strides, not bothering to avoid the puddles. I didn't know why I was running, whether I was rushing to get somewhere or just running away. What I did know was I wasn't moving fast enough to keep from feeling smothered by thoughts of Niki—my Niki—helplessly paralyzed and struggling for air.

I made it another half a block before my body gave in. I felt ill and dropped to my knees, puddle water soaking through my pant legs. I coughed up brandy and bile, making a puddle of my own in the weeds.

Why didn't she tell me? That asshole cut off her air, and she didn't even call. Why wouldn't she call? I wanted to go to sleep right there on the street, just curl up and go to sleep. I used to be *the* man. Nobody fucked with me. And now I'd fallen so far that I found my balls in the hands of some little wussy 'roid popper. I'd gone from puppet master to puppet, from fucker to sucker, from play*er* to play*ed*.

I'd gone full circle. I'd spent my childhood covering my ears while my father slapped the shit out of my mother. I was a weak helpless little kid, and all those years of wielding the power of the Koba Office of Police couldn't cover the fact that that's all I'd ever be, a weak helpless little kid who couldn't even protect his mother, or his wife.

Enough of this pathetic bullshit. I was back on the move, my feet stepping through the dark streets. Reaching the docks, I felt the stares of iguanas perched atop pilings, looking down their noses at me. I swatted at one, sending it diving into the drink—kamikaze style.

I found a skiff and untied the line before jumping aboard and waking the young pilot. She reacted quickly, starting the motor and putt-putting us toward deeper water. I told her to open it up. She reluctantly broke etiquette and gunned the motor, our rolling wake sure to bounce all the sleeping boat captains out of their slumber.

I just about lost my shit when she asked for the fare upfront. Then, when she aimed for a floating gas station, I did lose my shit. I laid into her with raving intensity. I didn't have time for this. I needed to get there fast. Wisely, she just tuned out my rants as she used my front money to fill up. Finished, she eased the skiff out onto open water and let the waves rock me silent.

I was so focused on my upcoming confrontation that I hardly noticed the rest of the trip, nor my walk up to and through the hospital. Before I knew it, I was there at her bedside, the sound of the air pump grating on me. With every fresh pump, my rage inflated until the words came bursting out of me in an uncontrolled torrent. I told her how stupid she was for jumping off a bridge. I blamed her for losing all our money, everything I ever worked for. I was out there every day, taking risks, hustling to get the money for that spine, and here she was, working against me. It was all her fault that I was under Ian's thumb. How was I supposed to save her when she pulled this shit?

She listened to it all, her eyes not meeting mine.

"When was he here?" I managed to ask in a strangled voice.

"Before you c—came this afternoon."

"What did he say?"

"He said that he'd k—kill me if I didn't get . . . you to do what he . . . says. He said I couldn't . . . get away." She smiled. "He's r—right about that."

I didn't find it funny. "Did he . . . ?" I pointed at the air hose. "Yes."

"Why didn't you tell me?"

"Why d—do you think?"

I knew why, but I couldn't bring myself to believe she'd go that far even though the facts were staring me in the face: she wanted to die. She couldn't do it herself. She wanted me to defy Ian so he'd come and make good on his promise. She let me think there was nothing wrong, nothing to worry about. I'd sat across the table from him, asking for money, not knowing he'd been here, in this room, with that tube pinched between his fingers. . . .

My insides were boiling. My hand was fucking gyrating. I shook the bed's railing, wanting to rip it off and slam it to the floor. "How could you do that to me!"

Niki's eyes targeted mine. She spat furious words that got mangled by the pump. I drowned out her garbles with shouts of my own. Curses flew out of my mouth like angry bees from a shaken hive. A nurse popped her concerned head through the door. I sprayed a few curses in her direction, and she went running for help.

Niki gave up trying to speak. She stared at the ceiling, feigning boredom. I shook the bed until I got her attention and launched into a fresh tirade, the words coming out of my mouth so fast that I had no idea what I was even saying.

Finally spent, I dropped into a chair and wiped sweat from my brow. The nurse was back with help. "It's okay," I told them. "I'm done."

Not taking my word for it, she asked Niki if everything was all right.

She said, "Yes." Then, after they reluctantly left, she said to me, "You know . . . I was going . . . to ask you the . . . same question."

"What's that?"

"How can you d—do this to me?"

I left the hospital when Vlad showed. I posted the former cop outside Niki's door, fronting him enough money to negate a fourth of my recent profits.

I walked out saying, "See what you've done, Niki. You've really fucked things up." The door closed behind me, shutting me off from her plug-pulling pleadings. Things would be different when she got her spine. She'd see I was right.

The rains were back. The city lights illuminated the long raindrops as they emerged from the darkened sky. I ducked into an all-night café and ordered up some eggs.

There was a vid screen hanging over the counter. The news was running a pic of the deceased Officer Ramos. He was a regular-looking guy. A real Everyman. Brown hair, brown eyes, and bronze skin. I recognized him now. He wasn't anybody I knew, but his face was probably one that I'd walked past a hundred times in the halls of KOP station. The gene eaters had really done a job on him. The gray pumpkin head I'd seen on the barge bore absolutely no resemblance to the smiling face on the screen. I read the scrolling headline, "Cop Crushed by Corroded Crane." Not a bad lie. It sounded plausible. Shit was always falling off those barges, and this way they wouldn't have to show anybody his gene-eaten corpse. They could just say he got pancaked beyond recognition. The press would drop it in a day or two, and the KOP brass wouldn't have to admit their ineptitude in failing to catch an offworld serial killer with a baker's dozen to his name.

I spiked the coffee with a splash from my flask, trying to soothe away that sick feeling I'd had in my gut ever since Niki's "accident." I thought of her watching Ian pinch off her air. My first instinct told me I should kill Ian. Eliminate the threat. What held me back was the knowledge that Ian was part of something bigger. I'd seen all those cops at Roby's last night. Some of them were the same ones that had joined in with Ian on that beatdown he laid on that sap cameraman. Ian was part of a cop clique, likely the leader. You couldn't take on one without taking on them all. I knew that better than anyone. I ran the biggest, baddest cop clique in KOP history for chrissakes.

I thought about the deal I'd made with Ian. The good news was Ian thought I actually wanted to be rid of Niki. If she only knew how that one backfired on her. She'd only made herself safer. If I'd known that he'd threatened her, I never would've asked for payment. As it was, Ian thought he had nothing to gain by killing her, and I'd be doing my best to keep him thinking exactly that. Things were going to get ugly. I had no illusions about getting involved with Ian. I knew Ian's type. Shit, I'd *been* his type. Once you got in with him, there was no getting out.

The eggs arrived, and I forced myself to choke them down despite the rebellion put up by my stomach.

I looked out the window. The sky was starting to brighten with the dawn. I could see the hospital from here. How could she do that to me? Maybe I shouldn't have saved her when she took her swan dive. Maybe I should've just let her die. That was what she wanted. That was what she told anybody who would listen. She had the shrinks convinced. Three separate ones came to me, each of them telling me she had the right to refuse medical treatment. It took all my powers of persuasion to bring them around to my way of thinking, a little cash flashing here, a little knuckle cracking there. It was hard enough getting her medical needs met; I didn't need a legal battle, too.

But why did she have to fight me like that? If that was the

way she was going to be, maybe I should just give Niki her wish, let them yank the plug and wash my hands of it altogether.

My eggs wanted to come back up. I sucked some coffee down hoping it might settle my stomach. Stop thinking like that, I told myself. I couldn't let them pull the plug. I couldn't lose her. This was Niki we were talking about. There was still hope for us. I was certain of it. Broken and battered as the two of us were, I knew we still had a future. We were meant to be together.

And there was no fucking way in hell I was going to let some punk wannabe enforcer take her from me.

I called Maggie, told her we needed to meet.

nine

THE smell of acid burned my nose. I moved around to the up-
wind side of the fountain and watched the small team of city
workers scrub the upper reaches of the statue from precarious
scaffolds surrounding the four intertwined iguanas. The iguanas were sculpted to look like they'd climbed each other's bodies until the whole lot of them had lifted themselves off the
ground. They were held up by their tails, which braided down
and disappeared under a pool of black water at the fountain's
base. The top halves of their bodies were stripped down to
bare stone as the city workers had already scoured away the
layers of molds and mosses. Their lower halves were still
coated with furry growth that looked like wooly pants.

I saw Maggie approach from the far side of the fountain
sporting designer duds and rain-speckled hair. The knot in my
stomach started twisting at the thought of having to fess up.

"My god, what happened?" were the first words that came
out of her mouth when she spotted my mummified hand.

"Did you get yourself scanned?"

"I'm clean."

"Good."

I had to be sure I wasn't bugged, so I'd gone down to an offworld tech shop to get myself checked out, and came up bug
free. It made me sick how much money the scan cost. If I had
to keep spending like this, I'd have no chance of making my
next payment. After breakfast, I'd called up to the Orbital and

asked what would happen if I missed a payment. They said that they'd keep the spine tanked for as long as it took for me to pay in full; only then would the bastards ship it down to the surface. I argued for half an hour, trying to convince them that they should ship the spine as soon as implantation was medically possible, but they held firm, telling me that their policy was to keep possession of all parts until receiving payment in full. The best they could do was to waive the additional daily tank storage fees until I paid up. The possibility of Niki lying there while there was a perfectly good spine ready for implantation made me sick. She deserved better than that. I *had* to make those payments.

"Did you break something?" she asked.

"Actually, it was Ian that did the breaking. He found out about me meeting the girl. He and Hoshi met me outside the Zoo."

Maggie's face turned angry. "How did he know?"

"One of the guards at the Zoo called him, one of his old buddies." It had been a long time since Ian had worked at the Zoo, but he obviously still had at least one supersized contact there. I could just picture Ian talking to the guard: "Anybody comes to see the girl, you call me right away. Got it, *boy-o*?"

"Oh damn," she said. "I'm sorry, Juno. I should've warned you that he used to work there."

"Don't worry about it. I knew he used to be a guard, too. His father used to brag about it all the time. But that was years ago. Neither of us had any reason to believe that he'd be tracking visitors."

Maggie nodded, her face tight.

This would be the tough part. I just had to spit it out. "I lied to you, Maggie, about Adela."

"What about her?"

"I didn't get a confession out of her. In fact, she was quite insistent that she didn't do it."

Maggie brushed it off. "That's okay, Juno. I understand."
And then she looked at my hand.

I wasn't going to let myself get off that easy. "It's not that. I
didn't lie because Ian broke a couple fingers. I . . ." I struggled
to find the right way to say it. "I needed the money. I thought if
I just told you that the girl confessed, I could get you to pay up
fast."

Maggie dismissed the whole thing, "Money doesn't mean
anything."

Only a rich person would say something like that. I was getting frustrated at how painless she was making this. I'd been
ready to spill to her about Niki, about how I couldn't afford the
payments, about how desperate I was to get her out of the hospital. I needed to make Maggie understand why I'd lied to her. I
needed to tell her. Yet I stood there, in the drizzle, unable to find
words, her quick forgiveness catching me totally off guard.

Maggie took my good hand in hers. "I understand, Juno. It's
okay."

"But—"

"I understand," she repeated.

I blinked rainwater out of my eyes and began to see that she
understood far more than I'd thought. She'd probably already
guessed that I'd lied about the girl, maybe picking up something in my voice when I'd tried to bullshit her. She was making it clear that she didn't care. She knew about Niki's accident
and knew the kind of financial pinch I was in. She wasn't going
to make me debase myself by saying it.

I squeezed her hands back. "Thanks, Maggie."

"Now, is there anything else?"

I filled her in on my late-night rendezvous with Ian, telling
her first about Liz and the offworlder, and then about how Ian
threatened Niki's life, and finally the deal he offered. I left out
the part about Niki not telling me.

Maggie listened to the whole story without saying a word until I was done. "So where do we go from here?"

"I don't think it's wise to kill him until we know more about the rest of his cop clique and what it is they're into."

"Christ, Juno." She was shaking her head. "We're not going to kill him. Killing him won't give us the evidence we need to exonerate Adela Juarez. She's going to die if we don't get evidence that'll free her. Besides, killing isn't what you're about anymore."

I didn't think I was "about" anything. But whatever it was that I was "about" I was pretty sure it didn't live up to Maggie's image of me. Ever since we'd worked the Vlotsky murder together, she'd gotten the notion that I'd turned a new leaf. I liked to think she was right. That I was still capable of good deeds and selfless acts. And when it came to that one case, maybe I *had* done some good.

"We have a chance to do something important here," said Maggie. "If we do this right, we can save an innocent girl and get some dirty cops out of KOP."

I nodded my head even though I wasn't so sure about Adela being innocent. I couldn't shake the first impression I'd had of her as I'd watched the interrogation vid. There was no way I could've misread her eyes. I'd spent most of my adult life looking into those same eyes. In my mind, Adela was still the one with the lase-whip in her hand.

"We together on this?" Maggie asked, her jaw set, her eyes fixed.

She had such purpose for someone so young, such drive. It was hard to understand where it came from, this unyielding determination to clean up KOP. I suspected it had something to do with her father's murder. I'd have to ask her one day, but not today. Today, I let her strength soak into me, my spine firming, the knot in my stomach uncoiling.

"We're together one hundred percent," I said. "It's you and me against the world."

Maggie walked in after a short stint at the office.

"Did you place it?"

"Yeah," Maggie said. "I pretended to shoo a fly off his head and dropped it in his hair."

"Good. Let's see what we're getting."

I made short one-handed work of setting up the recording equipment on the hotel bed. I'd spent the afternoon avoiding the hospital by getting the stakeout ready, picking a room in a high-rise but low-profile hotel, sneaking up to the roof and finding a primo spot for the receiver, placing it behind the aircon vents. You couldn't see it from the stairs, but it still had good line of sight to a relay tower. The reception would be good even in the rain. I checked to make sure that the unit was receiving a signal, then aimed the projection unit at the wall and flicked it on. The wall lit up with a view of the street that bobbed with Ian's footfalls. I found the volume control and turned it up just as Ian entered a shoe store.

"Well done, Maggie."

Maggie smiled. "That shoe store is just down the street from KOP station."

"He must've just left the office."

"You were right about the cam. The image quality's not bad."

After our meeting, Maggie and I had bought the cam from an offworld tech shop whose outrageous prices were indicative of the fact that the shop catered almost exclusively to offworld tourists. The offworld owner tried to talk us into a higher end unit, but I convinced Maggie that we didn't need to spend the extra coin, even though she was the one paying. Since the medical bills started rolling in, I'd become as frugal as my mother.

Besides, this unit had everything we needed. Even though it was the cheaper model, the unit still cost Maggie close to six month's worth of KOP paychecks. The flea-sized cam was designed to crawl through the hair and make its way to the hairline where it would attach itself to the scalp, a lot like the biomon I'd dropped into Niki's hair, except this one was even smart enough to match its shell to Ian's hair color.

Ian was going through the women's shoes, picking them off the wall and turning them over, looking at prices, stopping when he found the most expensive. He held the shoe up for the owner, who hustled into the back room.

Maggie tilted her chair back, putting her feet up on the bed. "What did you think of Adela when you met her?"

"She acted like a scared little girl."

"Acted? You don't still think she killed her parents, do you?"

"I do."

Maggie was incredulous. "How can you possibly think she did it?"

"I watched her confession. It looked genuine to me."

"If she really did it, then why would Ian be so sensitive about you interviewing her?"

"I don't know. Listen, I don't know if she did it or not; I'm just saying I believed her confession. She didn't admit to being abused, but I think that's what happened."

Maggie went from incredulous to annoyed. "Since when did you become such an expert at identifying abuse?"

And now I was getting a little annoyed myself. "Hey, you asked me what I thought, and I told you."

The conversation ended there.

Ian paid cash for the shoes and hit the street. Heavy rain blurred the image coming from the cam as Ian approached Surf, the seafood place with a fishnet over the door. He strode through the door and into the restaurant. Waitresses were busy folding napkins and setting tables. He snatched up a towel and dried his hair, making the camera view go black for a few seconds. He tossed the towel in a hamper and walked across the floor and into the kitchen, which was alive with the sounds of prep cooks chopping squid and lizard. Fresh spices hung from the ceiling; bundles of green leaves dangled down. Ian stopped and sampled the soup bubbling in a large pot over a roaring flame. He pulled off a couple leaves from a bundle of spice and dropped them in before moving on to the back stairs, sprinting up and knocking on a door at the top.

The door swung open a few seconds later. Liz had a robe tied loosely on, and her hair was up in curlers. The camera moved in close as the two exchanged a kiss. Ian held out the shoe box.

"You shouldn't have," said Liz as she took the lid off. "Oh, Ian, these are wonderful."

"I thought you'd like them. You have to try them on."

She sat down in the living room. Ian's view focused in on her partially open robe, taking a good long look at a half-exposed breast before dropping to his knees. She lifted her left foot, her robe parting, exposing her thighs all the way up to where they came together in shadow.

I could feel my pulse pounding as I watched Ian slip the shoe over her foot. He fiddled with the strap, running it around her ankle, his hands playing up her calf. She switched feet and Ian took his time putting on the other shoe, petting and stroking her toes and her ankle and then finally her calf. She stood up, her robe falling back into place over her legs, hiding all but her feet. Liz walked back and forth, stopping every couple steps to look down at her feet. "I love them," she said. "Thank you."

She threw her arms around Ian and moved in for a long kiss, the camera showing nothing but the corner of one of her curlers for a moment before Liz ran off to her bedroom, coming back a minute later with a handful of stockings. "You have to tell me which stockings match the best," she said to Ian.

Maggie asked me, "You up for room service?"

I looked at the time, thinking I should go to the hospital. Then I looked at Liz, who was pulling on a pair of fishnets. "Is there a menu in here somewhere?"

I swallowed the last bite of a very bland 'guana sandwich, typical hotel fare.

"He's waiting for somebody."

I nodded. At Ian's table were two place settings besides his own.

From the vantage of Ian's scalp, we could see most of the restaurant. He'd left Liz's place shortly after the fashion show, saying he had some business to attend to. He told her he'd see her later at Roby's.

I was starting to feel sleepy. I wondered if Maggie would mind if I took a nap. It could be hours, maybe days before we caught him doing anything, but then I decided I might as well try sticking it out until I saw who his dinner mates would be.

Ian ordered a drink and flipped through the menu. The restaurant was one of those touristy places on the Old Town Square. Its walls were covered with hand-painted jungle scenes that featured masses of thick greenery with lizards on every perch, each of them lit by magical beams of sunlight that twinkled through holes in the jungle canopy. It was the kind of thing that Lagartans would call classy, but offworlders would probably find tacky. Lagartans were always missing the mark when they tried to attract tourists.

The vodka arrived, and I watched as Ian brought the glass up to his lips. My mouth watered, but I resisted the urge to pull out my flask. I didn't want Maggie thinking poorly of me. Ian set an empty glass back on the table.

The view from the Ian-cam swung to the door, and in came a heavier-than-average man who waved at Ian. The guy looked familiar despite the fact that he had a painful-looking double shiner marring his face. I was already wracking my brain, trying to remember who he was as he took a seat across from Ian. "How's it going, Ian?"

Ian said, "Not bad, boy-o. How's your fucking face?"

The man shrugged and aimed his black eyes at the floor. The guy looked like shit, and it wasn't just the black eyes. It was the rumpled clothes, the dumpy body, the nervous face.

"Don't be a pussy," said Ian. "It'll heal."

"I know," he said. "But you didn't have to hit me that hard."

Holy shit. Did I hear that right? Ian was the one who gave him the coon face? Recognition overwhelmed me, the pear shaped bod, that same crappy shirt. What the fuck was going on?

Ian said, "Christ, Yuri. I was just trying to make it look believable. It's your own damn fault. If you hadn't been so fucking sloppy, I wouldn't have had to lay you out like that."

"I know, I know. It was my fault," Yuri responded, spineless.

"Are you going to order a drink or what?"

"Yeah." Yuri held up a meaty hand. When the waiter showed, Yuri looked at Ian's empty glass and asked him, "What are you drinking?"

"Christ, just order whatever you want. What does it matter what I'm drinking?"

"I just thought that whatever you were having might sound good to me."

"It's not like we're fucking lovers who have to drink the same thing. Just order."

The waiter stood by with raised brows.

"B—brandy," Yuri said in a weak voice.

Ian looked at the waiter and said, "I'll have another." When the waiter moved off, the cam squared on Yuri and stayed there until Yuri made eye contact. Then the cam's view moved from side to side as Ian shook his head at him. Yuri wilted and stared at the floor again.

I tried, but couldn't make sense of why Ian was having dinner with the cameraman, the one from the Libre, the one Ian and his boys had roughed up on the pier. Ian had just told him he had to make it look good. He said Yuri hadn't done his job right. What job? The three little circles on the cabin floor, made by a tripod. The scope of the Juarez case exploded in my mind.

"Where's Horst?" asked Ian.

"I don't know," said Yuri. "He said he'd be here."

"You didn't tell him we were meeting at the bar in the basement did you?"

"No. I told him we were meeting at the restaurant, just like you said."

"Go check the bar."

"He's not going to the bar, Ian. Horst knows we're meeting here."

"Don't make me say it again."

Ian watched as Yuri meekly complied, the cameraman's pudgy frame disappearing down a staircase a few seconds later.

Horst. He was the offworlder at Roby's, the one who was all hands with Liz. And he was coming to the restaurant. That wasn't good. I forced my scattering mind to focus in on the problem at hand. An offworlder's head was sure to be riddled with implanted tech. He'd be detecting our camera as soon as he got in range. "Shit." I placed the call. I could hear the ringing in my ear at the same time it was echoing from the projector. "Turn off the volume," I told Maggie.

Ian ignored the ringing and looked at the door. "About time," he said to himself. Just inside the door was the offworlder, waiting to check his raincoat and umbrella. *Pick up already.* Ian finally answered, his buff holo appearing in front of Maggie and me.

Maggie was up out of her chair, staring me down. I put up a finger to say, "Wait."

"Ian. It's Juno. We need to talk. Now."

"Okay, boy-o. What's up?" The camera on his head was aimed straight at the Holo-Juno that stood next to his table.

"You've been bugged." I said.

Maggie went wide-eyed.

Ian said, "What are you talking about?"

"You're in a restaurant with jungle paintings, and you were just sitting across from a guy with a bruised face. I can see everything."

"Where are you?" The camera view wheeled dizzyingly around the restaurant floor. The offworlder was approaching.

"Are you listening? You've been bugged. You remember Maggie shooing a fly away? She dropped a bug in your hair. I'm looking through the cam right now."

"You're shitting me."

"Ask the offworlder. He might be able to detect it." I clicked off. My guess was the offworlder had already picked it up. Those people seemed to have more circuitry under their skull-caps than they did brains. Maggie's cam was surely lost, and this whole stakeout setup was already shot—might as well take the opportunity to prove my snitch skills.

Ian led Horst into the men's. We caught a super-close-up of the offworlder a second before he picked the cam out of Ian's hair and the projector went blank.

Within seconds, my phone was ringing. Holo-Ian asked, "Where the fuck did she get this thing?"

"She's rich, remember? She said she picked it up from an off-world shop."

"Are you saying she's been watching me?"

"We've been watching you together, ever since you left KOP station. She just ran out to get some food when I called you. It was the first chance I got. Listen, Ian, I gotta go. I need to finish erasing our conversation from the recording before she gets back. She's going to be suspicious as hell. I don't know how long I'll be able to keep her trusting me."

"I'm not done with you, boy-o. Come to Roby's tonight," he ordered before hanging up.

Maggie was staring at me.

"Sorry about the cam," I said. "The offworlder would've found it anyway."

"You don't know that for sure. That unit was pretty high-end."

"Never underestimate an offworlder," I said with the authority of somebody who had been burned before.

Maggie sighed. "We got nothing."

"We got plenty, Maggie." I paused, prolonging the moment long enough to give proper emphasis to what I was about to say. "That guy with the bruised face, he was at the barge the other night. The unis caught him trying to sneak onboard to steal some footage. Josephs told me he was a cameraman for the Libre. I watched him get his ass kicked by Ian and company right there on the pier, and now we just heard Ian say something about how he'd been sloppy—"

"What are you saying?" she asked with a shocked face. "Are you saying Ian's involved in the barge murders?"

I nodded, my mind crackling with the possibilities. The plot was already forming in my mind. Horst: the offworld serial killer. Yuri: the documentarian. And Ian: the cover-up man. The three of them having dinner together: maybe a celebration dinner, or maybe they were getting together so Horst could pay them their fees.

Maggie's face knotted into a tight mask of concentration as she worked through the same possibilities. "That would explain why Ian's so determined to work the barge case."

"That it would," I said, stone sober. I was amazed at how quickly Maggie recovered from the bombshell. Here she just found out that her partner was likely involved in thirteen more murders than she'd thought, and already her mind was back in high gear. My worldview must have rubbed off on her more than I thought. She was finding it all too easy to believe the worst in people. That, or her opinion of Ian was so low that even thirteen murders weren't far beyond the reach of what she thought he was capable of.

"And you think Yuri is our filmmaking accomplice?" she asked.

I was already nodding before she finished the question.

"He must have vids of all the murders," she said.

I suddenly remembered to ask, "Hey, did you ever watch that vid, the one the rook found on the pier?"

"It was blank."

"Erased?"

"No. It was blank, never been used. Ian thought some tourist probably went down to take some shots of the old barges and then lost it in the weeds trying to change discs."

It sounded plausible, but I didn't believe it, and I could see in Maggie's eyes that she didn't believe it either. A tourist visiting the pier? The barges were hardly a top tourist attraction. And at this time of year? Way too rainy. I was shaking my head.

"He's full of shit," Maggie said hotly.

"Was the vid molded over?"

"No. Just wet." Which meant the vid hadn't been exposed to the rain for long, a couple days at most.

"So unless an offworld tourist went down there recently to film those rusted-out hulks in the rain, it was the cameraman who dropped the vid."

"And if that's the case, Ian was dead on about him being

sloppy. The cameraman must've realized he'd muffed it so he came back and tried to sneak onto the pier to retrieve it." Maggie's cheeks were flushed, and the smile on her face made her look like an animal baring its teeth. She had a lead, her first in a case she'd worked for months, and it led straight to her partner.

I took a hit off my flask and held it out for Maggie. I wondered how long I'd had the flask out.

She put up a no-thanks palm. "But why bother coming back if the vid was blank?"

My mind tangled up into a tight little knot. I thought about it for a minute and said, "I don't know."

"Maybe he was afraid we'd find prints."

"Did you?"

"No. It was clean. I don't get it. He had to know it was impossible to sneak around that pier without getting caught. There was a dead cop on that barge. A whole squad was crawling around down there. Why take the risk?"

"Like you said. Maybe he was afraid he'd left his prints on it. Maybe he didn't know it was clean."

Maggie gnawed on her lower lip, totally unsatisfied by the explanation. "It still doesn't make sense. Say we *did* find his prints on the vid. He could've beaten any wrap we tried to pin on him. There's probably a thousand ways he could explain it away. Especially if he really works for the Libre. He could say he lost it some other time. Who knows how many stories he's covered down on that pier? It's not like we found the vid in the cabin, or even on the barge."

Maggie's words barely echoed in my head. I felt like there was a doubled-up rubber band squeezing down on my brain. Why did Ian make such a show of knocking the guy around? Why not just have the unis escort him off the pier? But instead, he made a big production out of it, all under the guise that he was trying to keep the case from going public. Why? The answer was close, so close. . . . But I couldn't pin it down. I felt like I was trying to grab hold of smoke.

Maggie kept the theories coming. "What if he didn't know it was blank? Maybe the camera broke down on him without him realizing it, and he thought he had filmed the murder, but he really missed the whole thing. Or maybe he just got the blank vid mixed up with the real vid of the beheading. If he thought he'd dropped the beheading vid, he'd have plenty of reason to come back for it, even if it was the wrong one."

I took another swig of brandy and tried to tune her out. Her words were clogging up my thoughts. I closed my eyes and tried to relax away the clutter in my head. Fragmented ideas rattled around my skull. Maggie was still talking, her voice seeping into my consciousness. She was saying something about how it was just our luck that he dropped the blank vid instead of the real one.

It clicked. Instant understanding surged through my head like a drug. "Are we dumb? That son of a bitch," I mumbled.

"Who?"

"Ian."

ten

I TIGHTENED the slicker's hood then tilted my head forward and ran the water off in little streams. I needed to keep dry—couldn't afford to track water all over. I watched Maggie hustle through the drumming rain, stop on the porch, and knock on the door. Within seconds, she was inside.

I wished we could've done this when Yuri wasn't home, but the house had barred windows and dead-bolted doors. We wanted to get in and out with nobody knowing, and there was no way to break into that place without leaving some serious damage behind. Maggie wanted to do it official, warrant and all, but there was no chance. Our chain of evidence was so weak as to be nonexistent—a decorated police officer, an off-worlder, and a cameraman had dinner together, therefore they killed thirteen people and a cop. The judge would be liable to hold you in contempt just for wasting his time.

Ian was a smooth bastard. His transformation from candy-ass to badass boggled my mind. And he had a brain, which made him all the more dangerous.

He'd done some quick thinking on that pier. His videographer screwed up royally. After he shot his little snuff film, he probably had to clear his fat ass out of there in a hurry—there was a cop snooping around that barge. I could see the cameraman pumping his flabby legs in the dark, trying to carry all his equipment. He'd have a tripod in one hand and maybe a lens in the other, cameras and lights strung over his shoulders. I could picture the shoulder straps sliding off because he didn't have the kind of shoulders you could hook something on. There were no right angles on that body, just slopes and curves. He'd be running along, with his arms pinned to his sides to keep from dropping the gear that had already fallen from his shoulders down to his elbows. He'd be like an overloaded burro spooked by a thunderclap, galloping along with shit bouncing all over the damn place. He wouldn't have noticed the vid jarring free from one of his bags, or squeezing out of a pocket. The guy probably made it all the way home before he noticed he'd lost it.

Yuri came back for his vid, desperate to get it back, but by the time he got back to the pier, he found the place overrun with cops. He risked sneaking onto the pier anyway, bringing a camera with him, figuring that if he got caught, he could claim he was trying to get footage for his job.

And there was Ian, with the snuff film already in his shirt pocket courtesy of that young rookie cop who had found it in the weeds. Ian knew what it was, and he knew he needed to get rid of it before he and Maggie had their viewing. When he saw some uniforms with Yuri Kiper in tow, he thought quick. He played the tough guy and brought the hammer down on Yuri, acting like he was trying to keep the press out of KOP biz. He slapped the guy around and pulled a blank vid from his camera. Then a quick switch, and he hurled the real vid out into the Koba.

I gave it another minute before I came out from behind the shrub and tromped through Yuri Kiper's jungle scrub yard. I flattened myself against the side of his house and peeked through the window. Maggie was right where I expected her, in the sitting room, facing the entryway. The cameraman had his back to me. There'd be no problem getting through the front door, but his seat gave him a perfect view of the sitting room doorway. I'd have to walk past that doorway in order to make it to the back of the house. I'd be in plain sight. I didn't let myself worry about it. Maggie would think of something.

I moved along the wall and stepped up onto the porch. I slipped out of my shoes and then tangled with the slicker, finally managing to yank my splinted hand through the sleeve. I rolled my shoes up inside the slicker and set the whole pile on the ground alongside the porch. The door was cracked. How Maggie had pulled that off I wasn't sure, but I pushed my way through. I slid over the floor in my bare feet and edged up to the sitting room doorway.

I could hear Maggie's voice clearly now. "And how long have you been with the Libre?"

"Almost fifteen years, but I was just a gofer for the first couple," he responded.

"How did you learn to operate a camera? Did you go to school?"

"No. I just picked it up helping the other camera guys." I could picture him shrugging as he spoke.

"Do you work with the same reporter all the time?"

"No. When a story comes up, they assign whichever one of us is available. Why?"

"I was wondering how it was that you showed up on the pier the other night."

"I guess it was my turn."

"Who was the reporter?"

"Hoeg. Julia Hoeg."

"I didn't see her there."

"She was late, so I started shooting without her. That was when one of your cohorts saw me and kicked me off the pier."

"You mean that literally?"

He didn't answer.

"Tell me what happened to your face."

"Nothing. It was an accident."

"If an officer is responsible, you can file a complaint with KOP, you know." She was softballing him. She'd be turning up the heat soon.

"I don't want any trouble."

"Can I take a closer look at your face?"

"If you want."

"Come over here so I can see in the light. . . . Okay, now hold still."

I made a barefooted scamper past the open doorway, not bothering to look. I scurried through the kitchen and past a bathroom, then stopped at a bedroom that had been converted into an office. The room hummed with computer equipment that covered two walls. I couldn't hear Yuri and Maggie anymore, which was good. It meant they couldn't hear me either.

I didn't waste any time. I snatched up a tripod and studied its round feet, looking for bloodstains. I gave them a squirt of Luminol and turned off the lights, looking for the telltale blue glow of blood. Nope. I grabbed for another tripod but stopped when I saw that its feet were square. No other tripods. Damn.

I ejected the disc from a vid camera on the floor and held it up for my portable to make a bit-level copy of the data by beaming the ones and zeroes to a data chip in my pocket. Noises in the kitchen made me uneasy, but I kept working, knowing that Maggie was probably just stalling by getting him to make her some tea. I found three more cameras and repeated the process, each copy taking a nerve-wracking two minutes. I hoped Maggie had a lot to say.

I moved to his desk and pulled open the top left drawer, scoring nothing but a jumble of office supplies. I found more of the same in the next two drawers and then hit pay dirt on the bottom right. The drawer was full of vids lined up in neat rows. I scanned through the labels finding a complete row of station promos and next to it, a row of wedding vids. I ran my

finger from innocuous label to innocuous label, disappointed
even though I knew it had been way too much to expect that I
might find any vids labeled "Barge Murders." He'd have to be
an idiot to keep vids like that in his office. Even so, until now,
I'd been holding out hope that he was indeed a bona fide idiot.

I heard more footsteps in the kitchen and tried to ignore
them. *No wait. They're coming this way.* I spun around in the
desk chair just as the door opened. *SHIT!* In came somebody
slender, definitely not Yuri Kiper. He startled upon seeing me.
"Damn, man! You scared me."

I was frozen in my seat.

"They didn't tell me there was anyone back here," he said.

I recognized him from Adela's case files. Raj Gupta, ex-
boyfriend of our death-row dish. I forced my dry mouth into
action. "What the fuck are you doing here, kid? This is official
police business." I pulled my shoeless feet back under the chair,
hopefully out of sight.

"Hey, sorry, man. I just came to pick up a lens. Yuri always
forgets and brings it home. He and that cop lady didn't tell me
you were back here. Otherwise, I would've knocked."

"You work with Yuri?"

"Yeah. I work at Lagarto Libre. I'm an intern."

More connections fired in my mind. "Do you see the lens
you need?"

"Yeah, this is it right here." He picked it up from a bookshelf
then looked at me with his eyebrows up, waiting for permis-
sion to leave. Raj was a good-looking kid, dark hair, bright
smile, confident air. . . .

"You can go," I said. "But don't disturb them up front, you
got me? This is official police business. You just walk straight
out. Got it?"

"Yes, sir. I'll be on my way then." Raj walked out, closing
the door behind him.

I tried to swallow the lump in my throat. *Fuck me!* I stared at the closed door expecting a raging Yuri Kiper to come storming in any moment. *C'mon kid, just leave. Don't stop to chitchat. Just go.* With every uneventful second, my heart pounded a little softer and a little slower. Kid must've done what I said. Yuri Kiper was none the wiser—at least for now. I turned back to the drawer and tried to focus on the vid labels, skimming through them until one finally jumped out at me, its title: "Liz—Complete Works." I pulled it and sweated out the two minutes of copy time before putting it back in the drawer.

I shut the drawers and took one last look at the room to make sure everything was back in place. Looked good to me. I moved out into the hall and from there into the kitchen. I needed another distraction to help me get past the sitting room doorway. I placed a holo-free call to Maggie, then as we agreed, I hung up as soon as she answered. I tiptoed to the doorway and listened to the tail end of Maggie's fake phone conversation. "Yes, Mom," she said. "I'll be by after work, okay?" Then after a short pause, " 'Bye."

"Sorry about that, Yuri," she said. "Were you about to say something?"

"No."

"Listen to me, Yuri." The tone in Maggie's voice said it was definitely hardball time. "I know you and Ian have something going. I *saw* you having dinner with him." Maggie was pacing. I could hear her shoes clacking loudly on the floor with her overemphasized steps. "Ian told you that you were sloppy. Sloppy how?"

Yuri played dumb. "I don't know what you're talking about. That cop beat me up for doing my job. You should be grilling him, not me."

"Cut the shit, asshole." Maggie was full into it now. "The Libre didn't send you out to that barge. I talked to your reporter friend. She said she never got a call that night."

"She's lying." Yuri was sounding whiny.

"Why would she lie?"

"She never showed up. She's just acting like she didn't get the call so she doesn't get in trouble with management. These reporters don't like getting their hair wet."

Maggie's pacing stopped. "You expect me to believe that?"

"It's the truth," he said, quiver-voiced.

"I want to know why you were snooping around that barge. I want to know what kind of shit you and my partner are into. I want to know about the offworlder. You're going to tell me, Yuri, or I'll be back here with a warrant."

"But I didn't *do* anything."

"Liar!" The sound of shattering glass burst from the sitting room. I seized my opportunity and scrammed out the front.

I arrived at Maggie's first and sat on her front stoop, rain sleeting off the slicker. We Lagartans didn't use these things often, rain gear was for tourists. We'd rather tough it out than look like offworlders. Not that it was that tough. Even during the long stretch of winter, when our polar location hid us from the sun and left us in total darkness for twenty-two hours a day, even then, this place stayed balmy.

Maggie came up the walk wearing a conspiratorial grin. "Did you get anything good?"

"Don't know yet."

Maggie walked up to the door, which swung open for her DNA. I followed her through, my sopping shoes leaving little pools of water on the tile floor. Maggie snatched up a couple towels, tossed one my way. I stripped off the slicker, this time making sure I carefully slipped the sleeve over my splinting so as not to get knotted up again.

Maggie excused herself, and I settled in her living room, an almost cavernous room with monitor hide furniture and spot-less white carpeting. I wondered how much she must pay to keep this carpet mold free. Her family was loaded, descen-dents of plantation owners who made their fortune on the long since defunct brandy trade.

Maggie stepped in, wearing a fresh set of clothes and bear-ing a couple glasses of what was sure to be a rare family vin-tage. I took a deep swig, swishing the brandy in my mouth, savoring the flavor before swallowing it down.

"You scared him pretty good," I said.

"I wish you could've seen him when I smashed my tea glass. He was shaking, he was so scared."

"Did he say anything useful?"

"No. He held firm to his story, flimsy as it was."

"Ian's going to be fuming when he hears."

"Good."

I nodded, though I thought it likely that Ian had been ex-pecting Maggie to confront the cameraman. He knew that Maggie had seen him with Yuri and the offworlder. I wouldn't have been surprised if Ian had spent time coaching Yuri, preparing him for Maggie's interrogation.

"Shall we see what we got?"

We made quick business of going through the copied vids, frustrated by the results. Nothing but a series of vids shot for his job, interviews with local pols, footage of social events, countless hours' worth of humdrum garbage. The only thing that showed any promise was the last vid I'd copied, the one ti-tled "Liz—Complete Works," but all five vid files were pro-tected by an encryption scheme.

Maggie logged into the KOP systems and downloaded the latest encryption crackers and then started them up, checking each cracker's time estimates. "Damn," she said as she tossed a holographic timer my way. I reflexively reached for it, surprised when I succeeded in batting it down. Maggie must've had one seriously top-notch system to be smart enough to alter the hologram's trajectory when my hand blocked its path. A cheaper system would've just passed the holo through my hand. I mimed picking up the timer as if it were real, the timer's image moving along with my hands. I looked at the estimated completion date: December 18, 2790.

In hopes of cutting down the decryption time, Maggie tried offloading some of the processing work from her home system to the KOP databank servers. I held up the holo-timer for her to see, the new date: June 32, 2790. Not a whole lot better.

"This isn't going to work," Maggie said. "We're going to need some serious processing power." To the computer, she said, "Stop processing."

I watched the timer vanish from my hands. "Any other ideas?"

"Yeah. Let me see what services are offered on the Orbital."

Maggie got busy researching our options. I called Vlad, who assured me that nobody'd been by to visit Niki. He told me he was going to get sleepy soon and asked if it was okay for him to bring in his cousin Victor for the overnight shift.

"Is he trustworthy?" I asked.

"Like a brother," he said.

"Fine. Do it."

I decided not to call Niki. Let her fucking stew.

I sucked down the last drops of my brandy, thinking another sounded good, real good. I set off for the kitchen, hunting for that bottle. Maggie made it easy for me by leaving the bottle on the counter. I poured a full glass, took a couple long swigs, then topped my glass back off. I read the bottle's label:

ORZO

OAK AGED
2764

Damn. This was some good hooch. I decided I'd really take my time with this glass, try to enjoy it.

By the time I made it back into the living room, Maggie had it all worked out. There was an offworld company that could crack the vid files in under thirty hours. Maggie explained that they had a satellite network with a couple thousand sats, each one with far more processing power than it needed to do its job. They made a habit of selling off the excess processing time when they could find a buyer. For a job this big, they said they could dedicate a couple processors from each of the sats to cracking the encryption scheme.

"Sounds good. How much?"

Maggie showed me the numbers.

I was surprised at how low the numbers were. "That's cheaper than I thought it'd be."

"Are you serious?"

"Yeah. I thought it'd be at least twice that."

Maggie looked at me quizzically until it dawned on her. "The prices are in offworld dollars, Juno."

"Holy shit." I tried to do the math, multiply by two hundred and add ten percent . . . "Holy shit, Maggie. You can't afford that."

"My mother can."

I shook my head. Maggie and her mother butted heads all the time. First and foremost on the list was the fact that Mrs. Orzo didn't like her daughter being a cop. "You hate that woman."

"Not entirely. You have a better idea?"

I stole a look at my watch. It was almost midnight. Time to meet Ian at Roby's. "Yeah," I said.

eleven

ROBY'S gladiator-bouncer recognized me and opened the door as I approached. Just inside, a waitress offered me a towel, which I declined. I was liable to break into a nervous sweat at any minute, and my rain-soaked face and hair would do a nice job masking it.

Into the main room, the first thing that hit me was the drumming, slow and methodical. Over the beat, a violin whined in a spooky key. The tables were jam-packed, and people were standing along the walls, all of them watching the stage show that featured a man in a hooded black robe wielding a lase-bladed axe. *Fucking A. There's the murder weapon, right there.* That or one like it. On the chopping block was a lamb, held down by a pair of blood-spattered girls wearing virginal white. The drumming was getting more insistent as the executioner circled the lamb. Every couple steps, he'd stop and wave the axe back and forth over the lamb, letting the laser light from the axe's edge tint the lamb's wool bloodred. I ran my eyes over the audience, the whole lot of them looking like they were about to cream their pants. *What a bunch of crap.* My guess was the "executioner" was really just the local butcher, and the girls were likely his daughters. The way I saw it, the whole family was probably making a fortune dressing up to do their everyday job in front of a bunch of sick-fuck offworlders.

I made for the side room. My stomach felt toxic. That kid, Raj, he'd seen me at the cameraman's. If he'd talked to Yuri

and said he'd seen me, Yuri would've gone to Ian and told him
that a cop with a bandaged hand was snooping through his
vids. And if that was the case, the gig was up. Ian would know
I was screwing him, taking his money and going double-agent
on him, reporting everything I knew to Maggie. This time,
there would be little reason to believe that Ian would stop at
my fingers.

I took the measure of the back room—cops all over the damn
place, with a few offworlders mixed in. Horst was there, our
mystery offworlder, sitting with Liz at the autopsy table, talking
to her over a holo-cadaver. I looked Horst over, his slicked back
hair, his porcelain skin, searching for signs of the serial killer
within. Liz spotted me and winked. I nodded in her direction
then crossed the room, looking for Ian. I found him with Hoshi
in a secluded booth. Upon seeing me approach, Ian put up a finger, telling me to give him a minute.

I stopped and looked around, trying to find a spot to wait,
and saw Liz get up out of her seat and pull out a chair for me.
She was dressed more conservatively tonight, black heels, black
hose, black skirt, and a white top. I didn't move. She waved her
hand, gesturing for me to come over. I shook my head and
cocked it in Ian's direction, letting her know I was waiting. She
pointed emphatically at the chair she'd prepared for me, and I
suddenly became very compliant.

I weaved through the tables, mentally making note of every
cop face I saw. There was Froelich, Kripsen, Deluski, Yang, Wu,
Lumbela . . . I catalogued every one of them, remembering
which ones I'd seen here the last time. I reached Liz's table and
sat down in the seat she'd prepared for me. I was sitting to Liz's
right, across from the offworlder.

He looked at me across the midsection of the bisected holo-
cadaver. "Good to see you, Mr. Mozambe," he said.

I gave him a half smile in response.

"I understand you and Ian have come to an arrangement."

"That's right."

"I'm glad to hear it. He says you could be useful."

I half smiled again, the two half smiles equaling far less than a whole one. He stared at me, waiting for me to say something, but I had nothing to say. Liz moved uncomfortably in her seat.

What the—? The holo-cadaver moved. I jumped back, almost falling over in my chair. Horst was laughing, as were the customers at the neighboring tables. The cadaver was pulling the stitches out of its chest. Its eyes were still closed, and it looked plenty dead except its hands were pulling the stitching free in one long strand. I moved from startled to embarrassed to pissed, only stopping on embarrassed for a fraction of a second. I glared at Horst as the people at the nearby tables, having had their fun at my expense, returned to their conversations. Horst was still laughing, loud bellowing laughs that were amplified far beyond anything natural. The corpse pulled its ribs wide like doors to a cupboard and started playing show-and-tell with its organs.

I looked at Liz, who had a be-a-sport expression on her face. I tried out a full smile to show I had recovered, but it probably came out more like a full grimace.

I tried to picture Horst as the barge serial. Seeing him gleefully grinning at me, across this flayed corpse, his skin a full shade paler than the cadaver's, with hair blacker than oil, and eyes blacker still . . . It wasn't hard to imagine, not at all.

The waitress arrived with a plate of spit-roasted 'guana, and the holo-corpse disappeared. She set the plate in front of Horst on the cold steel table.

"Ah, now that looks delicious," he said as he waved the steaming scent in toward his nose. He peered at me through the steam and must've caught some steam of a different kind coming off my face. "You're not upset are you? It was just a joke." He stabbed his fork into the 'guana's flank and twirled a piece of meat free. He dipped it into the spiced juices and offered it to me.

I shook my head.

He dipped again before putting it in his mouth. "I love Lagartan food. You can't get anything like it in space. You can get the same spices, and you can find iguana meat in the specialty stores, but it's never the same. I'm always raving about the food, but you bring somebody to a Lagartan restaurant up there, and they think you're crazy. Half of them can't stomach the idea of eating reptile. And the half who can are repulsed by the sight of these creatures. They don't look like Earth iguanas, they say. Sure, there are a few adventurous ones who are willing to take a taste, but most of them say it's nothing special. I try to tell them it's different down here. It's so fresh. I bet this iguana was alive only an hour ago. Up there, your meat probably gets frozen and unfrozen two or three times before you ever get to stick a fork in it."

I nodded like I cared. Most offworlders were repulsed by our cooking. They'd see a 'guana on a plate with the head still on, and they'd get all queasy. Horst was one of the rare ones who'd fallen in love with the food. Even then, he'd probably only done so because he got to eat in all the nice restaurants where they made an effort to make the cuisine offworld-compatible. The average Lagartan survived on an unappealing diet of unspiced fat and gristle over rice.

I felt a hand on my shoulder, and Hoshi leaned in, telling me Ian was ready for me.

I got up without another word. Liz smiled at me and Horst nodded as he pulled a piece of bread apart for dipping.

I headed for Ian's table. Already, I could feel my face flushing with nervousness. *Get a grip!* I took deep breaths through my nose as I reached the booth and dropped into Hoshi's vacated seat. "She went to see the cameraman," I said.

"So I heard." Ian had ice in his voice.

I leaned forward, my hands on the table. "She didn't get anything out of him, but the guy's a miserable liar. She doesn't believe a word he said."

Ian nodded. I couldn't get a read on him. I waited uneasily for him to say something. He sipped his brandy . . . then bit his lip . . . then ran his fingers through his hair. . . .

He knows. I angled my feet toward the door, ready to make a break for it.

"I'm disappointed in you," he said.

"What the fuck are you talking about?"

"I'm paying you to get that cunt off my ass, and I'm not getting any results."

"The hell you aren't. You'd still have a camera in your hair if it wasn't for me."

Ian snatched my hand, his fingers clamping onto my splints. I reflexively punched with my free hand, my fist glancing off the top of his head. My fingers screamed as I tried to pull my right hand free from his grip. I targeted my left again, aiming low, anticipating that he might duck. My broken fingers shrieked in agony as he squeezed down on them. I threw my punch, but he blocked it effectively by lifting and turning his shoulder into my fist's path. He started twisting my hand. My fingers mashed together, bones rubbing in exquisite pain. I tried to pull my hand free, but his grip didn't budge. The bastard was strong as hell. I wouldn't doubt if—in addition to shooting 'roids—he had some offworld tech installed under those biceps.

"Stop fighting me, boy-o."

I stopped, my eyes blinded with tears.

"You were supposed to tell her I was clean."

I tried to talk, but I'd gone mute, my mouth just opening

and closing guppy style. He loosened his grip a tad, letting me speak. I looked at the other tables—everybody purposely averted their stares, except for Horst. He was looking right at me, chewing his food, his flawless face alight with amusement.

Between heavy breaths, I said, "I did tell her you were clean. She didn't believe me."

"You're proving my point."

"What point?"

"That I'm not getting my money's worth."

"I can't talk like this. Fucking let go of my hand."

He did.

My eyes started to clear, and I could breathe again. I clutched my hand to my chest. Waves of pain ricocheted through my arm. "Listen to me, asshole, it was too late to try that Ian's-a-good-cop bullshit. Maggie knows you're dirty. She's been watching you for months. She wants that squad leader job, and she knows that she won't get it as long as you're around. She wants to bring you down, and she's not about to listen to me telling her that you're clean. Besides, me saying somebody's clean doesn't mean a whole hell of a lot to anybody who knows my history. I'm the fucking dirty cop poster boy."

Ian was listening to me, really listening. He didn't know I'd been at the cameraman's. If he did, he and his buds would've hustled me out the back exit by now, and I'd be on my knees, begging for mercy until they fried a hole through my temple. It hadn't occurred to him that I might stay loyal to Maggie. What did a punk like Ian know about loyalty? He thought I was just a mercenary, out for hire to the highest bidder. He thought that, for all those years, I'd been nothing more than a hired hand to Chief Chang.

Confidence surged through me, making the pain in my fingers a touch more bearable. I waved a waitress over. "Get me a bottle and a glass. I want a *glass*, you understand me? Don't bring me one of those stupid-ass goblets." She scurried off.

Ian stayed silent, a vein bulging on his forehead.

My hand was pulsing. "Fuck, that hurts."

That brought out a grin from Ian. "Tell me why I should keep paying you."

"Because we had a deal, that's why."

"The deal was that you were going to get Maggie out of my hair."

"I did." I pointed at his widow's peak, where the camera used to be.

He glared at me, not enjoying the joke at all.

The booze arrived and I sucked down a pair of double shots, eager for the anesthesia to take effect. "The best I can do, Ian, is keep you a step ahead of her. We do that long enough, and she'll eventually give up."

Ian was still looking very displeased.

I took another hit of brandy. "I'll be honest, Ian. There are things she won't tell me. She doesn't trust me entirely, but I *can* keep you out of her reach. You can't keep her from sniffing around. She's already onto your scent. But if you let me do my job, I can see to it she doesn't find anything. I'll be with her every step of the way, steering her away from your trail. She interviews somebody, I'm there turning the questioning around. She starts tracking something big, I ring you up so you can erase your tracks. I'm your fucking guardian angel."

"You expect me to believe that a washed-up enforcer can protect me?"

"I protected Chief Chang for over twenty years. And his enemies were a hell of a lot scarier than Maggie Orzo."

I had him. He was nodding his head, seeing my reasoning. "I want this problem to go away," he said.

"It will. It will. It's just going to take some time. Now are you going to pay me or what?"

Ian nodded and shrugged at the same time. "We'll keep our arrangement a little longer."

I gave him an annoyed stare until he actually called up his account and transferred the funds.

Satisfied, I said, "Good. And if you touch my hand again, I'll fucking kill you."

Ian laughed. "You're unbelievable, boy-o. You sure got a pair on you."

"I'm serious."

"Sure you are," he said, like he was talking to a child.

I did my best to ignore the sarcasm. "I got something for you," I said.

"What?"

"I was on Maggie's home system last night."

"How'd you manage that?"

"I've been doing this kind of thing for a long time," I answered without really answering. "Anyway, I found a set of files that have your name on them."

Ian became fully attentive. "What's in them?"

"I don't know. They're encrypted. It'll take months to break them using Lagartan crackers, but I found an offworld company that can crack them open in less than thirty hours. It's going to cost you, though."

"How much?"

"A lot."

"How do I know you're not just going to pocket my money?"

I handed him a slip of damp paper from my shirt pocket. "That's the company's name and an account number. I've already uploaded the files to them. You pay them directly, and they'll start the decryption process."

"What's this other number?"

"That's the price."

He raised his brows at me. "I can't afford that."

"I know, but I bet your offworld friend can."

He looked at me dubiously.

"Listen, Ian, Maggie's been compiling dirt on you for months. Based on the file sizes, my guess is those are vid files. That camera in your hair might not have been the first."

Ian closed his eyes and shook his jar of a head. "I should just kill that bitch."

"You know that's a bad move right now," I said, thinking fast, more lies taking shape in my mind. "She shows up dead, and her family will find those files on her system and start wondering why she was surveilling you. You'd be suspect number one, and her family's got the juice to get a serious investigation launched. Play this my way, and I'll keep you safe until you get that squad leader post. Then you can get her transferred out of homicide—problem solved."

Ian gave a begrudging nod. "I'll talk to Horst." He crossed the room, placed his hand on Liz's shoulder and then began whispering in her ear.

I stayed in my seat, thrilling on my scam. Not only was I getting Ian to decrypt the camerman's vid files for me, but I'd gotten the technician at the offworld company to agree to doubling the price and splitting the surplus with me. I'd get that spine paid for one way or another.

Liz was up out of her seat and coming my way, leaving Ian and Horst to discuss my proposal. She took the seat across from me. "How's your hand?"

The pain had receded except for an insistent throbbing coming from my pinky. "It's okay."

She helped herself to my bottle, pouring a couple fingers' worth into her goblet. "Ian can be such a bully."

"What happened to him?" I wanted to know.

"What do you mean?"

"Did you know him before?"

"Yes," she said after a pause.

"Well, what happened to him? It's like he's a different person."

Her face changed. She looked over at Ian, where he was talking to Horst. For the first time, I felt like I was seeing *her*, the real her. She was watching her boyfriend, her eyes filled with longing, and not the puppy-love kind of longing. It was more the kind of longing you'd see on a widow's face.

I said, "So you're not so thrilled with the new Ian."

She snapped her gaze back in my direction, as if my observation surprised her. "I didn't say that," she said.

"You didn't have to. Why do you stay with him?"

"He means a lot to me."

"He *means* a lot, or he *meant* a lot?"

"Both," she said with more emphasis than necessary, like she was trying to convince herself more than me.

"One of these days, somebody's going to teach him a lesson," I said.

"And you plan on being that somebody?" she teased.

I didn't answer.

The real her was already gone. The mischievous flirt was back in full force. She played with a lock of hair that hung alongside her face. "I guess you know a thing or two about bullies."

I leaned forward, wanting to be close to her. "That's right."

"You have firsthand experience, don't you?"

"What makes you so interested in my past?"

"I like cops."

"I'm not a cop."

"But you used to be."

"Why do you like cops?"

She kept twirling her hair as she took a sip of brandy with her other hand. "Answer some of my questions first."

I nodded.

"As the chief's enforcer, it was your job to keep other cops in line?"

I nodded again.

"And how did you manage that?"

"I'd rather not say."

She took my left hand in hers and folded my fingers into a fist. She studied my misshapen knuckles, running her finger over countless scars. "That's okay. I think I can guess."

My hand went tingly at her touch. I was *alive*. At that moment, Niki was erased from my mind. I looked over at Ian, who was deep in conversation with Horst. He didn't seem to care that his girlfriend was flirting with another man so, I decided it was just fine to flirt back. I took hold of one of her hands from underneath and dropped my splinted hand overtop—a cool move that went wrong when I had to wince at a sharp pain coming from my pinky.

"Let me see that," she said.

I protested unconvincingly as she started pulling the wrappings free. With each layer of bandage peeling off, my mood turned increasingly sour as I remembered all the times Niki had nursed these hands, all the times she cleaned off the blood and sanitized the wounds. How I'd sit on the toilet and lean my head on her hip as she worked over the sink, or when there was too much blood, how she'd sit on the tub and hold my hand close to the faucet. All cleaned up, we'd go to bed, and she'd nurse my soul, telling me that I was doing the right thing. Paul Chang and I were running KOP, using our power to shape the city into a place that would attract offworld tourists and bring offworld money into our crippled economy. And even after Paul and I had lost our way and become nothing more than common thugs, concerned only with extending our own power and wealth, she never accused me of being such. She was my wife, and she supported me no matter what. No matter how misguided I'd become.

Liz had all the wrappings off and piled like spaghetti. Three of my fingers had stayed properly splinted while my pinky had sprung loose, unnaturally poking out to the side.

"This one's causing all the trouble," she said as she caressed it gently.

"Yeah. I'll have to get it set again."

Suddenly, lightning quick, she grabbed hold of it and snapped it back in place.

I yelped and jerked back in my seat. "What the fuck!"

Liz gave me a coy smile, and I felt her foot in my crotch. I felt dizzy as the pain washed over me. I just about blacked out while her toes probed my privates.

"What the fuck?" I repeated.

Liz just smiled at me. Then she made a show of dropping a hand down under the table. She rolled her shoulder, making it clear that she was touching herself. She let out a small moan. I wanted to reach down, grab her foot, and twist her toes until the pain equaled mine. I was furious . . . and confused . . . and repulsed. . . .

But I was also hardening.

"You'll have to come by my place sometime," she said. A second later, her foot was gone and a second after that, she was gone, walking back to the autopsy table and tickling both Ian and Horst's ears before taking a seat between them.

I took my time with the bandages, winding them back up, giving my erection time to do the opposite.

By the time I finished, Ian was back. "The files are decrypting as we speak."

"Good."

twelve

A LOOK at my watch told me the sun wouldn't be up for a few hours yet. I was at Maggie's with a glass of Orzo's oak-aged in my hand, and I'd just finished settling things with my offworld coconspirator. I had the satellite company's engineer take my share of the money and apply it directly to Niki's medical bills. It was more cost effective that way. If I'd had him deposit the money into my account, I would've been charged two percent to convert the offworld dollars into pesos, and then another two percent to convert it back when I paid the medical bills.

I still wasn't sure what I'd tell Ian when I got the files back. I'd intended on telling Ian that it would take a week to get the files decypted, which would've given me plenty of time to make some bogus files to give him or maybe just some primo lies to tell him. But instead, I'd been stupid. Somewhere between Ian's intimidation and my drinking, I'd lost track of that particular lie and told him the truth. Thirty hours. I tried not to worry about it. Considering all the things that could've gone wrong at that meeting, I'd gotten off pretty cleanly.

I brought up the case files on Maggie's home system— the barge murders, all thirteen of them. Before I dug in, I decided to organize my own thoughts. Using the phone system, I called up holo-heads of Ian, Yuri, Adela Juarez, her dead parents, and her boyfriend, Raj. I realized I didn't know Liz's full name, so I had the system provide a blank holo-head that looked like an egg with the word *Liz* written where her eyes would be. I was even able to access Horst Jeffers's holo. I didn't know much about Horst besides his name, but Maggie would report back soon. She was pulling an all-nighter at KOP station, catching up on her paperwork and tracking down background information on him.

I sat before the array of holo-heads and started drawing lines between them. Familial lines between Adela and her parents. A boyfried-girlfriend line between Adela and Raj, and another between Ian and Liz. I connected both Raj and Yuri's heads to Hector Juarez, their boss at Lagarto Libre. More lines between dinner mates Ian, Horst, and cameraman Yuri.

I called up a miniholo of a barge and ran a line between it and cameraman Yuri. Another line from the barge to Ian, who hung out in a club where the floor show featured a lase-bladed axe that was a perfect fit as the head-chopping murder weapon. One more line connecting the barge to Horst, an offworlder with the money to buy gene eaters. I decided to stop there, my 3-D diagram already looking like some incestuous family tree.

I stared at the diagram for long minutes, my mind scattering in every direction. I shrank the diagram down and tossed it to the side. I'd try to come back to it later.

I menued into barge murder number one. A moment later, I was in a small cabin with rusted walls. Three fold-down bunks hung from one wall, and on the opposite wall was a mold-covered nautical map. On the floor was a familiar looking block of wood, complete with a scooped-out hollow, bloodstains, and scorch marks on top. Other than the cabin itself, the scene looked identical to the thirteenth, the one I'd visited in person. There was even a collection of gene-eaten lizards on the floor. I knelt down over the holographic block of wood, dropping my chin into the hollow, imagining what it would feel like with that axe dropping down on the back of my neck. *At least it would be quick . . . Not like Niki.* The knot in my stomach constricted. I chided myself for thinking that thought. Niki wasn't dying. She was recovering nicely.

I jumped ahead a couple weeks to the second crime scene, which was altogether different. No block of wood this time. Instead, there was a table surrounded by thick ropes piled on the metallic floor. The table's surface was slick with gene-eaten blood. On the table sat a cockeyed metal bowl. I mimed picking it up, and the bowl's image moved along with my hands. I three-sixtied it, finding bloodstains on the rim only. When I looked at the bowl's underside, I could see the reason the bowl wouldn't lay flat. There were a half dozen eye rings welded on and they were lined up in two rows. Even stranger was the fact that the bowl's bottom was covered with wax drippings. What the hell was that about?

I pulled up Maggie's case notes to see if she'd come up with any theories. The cabin walls disappeared, replaced by walls of text. I skimmed through her notes, pulling out the most significant sentences and stacking them to the side, until I'd built a minitower of holo-texts:

"The bowl was of standard manufacture, except it had been modified with a series of rings welded onto the bottom."

"The underside of the bowl was spattered with wax drippings that suggest the bowl was heated by candle."

"Rope fibers on two of the eye rings prove that the rope was run through the rings to hold the bowl in place."

"Only the bowl's rim was bloodstained, indicating that it was placed facedown onto the victim."

"Lining the inside of the bowl was a brown-black substance identified as lizard excrement. The bowl's interior was also marked by a large number of short scratches likely caused by lizards that were at one time caged in the bowl."

"Eleven gene-eaten lizards were recovered from the scene. An analysis of their stomach contents revealed what appears to be chemically consistent with human flesh. Positive identification through DNA was rendered impossible due to treatment with gene eaters."

I tried to puzzle through the information, reach my own conclusions, but I gave up quickly and navigated into Maggie's summation with that same mild guilty feeling you get when you skip to the final page of a mystery. My eyes went straight for a sketch nested inside the text. One look at that sketch and there was no need to read what Maggie had written. The medieval pencil drawing said it all.

There was a woman chained faceup to a heavy wooden table. Strapped tight across her stomach was an overturned bowl. Standing alongside was a man with a candle in each hand, holding the flames close to the bowl, heating it up, driving the mice inside into a panicked insanity from which the only escape was to start eating.

My stomach lurched as I let the sketch sink in. I didn't know where Maggie had found that sketch, but substitute lizards for mice, and the killer had imitated it to a T. I had to put my drink down, the very smell of it suddenly making me nauseous. Even as the full weight of the horror came down on me, I had to pause to appreciate the inspired leap Maggie had made from the limited evidence, from nothing more than some rope and a bloody bowl to this, this . . . abomination.

And there were still eleven more case files. . . .

I cycled through Maggie's summations, which read like a how-to book of medieval torture. Burned at the stake. Sawn in half—vertically. Flayed alive, strip by strip, the floor littered with gelatinous gene-eaten people-jerky. I went through them one by one, each one more and more revolting. Death by impaling. Death by pendulum.

I turned it all off, the gory truth, the gruesome brutality. I just sat there with my agitated nerves and my disturbed thoughts. My mind kept imagining Horst, his creepy face in the glow of a lase-axe. Could I be wrong about him? No. The circumstantial evidence was piling up: Start with the fact that we knew the serial was an offworlder with the funds to buy gene eaters. Then think about how Horst went to the restaurant to meet Yuri and Ian—Yuri who filmed the murders, and Ian, who helped Yuri cover for his clumsiness by switching vids. Then there was the way Horst greeted me at the club. He practically welcomed me to the team, telling me Ian said I'd be useful. And don't forget the fact that he was willing to foot the bill to get the vid files decrypted. Why would he have done that if he wasn't running the show?

I thought about how Horst had toasted me with his smile full of charm. Who was this animal, this offworld monster who thought my home was his perverse playground? Who was this offworld coward of a serial killer who picked on nameless Lagartan victims rather than carrying out his sicko fantasies on his own kind?

I closed the case files and went back to the diagram I'd made and enlarged it, the interconnected holo-heads beginning to look like a molecule with heads for atoms. I called up thirteen blank holo-heads, the faceless victims of the most twisted shit I'd ever seen. Thirteen victims . . . no, fourteen when you included the unlucky Officer Ramos.

Fourteen. And those were just the ones we knew about. Who knew how many more crime scenes still hadn't been found on all those abandoned barges?

Looking at this molecule composed of human elements, I sought out the weak bonds. Bonds I could break, atoms I could co-opt.

There was Yuri. The guy always looked like he was going to

wet himself. His type was easy to break. A little intimidation and he'd start singing.

And there was Liz, Ian's less than faithful girlfriend, whose pillow talk could tear the whole thing apart.

Another possibility was Adela's boyfriend, Raj. He was her alibi the night her parents were murdered, but he didn't back her up under questioning. If I assumed Maggie was right about Adela being innocent, then Raj was a liar. He said she went home early, but if she had gone home around midnight as he said, she would've been there when her parents got whipped at two AM. She would've called KOP that night, not the next morning. Or more likely still, she would've gotten fricasseed along with her parents. I hated to admit it, but the notion that Hector and Margarita Juarez were lase-whipped to death by their daughter was looking more tenuous by the minute, confession or no confession. God, how was I going to forgive myself if Adela turned out to be innocent? I'd made the poor girl cry.

Raj. The kid was a big piece of the puzzle. I could lean on him, see who put him up to stabbing his girlfriend in the back.

But bracing Raj was too risky. He'd seen me at Yuri's. I couldn't brace him without risking Ian finding out. I had to keep Ian thinking I was on his side. And if I continued that same reasoning, I couldn't brace Yuri or Liz, either. I had to take it slow. If I did this right, I could keep squeezing money out of Ian indefinitely, money I needed. And it wasn't just the money. It was the offworlder. The deeper I got into Ian's circle, the more I could learn about him. That warped bastard had to be stopped.

For now, Maggie and I had to keep working on the fringes, digging deep, but not so deep that we blew ourselves up by striking a gas line. Make no mistake, Ian *would* eventually find out I was screwing him. The trick was to string that finger-cracking, tube-pinching, 'roid-popping son of a boy-o bitch along for as long as I could, all the way until Maggie and I were ready to bring the whole operation down.

thirteen

I MADE the trip home and emptied the arsenal I kept under the bed, dumping the full complement into a duffel bag I had to dig out of Niki's closet. I gave the duffel a final once-over: Three lase-blades with a range of ten centimeters all the way out to a full meter. One broad-beam lase-pistol. Two showerhead lasers, one set to spray, the other on pulse. One lase-rifle with remote targeting. Four charge packs. One trail-cam. One flycam. One AV recorder. A couple penlights.

I rolled my pant leg down over the ankle blade and strapped my holster on backward to make it lefty. It didn't feel right, so I dumped the holster and tucked my piece into my belt instead and headed out with the bag draped over my shoulder.

The rain had stopped, so I made for Tenttown on foot. Lights were coming on behind windows, telling me it was morning. I sloshed through flooded intersections whose drains were clogged with jungle. I left my neighborhood behind, not knowing when I'd be back. Those barge murders had me plenty spooked, and if everything went to shit, I didn't plan on being easy to find.

Maggie called. "I got the scoop on the offworlder."

"Good."

Maggie sounded tired, but her holo looked chipper as it skimmed alongside. "Horst Jeffers is a travel agent."

"A travel agent?"

"Well, actually he's more of a tour operator. His company is called Jungle Expeditions. They have an office on the Old Town Square."

"Do they cater to the Orbital or the mines?"

"Both. They have an office on the Orbital, but their main office is on Asteroid B3, which is where he's from."

It made sense that he was from the belts. He was always wearing traditional-looking clothes, albeit with a vampire flair. Miners usually dressed a bit more conservative than the off-worlders from the Orbital.

Maggie's feet disappeared below the water as I splashed through another ankle-deep intersection. "Are they on the up-and-up?" I asked.

"They appear to be. Their specialty is organizing deep jungle adventure."

"What does that mean?"

"I assume it means monitor hunts, fishing, that kind of thing. The guy's a successful businessman and by all accounts a personable one at that. Not exactly a loner, Juno."

"What are you saying?"

"Serials are usually loners."

"We can't be sure he isn't a loner. His bubbly personality could be nothing more than a digital implant."

"True," she admitted, "but it occurred to me that the killer could be one of his clients."

Horst Jeffers: Tour Guide for the Discerning Serial. Maggie could be right. "Is there a way we can get our hands on a list of his clients?"

"Not without walking into their office and demanding one. I thought that was a little too bold for us right now."

"I agree." *Stay on the fringes.*

"The only other thing I could think of was to talk to somebody at the Koba Office of Customs. Offworld visitors have to write in their tour operator's name on customs forms, so I thought they could compile a list for me. I must've talked to a dozen people before I got somebody who said she could get me the information in two or three days."

"Days? All they have to do is query the database."

"I know. But she needs to get approval."

Typical government bullshit. "Anything else to report?"

"No. Just that Ian's making it tough at work."

"How so?"

"Nobody will talk to me. I mean nobody. Not even Lieutenant Rusedski. They all ignore me like I'm not there."

"Just stay out in the field."

"I'll do that as much as I can, but there's always going to be a meeting or two that I have to attend."

"I say skip them."

She gave me an annoyed exhalation. "That wouldn't look very good on my record."

She'd never change. Career first. I was already in the outskirts of Tenttown. No more roads, just footpaths that wound their way through haphazardly placed tents. "Listen, I gotta go. I'll see you after you get off work."

To keep out of the mud, I walked across a series of planks laid end to end. At one point, I had to step off to the side in order to make room for a series of men with rickety wheelbarrows loaded down with sacks of rice. Once the sweat-stained group had passed, I almost tipped over trying to yank my feet out of the suctioning mud. The tents were getting denser as I penetrated deeper into Tenttown, each one now a mere meter from the next.

I took a set of rock steps down toward the canal, the smell of sewage coming through strong. I found a nice new-looking tent with the renter's red rag tied to the corner post. I popped my head in. "Got any openings?"

"Yeah," said the man inside as he rushed out to meet me.

I followed him as he led me around back. I weaved left and right to avoid having to step over tied tent stakes. He stopped at a faded blue tent and grinned rotten teeth. I looked the tent over, thinking that it wasn't as new as I'd have liked, but it looked solid enough. I couldn't see any frayed edges that told of leaks. "How about the inside?"

"Yes, yes," he said. He shook the tent by grabbing hold of one of the ropes. Out came a young woman holding her baby. The man waved me ahead and I peeked into the now vacated tent, deciding it would do.

We haggled over price while the woman, who looked like his daughter, went back in and began stuffing her belongings into a threadbare carpetbag. It didn't take her long to come back out. She didn't have much—the bag wasn't even half full. I momentarily felt bad about evicting her from her home but knew that she'd be glad to move in with her father if it meant they could earn a little money. Once her father and I settled, I went in and stripped off my muddy shoes, setting them on a rock by the entryway. I stepped from stone to stone to keep off the otherwise dirt floor and hung my duffle from the center post. Then I hoisted myself into one of the hammocks and sent the entire tent shaking and ruffling.

I swatted a mosquito, angry that I'd forgotten my bug spray. Hopefully it would start raining soon, putting enough moisture in the air to keep the little bloodsuckers grounded. I swatted another one . . . and another. *I hate this fucking place.* I began to wonder if it was a good idea to come here. Surely I could tough it out for a while. I'd grown up here, for god's sake. And my family's tent was a hell of a lot rattier than this one. Yet I knew that I'd softened after so many years of living high on the KOP food chain. I'd just have to suffer through it.

I called Vlad. "Did you get the new room?"

"Yeah. I got her set up in the morgue."

"The morgue!"

"Yeah. You don't want anybody to find her, right?"

"Shit, Vlad. I don't want her in the morgue."

"Listen, Juno. The morgue's perfect. It'll be the last place anybody looks, and the doors have locks."

"No, Vlad. Find someplace else."

"But—"

"Fucking listen to me, Vlad. You're going to find someplace else. You hear me?"

"All right, boss. Whatever you say."

"Do it now."

"You got it, boss. Hey, are you coming down anytime soon?"

"No. Why?"

"Well, she's been asking for you."

"What's she been saying?"

"Listen, Juno, I don't want to get in the middle of anything."

"Just tell me, Vlad."

"Well, she's in a real bad way. She just keeps crying, and then she starts choking like she can't clear her throat. I have to keep getting the nurses to come and take care of it."

"Can't they give her a sedative or something?"

"Yeah, but she refuses."

Unbelievable. "Okay, I'll come down."

"When?"

"Fucking later, okay?"

"Sure, you bet. Just call me before you come, and I'll tell you where we are."

"Right." I clicked off as the sick feeling in my gut reached epic proportions. I took a few hits off my flask and closed my eyes. Visions of Niki in the morgue haunted me. I tossed and turned as much you could in a hammock. I needed sleep. I tried changing the subject of my thoughts by thinking about the case and just found myself haunted by thirteen mutilated victims instead.

I turned my thoughts to Liz, and the way her toes had massaged me. I jerked off, concentrating on her cleavage, and then closed my eyes again, wanting desperately to sleep.

I woke up an hour later and thought I'd been lucky to even get an hour's worth of rest. I scarfed down a bowl of veggies and rice that my new landlord had brought over. I tried to ignore the occasional crunch as I bit down on a grain of sand. I wondered what Horst would think of the local cuisine if he had to eat like a Tenttowner. I found a bathroom, which was really just a hole in the wooden planking built over the canal. I took a whiz and tried to forget that the food I just ate was cooked with that same steeped-shit canal water.

I made my way to the hospital, finding Vlad in maternity and paying him before I went in to see Niki. I took a chair by Niki's bed. She was asleep. I felt desperate to get her out of here, where she'd be safe from Ian, but I had no choice but to keep her here with her machines and her doctors. I left her side and made my way up and down the ward, passing out thousand-peso notes to the staff like I was one of those street kids on the Old Town Square who would just about tackle you in order to pass you a flyer. I told every one of the staff, "Anybody asks for Niki, you tell him she checked out." I doubted it would do any good. My best hope was that Ian would continue believing that I didn't care about Niki, and that he couldn't go through her to get at me.

I returned to Niki's side. She looked worse than normal; her eyes were dark and puffy, and her complexion was more yellow than usual. I took her hand knowing I wouldn't wake her—she couldn't feel it. I was surprised by the warmth in her fingers. For some reason, I always expected her hands to be cold.

Why was she being so stubborn? Things would change

when she got her spine. Things would go back to the way they were. I'd quit drinking. Okay, maybe a glass with dinner, but no more bingeing. I'd quit freelancing for the rags. I'd just get a job, a regular job, with regular pay. We could sell the house and move into someplace smaller and less expensive. I could be a better husband. I could.

"Juno."

I opened my eyes. I was still at the hospital, still holding Niki's hand. I checked my watch—a half hour had gone by.

"You fell . . . asleep," she said.

"Yeah." I rubbed a kink in my neck. "Is this room okay?"

"Yeah." Her tone implied a ho-hum shrug. A baby started crying next door.

I said, "I hear you've been having a hard time."

She didn't respond.

"I know it's hard for you right now, but we can get through this."

"And what if . . . I don't w—want to get . . . through it?"

"You won't feel that way when you get your spine."

"And why n—not?"

"Jesus, Niki, you'll be able to walk, eat, run. . . . You'll be able to do whatever you want."

"How about kill my—myself?"

Anger started welling up inside me. "Dammit, Niki. Stop making this so difficult. I'm sacrificing everything to get you patched up. The least you can do is make an effort."

"I never asked y—you to spend all . . . your money."

"Our money."

"S—still, I never . . . asked you."

"What do you expect me to do? Just let you die?"

"Yes."

"Well that's not an option. Like it or not, you're alive, and you're going to stay that way, so grow up and deal with it already."

She stayed silent for a minute or two before saying, "You d— don't understand."

"Don't give me that bullshit, Niki. I understand just fine."

"No you don't. . . . If you . . . did, you wouldn't . . . make me suffer any . . . more." She was being ridiculous, once again putting on this woe-is-me crap that I'd been hearing for over two and a half decades.

"You think I don't understand? You think you've got all this secret pain. All these burdens that you and you alone have to bear. You think the whole world is living this dream life while you're the only one that's suffering?"

"If you only . . . knew."

Enough. I could feel the blood rushing to my face, surging from down deep. Anger shot up straight from the knot in my stomach. I practically hissed, "I'm not going to feel sorry for you. It's not going to work anymore."

She rolled her eyes.

"I'm serious," I said.

She looked away.

It was always the same shit with her. *I'm so tortured. You'll never understand.* Like her secrets were some license to feel miserable. She kept it all inside and then beat me over the head with it whenever it was convenient. And I'd let her do it. For all these years, I'd let her do it. I'd tell myself, maybe she'll open up one day, when she's finally ready, or maybe she won't, maybe some doors are better left shut. Truth was, she did go through a lot of hell in her life, but so did I, dammit. And so did everyone else on this backwater world. Yet she always acted like she was the only one, like the hell she went through was so far off the hell meter that she didn't have to listen to anybody. Well fuck that, fuck it to hell.

I leaned forward, forcing her eyes to meet mine. "I'm serious, Niki. I know your secrets. I *know*."

Her eyes went quizzical.

"I *know*," I repeated.

Her eyes widened in fear.

"That's right, Niki. I've always known."

"You're full of sh—shit."

"Am I full of shit when I say that I know your father raped you?" There. It was out.

"That's not t—true."

"Oh yes it is. And I know you murdered him, and your mother."

Her eyes were going misty. "No."

I couldn't keep from raising my voice as words that had been buried for decades erupted out of me. "You think I'm stupid? All this time you thought I couldn't figure it out? You thought I was just a dumb oaf who'd just believe anything you said? Shit, Niki, I was the one who covered it up. *Me*. If it wasn't for me, you would've gone to the Zoo."

Tears were breaking loose from her eyes.

"I've always known. So don't go thinking I don't understand."

She was full out crying now. She started to gag.

Dammit. Why does she have to do that? All the anger in me instantly melted. I rolled her on her side, putting some tissues by her mouth so she could spit out the mucus. I pinched a tissue over her nostrils so she could blow her nose. I kept her like that as she sobbed and choked. It went on for a long time, long enough to use up half a box of tissues. When the sniveling finally subsided, I laid her flat on her back and caressed her cheek. "We're going to get through this," I said. "It wasn't your fault."

fourteen

I crossed the Old Town Square, feeling great, better than I had in forever. The knot in my stomach was completely tame, and I hadn't had a drink for hours now. About time I got that off my chest. Year after year, I'd let Niki continue believing I didn't know about her father, thinking I was doing what was best for her. But now it was out, out in the open where she'd finally be able to face it and move on. I called the hospital and had them bring her some flowers, something nice I told them, not those wilted week-old flowers that die in a day.

I cut through one of the many narrow streets that ran off the square. I looked for numbers by the doors of the souvenir shops, but they were all hidden by cascading displays of monitor-hide handbags and oil paintings of regal-looking 'guanas perched on top of rocks or rooftops. I reached the end of the block and had to turn back before I spotted the Jungle Expeditions placard on the walk. I checked out the sign as I approached—sun-faded nature shots with words like *adventure* and *excitement* written in the gaps between pics.

I walked through a doorway into a courtyard covered by a series of tarps that were so pregnant with puddled water that they stretched in all the wrong directions, creating gaping holes in the coverage through which misting rain came glistening down. Souvenir stands ran around the circumference, their spaces overflowing with etched gourds and mini Lagartan-style skiffs made from seedpods. There was a staircase on the

far end that led up to a second tier where I could see a window
with painted-on jungle vines and tour prices. Standing alongside the door was a stuffed tiger, reared up on its haunches, one
of its paws raised like it was about to claw somebody's heart
out.

Tiger hunts? I took another look at the painted prices on the
window and found a variety of tiger safaris dominating the list.
I didn't think anybody did tiger hunts anymore. The tour oper-
ators quit running tiger shoots decades ago when the upriver
tiger territory was overrun by warlords. Not that the tiger
hunts were ever very successful in the first place. So few tourists
ever managed to bag one that they usually chose to spend their
offworld dollars elsewhere. From what I'd heard, even seeing a
tiger in the jungle was next to impossible. The foliage was too
thick to spot something that didn't want to be spotted. Tigers
weren't like the monitors who still hadn't learned to fear us humans. To hunt monitor, you could just about sit in a chair and
wait for one of the cocksure lizards to come right up to you. Being the top of the food chain for so many millennia had made
them dimwittedly overconfident. Looking around, seeing all
the monitor-hide jackets and gloves hanging on hooks, I found
it hard to believe us Lagartans hadn't yet slaughtered enough of
them to weed out their outdated king-of-the-jungle genes.

Tigers were another story. They weren't native. Their DNA
was heavily seasoned with an instinctual fear of man. They
were originally introduced over a century ago as a tourism promotion. They were supposed to give Lagarto a higher profile
among the Unified Worlds. We would become the haven for all
the extinct Earth species. All those offworld freighter crews passing through our system wouldn't be able to resist a trip down to
the surface to see tiger, rhino, gorilla, and every other species
that could be reconstituted from old DNA samples. The pols

pushed the plan through, telling everybody that happy days would be just around the corner.

What a crock of shit. The Bio-Regeneration Program was a total failure. Start with the fact that the rot shot their supersafari plans to hell by sending the gorillas, the elephants, and all the other plus-sized exotics straight back into extinction. Tigers were the only large mammals that actually took, and any benefit the tigers offered was easily outweighed by the havoc they wreaked on the frontier farms, always eating people's cows and goats. It became just one more reason why so many upriver farmers switched to raising poppies instead of livestock. What was supposed to create a boom for the tour companies instead turned into a boon for the warlords who ran the opium trade. Their toehold on the fringe towns became a foothold, and then when the government tried to take the land back by force, the warlords started spewing all this power-to-the-people bullshit and converted their foothold into a stronghold.

And now even Lagarto's lifeless deserts were more tourist friendly than the warlord-controlled territory where lase-rifle-bearing children called themselves freedom fighters and where the warlords made a habit of giving their rival O runners Lagartan neckties—cut the throat and then reach in and pull the tongue down through the opening.

And I was supposed to believe Horst Jeffers had revived the tiger hunt business? No. I wasn't buying it. The tiger hunt business went under for a reason. Unless he had a damn tiger farm out there where his customers could pop them in their cages, tiger hunts were a cover. Only a damn fool would want to spend his vacation in the fringe towns where you were more likely to get a Lagartan necktie than a tiger pelt.

I kept one eye on the Jungle Expeditions door and used the other to paw through a set of monitor-hide belts. The hawkers

eventually stopped pestering me after I gave them a long dose
of total disregard. I made my way around from stand to stand,
focusing on belts, thinking I could use a new belt, but not
wanting to take the time to make a purchase. I had to stay
ready to leave in a hurry should that powder-skinned Horst
Jeffers show up.

It wasn't much longer before a trio of offworlders came out
and walked down the stairs. A dozen-odd hawkers were ready
to greet them by the time they reached the bottom. The hawkers descended on them, a mob of trinket-wielding parasites.
The offworlders tried to ignore them but couldn't keep their
resolve for more than a few seconds. One of them became so
uncomfortable with the invasion of his personal space that he
stepped away from the group, playing right into the hawkers'
divide-and-conquer strategy.

A local emerged from the Jungle Expeditions door, and with
a scowl, saved the offworlders from making some overpriced
purchases. The parasites scuttled back under their rocks as he
came down the stairs. "All ready?" He smiled.

The trio of tourists followed his lead. I dropped the belt I'd
been mock studying and fell in behind them. The local led the
way, with one of the offworlders hanging on his shoulder, talking his ear off, asking questions nonstop. The other two lagged
behind. They were looking around, taking in the sights, both
of them trying to enjoy the walk. I trailed behind, following at
a comfortable pace.

We crossed the Old Town Square, stopping twice, first so
the tour guide could point out the church that sat at the head
of the square, and second so he could give a spiel on the
square's history. They listened to his rehearsed shtick and
laughed at his well-worn jokes while I stayed a short distance
away and pretended to be interested in some jewelry. The offworlders stood side by side, wearing their I'm-a-tourist slick-

ers, their faces hard to see, hidden by steam that came off their
tech-heated quick-dry skin.

They were on the move again, walking in the same formation
as before. Based on their multicolored threads, I figured these offworlders were from the Orbital instead of the mines. The offworlders on the Orbital were always coming in contact with the
latest trends and these three were sporting some ultrabright
reds, greens, and yellows under their slickers. As I kept looking
at those flashy clothes, I started thinking that these three might
actually be from one of the freighter crews instead of from the
Orbital. Those over-the-top colors were plain gaudy, even by Orbital standards.

They were probably from Pivon, the planet closest to Lagarto, only five years by freighter. They could be on their way
home, docking with Lagarto Orbital-1 for a final restocking of
raw materials that had been slingshotted in from the mining op-
erations out in the belts. People said the Orbital was a major
stop on the trade routes. I wouldn't know. All I knew was that
looking around these streets and seeing the opium-ravaged
derelicts holding out their hands, I found it mighty hard to
fathom that there was a flourishing economy going on up there.

We took an arched bridge across the canal and headed toward the Phra Kaew market as the rain picked up its pace. The
offworld trio didn't seem to mind, thick steam venting out the
top of their slickers, making them look like walking cigarettes.
We were about to reach the covered portion of the Phra Kaew
market, and I was beginning to think this afternoon would be
a total waste if it turned out I was following them on nothing
more than a shopping spree. Just then, they took a right. I resisted the urge to speed up and took the corner at my regular
pace. They were gone, all four of them. I strained my eyes,
stretching my gaze in all directions. They were gone, but I had
a good idea where.

I passed the door without a knob, remembering it well, the secret knock that changed every ten days. I'd gotten so frustrated keeping up with their rotating knocking codes that I'd gotten Jae, the owner, to give me a knock of my own.

I turned right, then right again, and stepped into a dark alley with a low-hanging roof that made it feel like a cave. I could hear the rustle of fleeing lizards in the weeds. My feet crunched on broken glass. Opium smoke tickled my nostrils. I kept walking with confident strides—no telling how many O heads and glue huffers were camped in this alley, and until my eyes adjusted, I didn't want any of them jumping me. I could see a light up ahead, and I made for it, my eyes starting to make out shapes along the walls that looked like caved-in boxes and piles of rags that could be people. I made it to the light and rapped on the back door, using my old code. Nothing. I rapped again, this time louder, and the door swung open.

"Idris?" I said.

"Juno? Is that you?"

"Yeah."

"Shit, let me look at you, boy."

I stood there, letting him once-over me.

"Fuckin' A!" said the old man with a broad grin. He slid a cinder block over to prop the door and laid a hug on me. "Juno Mozambe. Where you been, motherfucker?"

"I lost my shield."

"Yeah, I heard about that, but that don't mean you got to stop comin' by, do it?"

I shrugged.

"Shit, Juno, you done made my day, you hear me? I wish things could go back to the way they was. Things just ain't the same anymore. You was a righteous collections man, Juno. You was always fair, everybody said so. And Idris don't ever forget the fact that you took care of him. Shit, you always was willin' to throw a little cash Idris's way."

"Glad to do it. You tell Jae that I said you need a raise. Had he paid you properly, I wouldn't have needed to look out for you."

"You wanna come in? You can tell that pimp off your own self."

"No thanks. How's things?"

"They ain't the same, I'll tell you that. Now them cops got this new guy, some fuckin' street cop with his blue uniform comin' by and collectin' now. The guy's a real A-hole, too. He always be demandin' a BJ from one of the girls when he come a collectin'. That shit ain't right, Juno. It ain't professional. He's supposed to pay for that shit."

"What does Jae say about it?"

"Shit, that pimp don't do nothin'. Jae gone soft, man. That cop boy start sayin' he goin' to raise rates if he don't get his BJ, and Jae just give in. That cop don't even have to ask no more. Jae give him his payoff, and he just goes and grabs one of the girls. The girls ain't happy about it. They come a-complainin' to me, but what can I do? I'm just the houseboy."

"I wish there was something I could do, but I don't have any standing down at KOP anymore."

"Shit, man, I know. I wasn't askin' you to do nothin'. See, I was just shootin' the shit, that's all."

I snagged a wad from my pocket and put it in Idris's palm.

"That's what I'm talkin' about," he said grinning broadly. "Since you been gone, Juno, KOP's gone to shit, you know what I'm sayin'? These A-holes don't know what they's doin'. They don't understand the business. They just want they's scratch and they's snatch, and they want it now. Shit."

"If you ask me, Idris, you should be running this shithole."

The guy lit up. "You ain't serious."

"I am serious." And I was. "You know the business as well as anybody. The girls respect you. You should get a mutiny going and toss Jae out on his ass. You and the girls could turn this place around."

"Shit! Ha! I missed you, Juno. I really did. Ha! Can you imagine me runnin' this place? Shit, Juno, that ain't me. I can't pull that shit off."

"I don't see why not."

"Ha! You always was the man, Juno. I wish you was still runnin' collections. I really do."

"Listen, Idris, I can use a little info."

"Whatever you want, Juno, but you got to promise you won't be no stranger, you hear me? You got to come by more often."

"I will."

"Now what you need?"

"Did you see the three offworlders come in a few minutes ago?"

"You mean those fuckers that's dressed up like parrots? Yeah, I saw them."

"They been here before?"

"No, they's first-timers."

"What about their guide?"

"Gomez? Shit, he be here a couple times a week. He work for this offworld company on the Square."

"Jungle Expeditions."

"Yeah, that's it."

"What kind of shit are his clients into?"

"The one's he bring here is mostly just lookin' for straight pussy. Sometimes he bring one along who want a little kink, but you know we ain't one of them specialty houses."

"Do you have an exclusive arrangement with him?"

"No. He always shoppin' around on price and shit. We get most of his straight pussy business though."

"Where else does he go?"

"Listen, if you lookin' for some weird shit, you should check out Kaiser. He another one of them guides that work with Gomez, but he the one that take the special orders."

"What kind of special orders?"

"Shit, man, them Jungle Expeditions folk cater to the dowack-ados. They get some regular customers, too, like them parrot motherfuckers in there, but they's main business is in kink. They's customers is regulars at the Red Room and the Cellar Dweller. From what I hear, they does some big kiddie biz. They's also into rape sims and all that bondage shit. I heard they even done some necro."

"Necro?"

"Ha! I told you they was some dowackados, didn't I? Didn't I?"

"Thanks, Idris."

"Anytime, Juno. You needs anything else?"

"I'll let you know."

I walked out the way I came in. Nobody bothered me, not after they'd seen me chatting with Idris. It was courtesy of Idris that they got to stay in this alley. Piss him off and they could find themselves evicted from the alley, and this alley was primo, being covered and all.

fifteen

I REACHED the fifth floor and Maggie was already there, waiting at the end of the hall. We walked toward each other, meeting in the middle.

"Sorry it took me so long to get here."

"No problem," Maggie said as she led me down the hall.

"How was work?"

"The same. How was your afternoon?" Maggie knocked on door number 511.

"I got some dirt on Jungle Expeditions. That jungle adventure crap is just a cover. They do sex tours."

Maggie nodded, not surprised at all. The door swung open, revealing a slightly heavy woman wearing a frumpy number. Maggie held up her badge. "Are you Inez Shenko?"

"Yes," she said as she fiddled with her dated hair.

"I'm Detective Orzo, and this is Detective Mozambe. Can we come in?"

"Yes, of course."

We entered her apartment, a plain-looking place with a decent view of the river.

"Can I get you some tea?"

"Please," said Maggie.

Inez Shenko went into her kitchen.

My eyes inventoried the sitting room—floral print upholstery, cheap plastic angel figurines in glass cases, no vid system, no sign of a man. *Total square.*

Inez came back in after having put some water on the stove. "How can I help you, officers?"

I hoped this line of investigation would yield some results. We decided to start with the only victims we could identify: Margarita and Hector Juarez. If it wasn't their daughter who did them in, it was somebody else, and lase-whipping them in their own home didn't match the MO of our offworld serial killer with the medieval fetish.

Maggie said, "I appreciate your willingness to speak with us. We'd like to talk to you about the Juarez family."

"I've already told everything I know to Officer Davies."

"Yes, we know. But I'm sure you're aware of the fact that Adela Juarez is due to be executed on the fifth."

"Yes."

"Well, it's standard procedure for us to conduct follow-up interviews just to make sure we have everything in order before we turn our records over to the Koba Office of Records."

"I see."

"So if it's not too great an inconvenience, could you please tell us how you know the Juarez family?"

"Sure," she said. "I went to school with Margarita, and we've been friends ever since."

"Did you see her regularly?"

"We'd get together a couple times a week and have lunch or go shopping." She targeted Maggie as she said, "Sometimes we'd treat ourselves to a spa." She said it like she was confessing a dirty little secret, like visiting the spa was the biggest curve in her otherwise square life.

"What can you tell us about her husband?"

"Well, Hector worked a lot. He had a very important job, you know."

"Yes, we know. Why were they going to divorce?"

"They grew apart. He was always working, and she got lonely."

"Who initiated the divorce?"

"That was Margarita. Hector was very upset about it."

"He still loved her?"

"I suppose so, but the way Margarita talked, he sounded more interested in keeping his money than he was in keeping her. Excuse me." She got up to tend to the whistling teapot.

Maggie and I waited silently until Inez came back with three cups of mellow green tea. "Where were we?" asked Inez.

I spoke up for the first time. "You were saying that Margarita was going to take Hector's money in the divorce."

"Only what she was entitled to," she responded, semi-offended.

Maggie blew on her tea. "How well did you know Adela?"

"Oh, I've known her since she was a baby. She was always a good girl. I think it's horrible that they're going to execute her."

"You don't think she killed her parents?" I asked.

"No, I think she did it, but can you blame her? She just lost her head. She didn't know what she was doing. That lawyer she had did her a real disservice. He should've claimed temporary insanity."

"I don't understand," I said.

"Didn't you read Officer Davies's notes?"

I had read Ian's notes, but they claimed Inez thought Adela Juarez was a bad seed, a wicked little girl who couldn't be controlled. I sheepishly grinned. "Well, I didn't read them in their entirety."

She shook her head at me like a disapproving schoolmarm. "Margarita was having an affair with somebody younger. She was so lonely."

"Who was he?"

"She told me his name, but I didn't know who he was until after she died. If I'd known, I would've done something, taken her to counseling or something."

"Who was he?" Maggie asked.

"Really, I don't know what Margarita was thinking."

"His name?"

"Raj Gupta," she whispered. "Don't you see? Adela must've found out about it."

Maggie and I waited at the Gupta household for Raj to show. His parents were treating us well, serving us black tea and crackers. "He should be home momentarily," they had said. That had been over an hour ago.

I sipped my tea, wired on something other than caffeine. We'd found a loose thread in the Juarez case, and his name was Raj Gupta. Ian hadn't tied it all up as tight as he thought. Maggie and I were itching to pull on the thread, see if any fabric would come with it. We needed to find out why Ian would protect the kid. Assuming Ian framed Adela, why wouldn't he let Inez Shenko's statement stand? What better motive could he ask for? Adela's mother was screwing her boyfriend for chrissakes. But Ian went against his own interests in falsifying the report by leaving the affair out.

I squirmed in my seat. We were taking a chance talking to Raj, a big chance. If it got back to Ian that Raj had seen me at the cameraman's . . .

A door opened, and in he came. He recognized us at once and smiled politely. He took his wingtips off at the door—very adult shoes for such a young kid. Mrs. Gupta told her husband to make room for Raj on the couch.

"Actually, we'd like to talk to him privately," I said.

The Guptas stepped out graciously. "How can I help you, officers?" said Raj.

Maggie took a sip of tea. "We'd like to ask you a few questions, if you don't mind."

"Of course not," he said with a slick grin.

"It's just a formality, Raj. We're just trying to get our paperwork all straightened out."

"No problem. I'm glad to help. Hey, what were you doing at Yuri's yesterday?"

"I'm afraid that's police business."

"Okay, no problem," he said without the slightest hint of nervousness.

Maggie put her teacup down. "You work at the Libre?"

"That's right."

"What do you do there?"

"I'm an intern. I do whatever they tell me."

"Do you get paid?"

"No."

"Then why do you do it?"

"For the opportunity."

"You want to be a reporter?"

"Yeah."

"Do you go to school?"

"No."

"How can you be a reporter if you don't get a degree?"

"You don't need a degree. The camera loves me."

I wanted to slap the smug little bastard. Maggie kept her tone neutral. "You were dating Adela Juarez?"

"That's right."

"How did you meet?"

"We met at the Libre. She'd come in with her father from time to time, and we'd talk and stuff."

"How long were you dating?"

"Maybe three or four months."

I saw something from the corner of my eye. When I turned

to look, it disappeared back into the kitchen. I kept my eyes fixed on the doorway.

Maggie kept up the questioning. "How do you feel about what's happening to Adela now?"

He didn't hesitate. "She's getting what she deserves."

"You think she killed her parents?"

"I know she did."

"And how do you know?"

"She tried to get me to *lie* for her. She wanted me to say that she was with me all night."

"And was she with you all night?"

"No."

"Was she with you at all that night?"

"Yes. She snuck over and I let her in through my window. We did it a couple times in my bed and then she left."

"When did she leave?"

"I don't know. I was sleeping."

"Then how do you know she left?"

"She was gone when I woke up. She called me in the morning, when the police were at her house, and she told me to tell them that she was here all night."

"Maybe she was."

"She couldn't have been. Detective Davies said she killed her parents at two in the morning."

"How do you know she wasn't in your bed at two? You just said you were asleep."

"I never told Detective Davies that she *wasn't* with me at two. I just told him that I couldn't say she *was*."

"Didn't you want to protect her?"

"Not after I found out what she'd done. You think I want a crazy bitch like that as a girlfriend? I date a lot of girls, but I draw the line at murderers."

Maggie paused to rub her temples. A real piece of work this

kid. I returned to watching the door. It was back, a tuft of frizzy hair poking out. Slowly, the hair moved further into the doorway, followed by a pimply forehead, and then finally an eye. She saw me looking right at her and ducked back behind the wall.

Maggie saw her, too, but she kept her attention focused on Raj, whose back was turned to the doorway. Maggie asked why he thought Adela did it.

"She was pissed that they were divorcing."

"You think she killed her parents just because they were divorcing? Doesn't that seem a little crazy?"

"Surprised me as much as anybody," he said.

No longer afraid that she was going to get in trouble, Raj's puberty-stricken sister poked her head fully into the doorway. I threw a wink her way, getting a smile full of braces in return.

"Well, thanks for going through all that again," Maggie said. "So you said you like to date a lot of girls?"

"That's right."

"Did Adela know?"

"I don't think so. You think I'd tell her?"

"How do you think she would've reacted if she found out?"

"I guess I'm lucky she never did, or it might be me that got whipped to death."

"Were you ever serious about Adela?"

"Listen, I thought Adela would be a lot of fun. I mean you've seen her, right? She's hot as they come, but she had . . . *issues.*"

"What kind of issues?"

"She was all clingy, you know what I mean? We went out a couple times, and it was like we were married or something."

"If it bothered you so much, why didn't you just break it off?"

"She was my boss's daughter. I wanted to let her down easy."

"By having sex with her?"

"Like I said, she was hot."

"How many other girls were you seeing?"

"I don't keep count," he said, self-satisfied.

"Did Adela know any of these other girls?"

"I don't think so."

"How about Margarita Juarez? Adela knew her, didn't she?"

Raj went instantly icy. His smarmy grin frosted over. Behind him, his sister covered her delighted mouth.

"What?" he asked.

"You heard me," Maggie said with steel in her voice.

He laughed. "You must be crazy."

"Quite a triangle you got yourself into, Raj. Did Adela catch you in bed with her mother? Or maybe Hector found out about you. I can't imagine his surprise, finding out that not only were you deflowering his precious daughter, but you were also poking his wife."

He was nervous now. His face was flushed, and he sputtered out the words, "You can't prove that."

I checked out the sister. She was loving every minute of it. She was giggling, her hands clamped over her mouth.

Maggie decided to push him. "Maybe you're the one that killed them, Raj. Maybe Hector found out about you, and he was going to fire you. There goes your dream of working in front of a camera. It's not like there are any other news agencies on this planet. Lagarto Libre's the only game in town."

He shook his head no.

"You had to kill him, didn't you? He was going to ruin your life. And you had to kill Margarita, too. If you hadn't, she would've told on you."

Raj kept shaking his head, and now he was biting his lip. I sat on the edge of my seat, reading the signals he was giving off—hand wringing, foot tapping. He kept reaching up to scratch a nonexistent itch on his cheek. He was close to tipping. *Keep pushing, Maggie.*

Maggie switched to a motherly voice. "Just tell us the truth, Raj."

"No," he said. "I'm not going to talk to you anymore." He was shutting down.

Maggie is screwing this up. Stop fucking around with the nice tone and push him, hard.

"C'mon, Raj, just tell us the truth," she said lamely.

I looked at Raj. He had his arms crossed. He was clamming up tight. "I'm not saying another word," he said.

Son of a bitch. I'll do it myself. I tried to put my finger in his face, forgetting my fingers were all wrapped up tight. I had my whole shaky karate-chop hand pointing at his nose. "You better start talking, you little shit. Adela's going to get gassed, and I don't have time for your bullshit—"

"Mom! Dad! They're harassing me!"

"Be quiet you little—"

"Mom! Dad!"

Shit.

The sister disappeared an instant before Mr. and Mrs. Gupta came rushing in. "What's going on here?"

"They're harassing me," Raj griped.

Maggie was glaring at me. *Fuck me.*

"Call our lawyer," said the father.

"No need to do that," I said. "We were just leaving."

I followed Maggie to the door, utterly defeated. I took one last peek back—mother and father standing together, behind their son, and way over, in the corner, was the sister, making very deliberate eye contact with me.

Maggie laid into me the instant the door closed. "Dammit, Juno. I had it under control. What were you thinking?" I circled around to the side of the house as Maggie kept jawing.

"Don't forget that *I'm* the cop." I ignored her and picked my way into the overgrown jungle that clung to the side of the house. "Where are you going?"

"I'll be right back." I got soaked by large drops of water that shook loose from the vines above as I rustled my way alongside the house, breaking through any vines that tried to hold me back. I made it to the back patio and looked at the windows, trying to guess which one was hers. She made it easy by flicking her light on and off. *Smart girl.* I crept up to her window and attempted a one-handed chin-up, winding up on my ass. I found a patio chair and pulled it over to the window then stepped up, reached my hand through the bars, and rapped lightly on the glass.

Raj's little sister opened the window with the biggest brace-faced smile I'd ever seen. She handed me a vid then put her finger to her mouth and shushed.

sixteen

My phone rang: Ian.

Maggie paused the vid we got from Raj's sister, and Margarita Juarez's bobbing head stopped in fellating freeze-frame.

"Yeah," I said.

A holographic Ian overlaid the scene, his appearance blocking the blowing. "Hey, boy-o, it's time for your report."

My nerves hummed. I'd already planned out what I would tell him, but that didn't stop a surge of doubt from suddenly running through me. Maybe I was forgetting something. Maybe I'd say the wrong thing. "Maggie interviewed Inez Shenko. Remember her?"

"Yeah. Did you go with her?"

"Of course I did. Inez told her about the affair between Adela's boyfriend and her mother."

He said, "Damn." He sounded frustrated, yet his holo kept up its brainless grinning. Most of the time these canned phone holos were a real nuisance, always looking happier than you'd ever seen that person look in real life, but with Holo-Ian it was totally eerie, him standing there with that plastered-on smile. "Anything else?" he asked, sounding like he was asking through clenched teeth.

"Yeah. After Shenko, she went to visit Adela's boyfriend, Raj, but Maggie didn't get shit out of him. He denied the affair, and the parents threatened to lawyer up. Still, you might want to talk to him. He looked a little shaky when Maggie started pushing him."

I waited for his reaction, my ears tuned to his mood, trying to pick up any sign that he was getting suspicious.

"Okay. Is that it?" he said.

There was no hint of suspicion in his voice. I had him. I was getting nervous for nothing. It was time I nudged him. I braced for the worst as I upped the ante. "Yeah, but it might help if you told me why you're covering for the kid. It's hard to steer the questioning down a safe road when I don't know where the cliffs are."

I held my breath as Holo-Ian took a long time answering. "Not over the phone, boy-o. Come to Roby's."

"Will do."

Holo-Ian vanished, leaving us staring at Margarita taking a mouthful of Raj Gupta.

Maggie started the vid again. "Do you thing it's wise to meet with him again?"

"I think so. Nothing's changed since last night."

"Except we interviewed Inez and, and lover boy." Maggie threw a disgusted gesture at the vid.

"So?"

"Ian covered for Raj once before, so who do you think Raj is going to run to now that he's feeling the heat?"

"So what if he does? I just told Ian you interviewed him."

"But they might get to talking, and Raj might tell him about how he saw you at Yuri's."

"I was just thinking about that," I said. "Let's say Raj does tell him I was at Yuri's. If Ian confronts me on it, I'll just admit it. I'll tell Ian I *was* there, that I was observing the interview."

Maggie shook her head. "But Yuri and Ian have surely talked since then. Yuri must've told Ian that I interviewed him alone."

"Right, so I'll say that I was observing the interview without Yuri's knowledge. I was watching from the kitchen, and I got bored for a minute and wandered into that room with all the vid equipment."

"Why would you watch in secret? Why not interview him with me, like we did Inez and Raj?"

I need a drink. Things were getting too complicated. I took a deep breath and set my brain to concentrating on the problem. I dug deep, looking for that perfect lie. I waded through all my years of being the right hand to the greatest manipulator in KOP history. All those years of cover-ups and backroom politicking . . .

"Got it," I said. "Lieutenant Rusedski scolded you already for inviting me to the barge, right?"

"Yep. And thanks for that, by the way."

"No problem. But you would've gotten into more trouble if you had let me sit in on Yuri's interview, right? You made me hide out because you knew that Yuri would talk to Ian, and you were afraid that when Ian found out I was there, he'd tattle to the KOP brass about you bringing a disgraced cop into official police business, *and* that was after you'd been warned. It'd put your promotion in jeopardy."

Maggie nodded agreement. "And I let you attend the interview of Inez Shenko because . . . ?"

I grinned as the pieces fell into place. "Because you had no reason to believe Ian would find out about it. Inez isn't mixed up in any of this. She was hardly going to go call Ian."

Maggie leaped ahead of me. "And I let you attend Raj's interview because he'd already seen you at Yuri's. What harm would there be in letting him see you again?"

"Right." I ran through the pile of lies in my mind, looking for contradictions and finding none. "Piece of cake."

"And what if Raj finds out that his sister gave this vid to us? You didn't tell Ian about that."

"That would be a problem," I agreed.

"You need to cut ties with Ian."

I nodded like I was thinking it over, but I'd already decided to go. Ian was starting to trust me, and I was already running scripts through my head, things to say, ways to ask questions without sounding like a snoop. If we were going to bring him and his cabal down, we'd have to take some risks.

Plus I wanted to keep Ian's money flowing into my pocket. I had a spine to pay for.

The vid was still running, and Raj was now jackhammering Adela's mother from behind. Raj was wearing a loincloth, which was just plain silly since it didn't cover anything, like trying to cover the flagpole with the flag. I was certain they were on the Juarez's bed. I recognized the bedding, the wallpaper, the nightstand, all looking better in their pre-lase-whipped state. Raj and Margarita had some guts doing this in her bedroom. What if Hector came home? Or Adela?

We refocused on the vid. We wanted to know who was working the camera, zooming it in and out, panning left and right. He'd talk from time to time, saying things like, "Oh, that's hot," and "That's right, suck it." We kept watching, scene after scene, looking for that one glimpse of the man.

Maggie kept the vid rolling. Raj and Margarita cycled through positions like they were Kama Sutra obsessed. Margarita was getting more adventurous with each session. The first few sessions featured a nervous and deliberate Margarita Juarez. But then, by the time they'd had a dozen-odd sessions in the bag, she'd completely transformed herself from a shrinking violet into a Venus flytrap. Instead of just lying there like she was at the beginning, she was now ordering the loincloth-clad Raj around,

a greedy glutton with an unquenchable appetite for his young
flesh. Raj, on the other hand, had the endurance of a marathoner.
The kid could go forever before letting loose, and even then, his
loincloth would only drop to half mast for a couple minutes before he was ready to run it back up for another go round.

Maggie and I were long past the discomfort of watching the
erotic material in each other's presence and had now entered a
phase of total pornographic overload. We had to keep it rolling,
though. We needed to know who was working the camera.

After another half hour of muff-diving, titty-fucking, anal-
popping action, I was tempted to tell Maggie to turn it off,
thinking he would never show himself. I was pretty confident
it was Yuri Kiper anyway. We already knew he'd filmed the
barge murders so picturing him as the debaucherous director
wasn't a big leap. It was like the guy was putting a portfolio together to be the devil's personal filmographer.

Finally, the camera operator showed himself. He stepped in
front of the camera to readjust the shade of a floor lamp, aiming the light at the bed. His back was turned. We couldn't see
his face, but we already knew it wasn't Yuri Kiper—this guy was
too thin. He turned back toward the camera and gave us a clear
view. *Unbelievable.* I didn't know why I was so surprised. . . .

Husband, father, and vid-station exec Hector Juarez.

It was Friday night and Bangkok Street was hopping. Roby's
had a line outside the door, mostly offworlders, steam fogging
out of the gaps in their slickers. I walked past them and cut
ahead of the line despite their protests. The bouncer ushered
me in as they clamored at my back. They'd probably assume I
was there to clean the toilets. How else would a raggedy old
local get in before them?

I forced my way through the crowd. I couldn't even see the

floor show because there were so many bodies packed in. The crowd thinned as I made it past the bar and into the side room. I scanned the room and picked up the wave of Ian's hand from the far side, where he was sitting with a group of cops. Again, I tallied the names, putting together a mental roll call of Ian's crew. They dispersed as I approached, and I took the seat opposite Ian at a table designed to look like a huge razor blade.

"Hey, boy-o, have a drink," and before I could say no, he poured some brandy into one of those damn goblets.

"Cheers," I said and took a swig of brandy that tasted like it had been infused with aluminum foil. *Cheap-ass goblets.* "Where's your girlfriend?"

Ian ignored the question altogether. "So you think I should tell you about Raj Gupta?"

"It's up to you, Ian. I'm just saying that it'd make my job a lot easier."

"And you think I can trust you?"

I looked across the room toward the door that led back to the bar. Hoshi was standing there with Freddie Lumbela, the two of them yukking it up. "It's up to you, Ian." I glanced at the fire exit; two more hommy boys swapping stories. A hinky feeling crept up from my gut. Standard KOP procedure—cover the exits. I kept my voice level. "Give me the lowdown on the kid, or don't. It's your choice."

"Tell me why I should trust you," he said with his jaw clenched, sinewy neck muscles buttressing down to his shoulders.

Adrenaline was already pumping through me. The urge to flee dominated my senses. I saw the waitress walk out and saw an opportunity. "Quit the third degree already. Either tell me or don't. I don't give a shit." I took a swig from my goblet and made a sour face. "I can't drink this garbage. Where did that waitress go? I'll be right back," I said. "You can think about it while I run to the bar to get a glass. Want anything?"

He shook his head.

I was up out of my seat, moving for the door that led to the bar. I weaved around tables toward the blaring demonic screech of music pulsing from the main room. Hoshi and his cop buddy saw me approaching and straightened up, their conversation suddenly over.

My fingers twitched as I looked for signs of aggression in their body language. My vision narrowed. The room got smaller. The walls closed around me, and I could feel the hollow stares of the skull sconces. Hoshi was looking past me, looking to Ian for direction. I kept walking with purposeful steps, my left hand reaching back for my piece.

Hoshi stepped into the doorway with his arms crossed. Then picking up the cue, Freddie Lumbela joined him shoulder to shoulder, the pair of them barring the door. I slipped my hand under my untucked shirt, feeling the cold metal tucked into my waistband. I wrapped my fingers around the grip and pulled it free an instant before arriving at the doorway. I brandished my piece unnaturally as a lefty, looking more like a joke than a threat.

"Step aside," I said with an enforcer's authority.

"Why you getting so spooked, Juno?" asked Hoshi without budging.

I chanced a look back over my shoulder—four, maybe five guys coming this way. My finger twitched on the trigger as I prepared to fry my way out of here. "Move. You know I'm not joking."

Freddie Lumbela stepped aside. He'd been a cop long enough to know my reputation. Hoshi stayed in place, blocking the right side of the broad doorway and staring me down. I went left and slipped past him, keeping my piece trained on his chest as I backed into the crowd at the bar, bumping my way backward through people who muttered angry complaints until they saw my weapon and moved aside. I kept backing away from the door while Ian and crew stood there like they were posing for a group photo. I set my mind on taking a mental snapshot, adding their names to the exposure . . . Kripsen, Deluski, Lumbela. . . . I kept backing my way through, leaving a wake of parted partyers behind. *That was too easy.* I was halfway to the front door before I did the math. There were five of them standing in that doorway, watching me go. *I counted six or seven a minute ago.* I took another step back, and another, as I processed the information. The missing one, maybe two, they would've gone out the side room's fire exit, then run around the block to the front door and reentered the club where they could approach me from behind. They'd be here soon, and I was backing right into them.

I looked at Ian one last time, his arrogant face, and bolted onto the main floor. I beelined for the stage. There had to be a way out behind it, maybe one of those big cargo loading doors. I bumped tables, spilled drinks, tripped over offworld feet. I didn't look back to see if they were in pursuit—didn't need to know that they were tearing across the club waving badges and weapons. I hit the stage and vaulted up. I raced to exit stage left; a performing dominatrix was in my way: I aimed to the right of her, but she dodged in the same direction, and I plowed into her, the two of us tumbling to the floor. I landed on top of her and winced as her spiked leather dug into me. She wriggled out from under me as I scrambled for my footing. Lase-fire crackled over my head as I disappeared behind a curtain that flamed up an instant later.

I crashed through a set of dominatrix extras, catching a whiff of cheap leather. I saw an exit sign and bulled my way toward it, flinging stagehands out of my way. I slammed my body into the crash bar and erupted out into the alley. I didn't think about which way to run, I just ran. My lungs blazed as I hoped to reach the corner before I heard them come through the door behind me. If I could reach the corner first and get around it, they wouldn't know which way I'd gone. They'd have to split up. I heard the door smash open behind me a full second before I made it around the corner. *Fuck*. The whole lot of them would still be on my tail.

I was on Bangkok Street, my feet speeding through a crowd of drunken bar hoppers that wobbled out of my way. I couldn't keep this up. My legs were already getting heavy, and my chest felt ready to explode. I sprinted into a trashy souvenir shop that had a stuffed monitor on its haunches guarding the door. I dashed down an aisle crammed with cheap wood carvings and machine-painted ceramics. When I reached the aisle's end, I threw a shoulder into the shelving before hurtling through the back door to the sound of toppling knickknacks.

I ran left, sending a group of teenage opium smokers clambering. I took a couple more steps and had to stop to keep from collapsing. I turned around and fought to keep from vomiting as I aimed at the door. The door flung open and I squeezed off a stream of lase-fire. I tried to keep my left hand steady, but between having to shoot lefty and my wild breathing, the beam wavered all over the damn place. As bad as the aim was, it was still effective enough to force Ian and Hoshi back into the store. The door swung open again, and I squeezed off a sustained burn that fried a path of raindrops out of the air. I stepped backward down the alley, my eyes trained on the door as I began to catch my breath. Again, the door swung open, and I squeezed off another burst that scorched the brick walls with a scribble of black as my aim fluttered hopelessly about.

I took off for one last fast-paced sprint. My feet kicked up puddle water, splashing the O heads who had plastered themselves against the alley walls to keep from getting in my way. I got back out onto Bangkok Street and slowed down to a walk. Ian wouldn't be far behind, but I decided to try melting into the crowd of dark-haired, brown-skinned Lagartans, most of whom were wearing their cotton whites just like me. I walked as fast as I could without running. My phone rang. I didn't have to look at the display to know it was Ian trying to run a trace that would lock down my position. I dropped it on the street—should've dumped it as soon as I'd started running.

I kept moving, not looking back. I saw Froelich, one of the hommy boys who had been guarding the fire exit. He was standing tiptoe trying to pick me out of the crowd, but succeeding only in making himself stand out. I avoided him easily by ducking behind a series of street vendors with canvas tarps tied to lampposts that shielded me from his view. I turned left, down one of the side streets. I tried to stay under the tarps as I passed by the vendors' booths—first a florist, then a souvenir hawker, and finally a snail-selling street vendor who tried to entice me by ladling snail juice over a steaming snail pyramid.

I came out into the open. My back muscles tightened in expectation of lase-fire. I told myself not to look back. The crowds were thinning and looking back would make me easier to pick out. I kept my feet moving at a controlled pace and hit the end of the block. I turned right, the buzz of Bangkok Street falling away behind me.

seventeen

I'D spent half the night at the hospital, the other half in my tent, lying awake in my hammock, my head full of racing thoughts. I was surprised that Ian never showed up in the maternity ward. I didn't know if he'd checked in on Niki or not, but if he had, he must've believed that she had indeed checked out. That, or he still thought I didn't care what happened to her. Either way she was safe, at least for now.

I was worried about Maggie. I'd woken her up when I called her from the hospital and told her she should get out of the house, but she refused, saying she'd be safer staying inside where her alarm system would keep her well protected.

It was getting noisy outside my tent as I began to hear the early risers clearing their throats of night phlegm, and shortly thereafter came the ring of pots and pans bumping together. Suddenly, there were crying babies and zippering tent flaps all around. Hushed conversations were getting gradually louder as there were fewer and fewer sleepers to be mindful of. I could hear the hollow clangs of gas cans and plastic milk jugs as Tenttowners made their way down to the canal to fill up with filthy water. Dozens of propane stoves came alive, sounding like a chorus of exhaling emphysema patients.

Three generations of Mozambes had lived this same harsh existence until I said enough and got myself out. My family emigrated from Earth, one family among thousands who set off on the fourteen-year journey to Lagarto at the peak of the brandy boom only to find that the boom had gone bust by the time they landed. With no jobs or homes waiting for them, they were all left to rot here in Tenttown.

The tent shook. I reflexively grabbed for my piece with the wrong hand. I pawed at it with my splinted fingers once, twice before realizing that I needed to switch hands.

I heard Maggie's voice. "Juno. Are you in there?"

"Yeah. Come in." I rested my piece on my chest and flicked on the battery-powered lantern as Maggie unzipped her way in and looked for a dry place to set her bag, one of those high-priced soft leather suitcases. "You can hang it there," I said, pointing to a hook on the center post.

She hoisted it up over her head and hooked it through one of the handles. "Got an extra hammock?"

"Take your pick."

Maggie took a swinging seat. "My partner dropped by last night."

"Are you okay?"

"I'm fine, just a little shaken up. He started shouting threats through the door. I pretended I wasn't home, which must've made him angry because he started throwing rocks through my windows."

I didn't even want to think about what he might have done to my house. "Was he alone?"

"I don't know."

"Did he try to come in through the windows?"

"If he had, he'd be dead. He must've taken off pretty soon after the alarm went off. I waited until the rent-a-cops arrived and then I snuck out the back."

"Did you ditch your phone?"

She nodded and swung her legs up onto the hammock.

I had my landlord bring in some food for me to share with my new roomie. Maggie and I hung in our hammocks and

forked through our eggs unenthusiastically. I thought I should
be mad at Maggie for getting me into this. It had seemed simple enough at the start. All I had to do was talk to the Juarez
girl and get a confession. I'd score a little cash, and that would
be it. And now I was living in this pit with a bounty on my
head. Yes, I should've been mad at Maggie, but I wasn't, not in
the slightest. Niki had used up all the anger I had. It was her
fault. She was the one who had me scrounging for dough.

Hours passed before somebody came out of the house. It was
the sister. And when she stood under the porch light, we could
see she was sporting a fresh black eye. She walked down the
block and stepped into a bodega a few doors down, coming back
out a couple minutes later with a candy bar. She inhaled it on the
way back and stuffed the wrapper in her pocket before going
back inside.

Another hour passed before Raj finally came out. He strutted down the sidewalk, right past the burned-out opium house
where Maggie and I were hiding. Maggie and I filed out the
door, leaving the stink of O-head piss behind. She and I fell in
behind Raj as he crossed the street. We followed ten paces
behind, closing the gap as he approached a minialley between
a liquor store and a pharmacy. Maggie and I timed our sprinting approach so we would catch him as he passed what we
hoped would be a nice place to have a private little chat. He
spun around too late, and I had him in my arms, pulling him
into the gap between the stores. He flailed his arms, trying to
shake loose of my grip. I slammed him into a brick wall, stun-
ning him still.

Maggie surveyed the alley. "It's clear."

I shoved my bandaged forearm under his chin and pinned
his neck to the wall. I clamped my free hand over his mouth to
cover his calls for help. I started baby-talking him. "Where's

your mommy and daddy now? They're not here to protect their little baby boy, are they?" Raj put on a defiant face that I broke through with a little more pressure on his windpipe.

"Take it easy, Juno," Maggie said.

I paid no heed to Maggie and stared deep into his eyes, keeping up the pressure until he turned good and red. I counted to five in my head then loosened up so he wouldn't pass out. Raj started sucking air through his nose so hard that his nostrils almost pinched themselves shut. "I'm going to take my hand off your mouth," I told him. "You start screaming, and I start squeezing, understand?"

He nodded his pinned head.

I took my hand away but kept my forearm under his chin. "You put that shiner on your sister, didn't you?"

He opened his mouth to talk but couldn't speak. I relaxed my forearm a little more and let him catch more breath. "She's lucky that's all I gave her," he finally wheezed.

"How did you know she gave us the vid?"

"She told me. She's so fucking stupid. She stole that vid out of my room and then bragged about it."

"What do you say we get back to how you were banging your girlfriend's mother while her father watched?"

"What about it?" he said in a defeated voice.

"Tell me about Hector and Margarita, from the beginning."

"It was Hector's idea. He came to me months ago. He saw I had a way with the girls, and he started asking me questions about them. Just innocent stuff at the beginning, but then he started asking me about what kinds of things I liked to do with them. That's when he told me he liked to watch. I got all weirded out thinking he wanted me to let him watch me with my girlfriends, but then he explained how he wanted to watch me doing his wife. He told me that if I did it, he'd hire me as a junior reporter after my internship was over."

"He offered you a job if you'd have sex with his wife?"

"That's pretty much it. He asked if I'd be into it, and I thought why the hell not. Rita looked like a nice piece of ass."

"How about her? Was she into it?"

"Not at first. Once Hector got me onboard, he had to talk her into it. It took weeks before we all got together that first night. She was all nervous and shit. But by the time we finished, she was into it. Believe me, she was into it." He flashed his pearlies.

"Why were they going to divorce?"

"That was Rita. She was the one that wanted to divorce. She started seeing me without Hector. I guess she eventually decided she didn't need him anymore. She'd get a hotel room, and I'd come over and bone the shit out of her. That lady was an animal. I'd have to put my dick on ice afterward." More pearlies.

"And you were doing all this *while* you were dating her daughter?"

Raj grinned even wider. "Yeah. I figured that tight little pussies probably ran in the family." He leered at Maggie.

I slapped that look off his face. "Show some respect," I ordered. "What did her parents think about you dating their daughter?"

"You think I'm stupid? I kept them in the dark."

"And how did you manage that?"

"I told Adela that if she wanted to see me, she had to keep it secret. I told her that her father didn't like me, and he'd fire me if he found out we were seeing each other."

This kid was fucking unbelievable. At nineteen, he was already a master manipulator. "Who killed Hector and Margarita?"

"Adela did."

"Bullshit."

"She did. She must've found out about me and her parents, and she went nuts."

"You're full of shit, Raj. You expect me to believe that when Adela found out about your little ménage à trois with her parents, she decided to kill them only *after* sneaking off to hump your sorry ass a couple times?"

"No. She must've found out that night when she went home. Detective Davies found that same vid my sister gave you loaded up in the home system. My guess is Adela walked in on Hector whacking off to the Raj and Rita show, and then she just lost it."

"What's your relationship with Detective Davies?"

"I barely know him."

"You know him well enough to call him and tell him about our visit last night."

"I thought he might be able to get that vid back again."

"What do you mean by again?"

"When Detective Davies told me about the vid he found in their home system, I begged him to keep it quiet. I didn't think it would be good for my career if my new boss found out that I was doing the old boss's wife. He gave it to me, but then my sister stole it and gave it to you. I asked him if he could get it back again, or maybe just destroy it."

"Why did Detective Davies agree to help you the first time?"

"What would it hurt? He had his killer already. He knew I was going to be a reporter someday. He said that he'd ask me to return the favor one day."

I looked over my shoulder at Maggie. "Are you believing this?"

She didn't respond, but I could see the uncertainty in her face. If Adela really had killed her parents it, then why would Ian be so sensitive about me talking to her? He broke my fingers, dammit. But there were other possibilities. Maybe he was just worried that I'd find out about his little arrangement with

Raj. But that was hardly a big deal. All he did was save the kid some embarrassment by burying the vid. It was the kind of thing cops did every day. But this time, there *was* a promotion on the line. A black mark in his file, no matter how small, could make the brass favor Maggie over Ian. Or maybe he was just afraid of me digging into his other cases, like the barge murders. Was it possible that Adela did do it? She *did* confess. And she didn't just say the words and sign the papers. She was *believable*.

I had to be sure Raj was telling the truth. I balanced on one foot as I slid my left hand down to my ankle strap and pulled out my blade. "You think the camera loves you, do you?" I powered the blade up. The red blade sizzled into life.

Maggie was tugging on my shoulder. "That's enough, Juno."

I raised the blade's tip to his face. "What will the camera think if I split that little nose of yours in half?"

Maggie was yelling at me, telling me to stop. The kid was squirming under my grip, but I had him firm. I waved the blade across his face, close enough that he could feel the steam of flash-fried drizzle.

"I don't believe you," I hissed.

"It's true," he screamed.

I aimed the tip of the blade at his eye. "Tell me the truth or you'll be doing the news with a glass eye."

He was crying now. "I did tell the truth. Please don't . . . Please!"

Tears evaporated off his cheek as I moved the tip closer. "Tell me the truth."

"I did tell the truth," he sobbed.

Maggie was still tugging my shoulder. "That's enough. Stop it," she said in my ear.

I dropped the kid, letting him tumble to his knees. I turned off the blade and slid it back into my pocket. Maggie and I walked away, leaving the kid blubbering. We didn't get more than a block before Maggie stopped me. "What the hell was that about?" she asked.

"I had to be sure he was telling the truth."

"This is *my* investigation, Juno. We're doing this my way, and my way doesn't include burning a kid's eye out."

"Relax, I wouldn't have done it," I lied.

"We're not going to torture suspects! You hear me?"

I shook my head and started walking again.

She grabbed my wrist and yanked me to a stop. "Don't you walk away from me when I'm talking to you!"

I turned away. I didn't need a lecture.

She kept at me. "I'm sick of this bullshit, Juno. One minute you're sitting there behaving yourself and the next you're like some damn psycho. Don't you have any self control?"

The knot in my stomach clenched. Pent-up rage welled up from my gut. "Dammit, Maggie!" I yelled back almost incoherently. "Ian pinched my wife's air hose shut 'til she turned fucking blue! If I have to carve that pervert's eyes out to get to the truth, I'll do it, and I don't care what you say!"

Maggie didn't respond. The two of us just stood there fuming at each other, avoiding each other's eyes. We finally started walking again, covering the blocks in silence, the drizzling rain cooling my hot head. My stomach was knotted to the point of cramping. I forced myself to walk upright, stretching my stomach muscles until they stopped seizing. I wondered how long I could live like this. Something had to give, and soon.

"Did you believe him?" I asked when I finally felt calm enough to talk without raising my voice.

"Yes."

"You think Adela killed her parents?"

"No. But I think Raj believes she did. Ian probably convinced him. How about you? What do you think?"

"The same."

We stopped at a café, and I used the owner's phone to call Vlad. Still no sign of Ian. Then I called up to the Orbital and downloaded our now decrypted vid files. Maggie paid the café's owner to let us go upstairs and use their home vid system.

I settled on the sofa, a foam futon with a cheap faux-brass frame that was splotched with patches of faded metal. Maggie sat next to me after having tried the armchair, which was so mildewed it had made her sneeze. Once Maggie finished backing up the files to her home system, she started the first vid.

The room shifted. Gone were the crucifixes and the glittery Virgin Mary display. Gone were the family photos and the ratty furniture. Suddenly we were sitting in an overwhelmingly pink bedroom. It was so pink, it felt like one of Niki's corner-store romance novels had exploded in here. There were red scarves draped over the lamps and sweetheart pillows stacked high on pink satin sheets. Two white vases filled with red roses stood at the foot of the bed. The vases were so large that they were gaudy by definition. Noticing the small round windows, I realized it wasn't a bedroom at all, but a cabin on a boat, a nice boat.

Liz came in, stark naked. I remembered the label Yuri had put on the vid disc I'd copied, "Liz—Complete Works." She stepped in front of the camera and smiled shyly. The vid froze on her smiling face, and the words *Liz Lagarto* popped in over her head.

Maggie shook her head. "Christ. I don't think I can take any more porn."

I felt empty with the realization that Liz was a porn star, with a tacky name to boot. I didn't know what my feelings for her were, but I was already feeling jealous of the men I'd soon be seeing. She was masturbating now, vibrating her way around the bed.

"Mind if I speed this up?" Maggie asked.

"Please," I responded, hoping she couldn't see the bulge in my pants.

Maggie set the vid to 4X, and we watched Ian's girlfriend get off at quadruple speed. *Un-fucking-believable.* I hit my flask hard, wanting to soothe the knot in my stomach that was now screaming at me, telling me how bad I'd screwed everything up. I was back to living in Tenttown. I was being hunted by Ian and his gang of dirty cops. I was watching porn with a woman I thought of as a daughter. I was spending money I didn't have in an effort to keep my suicidal wife alive. And now I had the hots for Ian's girlfriend, a porn star for chrissakes. I felt miserable as I watched Liz Lagarto in what was now a quad-speed four-way, my pants getting more and more uncomfortable with every passing second.

I passed the flask to Maggie, who took a deep swig then said, "This is the most action I've gotten in months."

I chuckled, and she chuckled back. The nervous chuckles quickly escalated into outright laughter for no apparent reason other than we needed it to. Then when the coffee shop owner walked in on a high-speed cum shot and ran out covering her eyes, our laughter turned into bent-over, tear-rolling hysteria.

We were well into the third movie when I asked Maggie to slow the speed down to normal. Liz Lagarto was in a bamboo hut that looked like the huts you'd find in the fringe towns except you could tell it was just a cheap set piece. She was playing the role of some Tarzan-like jungle girl who needed taming.

"Now, freeze it," I said. I got up and walked past Liz, who was wearing a tiger-skin outfit that was so skimpy it could have been made from a cub. "I know this guy," I said as I stepped up to the stuffed tiger that was being used as a background prop. I was sure it was the same one, standing upright with one claw raised. "Horst has this tiger standing outside his office on the Square."

"You know what these movies are?" Maggie asked rhetorically. "Have you noticed how Lagartan they are? Liz Lagarto in the jungle. Liz Lagarto on a riverboat. Liz Lagarto in a brandy cellar. How much you wanna bet they're promotionals for his tour company? I bet he distributes them for a tidy profit, but his main purpose is to feed his sex tour business."

I realized she was right, and I said so. I went back to my seat thinking Horst had found quite the market penetration strategy.

Maggie started the vid running again. "You've got to be shitting me," she said upon recognizing the loincloth-wearing jungle boy who entered the hut—Raj Gupta.

I was speechless. Jaw-drop dumbfounded. That little shit, he didn't tell us he'd starred in a porno. He said he hardly knew Ian, but here he was getting his loincloth lifted by Ian's girlfriend. And what was it with this kid and loincloths? We interviewed him twice, *twice,* and we still hadn't gotten the full story. Right then, as I watched him get a lubing à la Liz Lagarto, I was seriously wishing I'd taken the opportunity to do some facial carving when I had the chance. "Are there any women on this planet that he isn't banging?"

Maggie said, "I might be the only."

My flask was empty by the time we started number five. I just wanted to get it over with. I was OD'ed on porn. What had started off erotic had quickly turned laughable, and now it had become just plain tedious. It was true that we'd learned a little more about Raj and Horst. And it was also true that we'd learned a hell of a lot more than we ever wanted about Liz, but our main goal in ransacking Yuri Kiper's office was to get us closer to the barge murders, and on that score we'd come up empty.

Maggie had the system cranked up to 8X now. The plot was easy to follow, even at eight speed, and without hearing any dialog. Liz Lagarto, married to a less than adventuresome husband, seeks out an affair with a charismatic neighbor played by a dark-skinned, middle-aged local who had starred in two of her other movies. He introduces her to the rough trade, starting with a little pinching during sex and quickly moving up to spanking and nipple clamps. Each time they have sex, she encourages him to push a little further.

Maggie slowed it down to regular speed as the degradation began to hit disturbing levels. They'd moved far beyond kinky and were now into the realm of the truly perverted. He was keeping her locked in his basement now, chained to a post with a dog collar on. When she cried, he'd tell her she was a sinner. "Thou shalt not commit adultery."

This was the first thing we'd watched that smacked of the S&M culture that all our suspects seemed to be a part of. I paid rapt attention despite the mounting revulsion.

Liz groveled as he came in and told her that today was her day of reckoning. He had a bed in the basement, and he cuffed her to it. He started in with electric shocks to her privates. How could she submit to this? Liz was panicked, straining so hard at her cuffs that her wrists bled. I squirmed in my seat when he razored her thighs and then her breasts. *Make it end.* Bile rose up in my throat as he snuffed out an entire pack of cigarettes on her back, making a connect-the-dots cross. *This can't be real.*

I looked over at Maggie, who was looking as pale as I felt. "This can't be real, Maggie."

"God, I hope you're right."

I didn't know what was worse, the fact that a human being would make a movie like this or the fact that there were people who got off on it.

He turned her over so she was face up. "Cheating on your husband is a sin," he said. "Now you die."

Liz struggled against her restraints. She yanked so hard that she dislocated her shoulder and cried out in pain. *It's all a fake. It has to be.* But there were no cut shots like you saw in regular movies, the kind of thing where you see the attacker stab down, then you see the victim bleeding, but you never see the knife go in. He grabbed her by the hair and held a knife to her throat. I kept telling myself it couldn't be real, but when I looked at her eyes, I saw pure terror. She was hyperventilating. It looked so *real*. I wanted to believe she was acting, but I'd seen her movies, and she wasn't that good an actress.

But it had to be fake. She was wearing an open-backed dress the first time I saw her. I would've seen the cig-burn cross on her back. He dragged the blade across her throat. Blood went spurting. She jerked against her restraints, once, twice, spraying blood all over her attacker. One more spasm and she went still, her eyes staring off in death. *It's not real. It can't be. Liz is alive.* But it was all so believable, all one long shot, no cuts.

I stared at her corpse as I told myself she was fine—she was *alive*. But she wasn't at Roby's last night. . . . No, I told myself, I copied this vid almost two days ago. I'd seen her since then.

The vid was still running. Her murderous boyfriend circled the bed, studying his handiwork, his face speckled with blood. She looked like a real corpse. Her chest didn't move, and she didn't blink. Her skin turned ashen. How did they do this? Flies were buzzing around the scene. Scavenging geckos were coming out of the walls, their noses tuned to the scent of decay.

The murderer kneeled on the bed. *No, don't tell me!* He unzipped his pants.

I covered my eyes. "Turn it off already!"

The scene blinked out, and the room returned to normal.

We were left staring at the café owner's Virgin Mary shrine.

I focused on it, trying to purge the images from my mind. I studied the brightly painted Mary standing in front of a mosaic background of sparkly glued beads. I never was the religious type, yet I felt the urge to ask for forgiveness, just for having watched.

My phone rang. My new anonymous phone.

eighteen

MAGGIE and I sped down the hospital corridor. I didn't see Vlad posted by her door. I sped up, Maggie staying on my wing, our shoes echoing off the linoleum. We thundered through Niki's door. Niki was there, right where she was supposed to be. Her startled eyes said that if she could have jumped she would have. Maggie was already rushing over to her when Vlad came bursting out of the bathroom, his piece raised. He stopped half a second before frying a hole through my chest.

"Shit, Juno," he said, "I almost killed you. You should've announced yourself before barging in like that."

I grabbed Vlad's arm and yanked him out into the hall. "Why weren't you guarding the door? I thought you'd ditched her." The only thing keeping me from yelling was the fact that I hadn't yet caught my breath.

"Relax," he said. "I didn't think it was too smart to be hanging around outside her door. Might as well put a big sign up that says, 'Here's Niki.'"

"Right," I said as I tried to collect my haywire self. "When was he here?"

"About a half hour ago. One of the nurses came down to tell me, and I called you right away. She said he got very belligerent with the desk nurse upstairs. She told him Niki checked out, but he wasn't buying it."

"But he left?"

"Not until after he threw up a big stink. Listen, Juno, I don't think this is going to work much longer. If he comes back with a wad of bills, I don't think he'll have to ask around long before some orderly tips him off."

Vlad was looking at me, waiting for me to tell him what to do. I had no idea what to tell him, none whatsoever. "I'll figure something out," I said unconvincingly as I walked back into Niki's room.

Maggie had Niki turned on her side so she could check the skin ulcers that had formed on her backside from lack of movement. I took a look myself. They looked good. The staff was doing a nice job keeping them under control. There was nothing more life-threatening for Niki than those ulcers, which were sure to get infested with maggots if they broke open. And then, if they didn't heal quickly enough, the rot would set in, and once the rot set in, it was only a matter of time.

Maggie eased Niki over onto her back. Niki looked me straight in the eye. I stroked her cheek, which was just about the only place she could feel my touch. The door flew open. Vlad was there with a nurse I recognized as one of the nurses who took care of Niki when she was in Intensive Care. "He's back, boss. He's got a whole crew of cops with him, and they're going from room to room."

The nurse took the purple 10K bill Vlad held out for her and stepped away in a hurry.

"Shit. Let's move her. I'll get the bed, you get—"

Vlad interrupted. "No way, boss. I had them move her twice. It takes a whole team."

"Well get them in here. NOW!"

"There's no time, boss. It's a big production."

I was so panic-stricken, I was practically panting. "What am I supposed to do? Just let them come and kill her?"

Vlad looked down at the floor like a kid who just got in trouble.

"Yes," said Niki in her ventilator voice.

I wheeled on her. "Shut up, Niki. Now's not the time."

"Seems to me . . . now's the p—perfect time."

"Shut up already!"

Maggie aimed a stern look at me before comforting Niki. "It'll be okay," she said to her. "We'll think of something."

Vlad poked his head out the door and looked both directions. "Nobody yet. They must still be upstairs."

Fucking fuck! I was about to freak out. My blood was boiling. My bobbing hand was waving like a blade of grass in high winds. My stomach burned like I'd swallowed a hot coal. I grasped for a little sanity and came up empty. *SHIT!*

Vlad looked out again. "There they are. They're at the far end of the hall, two of them."

From somewhere in my gut came the answer, like it was always there. *Today's the day I die.* I pulled my piece and spat orders. "I want Maggie and Vlad in the bathroom. It's me they want. I'll take the fight to them in the hall. Don't come to help. If they get me, they get me, understand? They'll leave once they have me."

Maggie was shaking her head no.

"It's the only way, Maggie. If any of them come in, I need you and Vlad to ambush them from the bathroom. I'm counting on you."

Maggie kept shaking her head.

I grabbed her hand. "I need you, Maggie."

"No. You can't just provoke a firefight in a hospital." She pulled Niki's blanket off and started wrapping it into an oblong ball.

"What are you doing?"

"We're in maternity, right?" She took the bundled blanket and tucked it under Niki's arm.

"This won't work."

"Yes it will," she said. "Now go get another blanket to cover this equipment."

It won't work. It won't work. It won't work. I was looking at Maggie. She was staring me down, her face hard as iron. I tucked my piece back in my belt. "You better be right."

"A blanket. *Now*."

"I got it, boss," said Vlad. He took a peek out the door and slipped out.

Maggie started pulling tubes and wires, unhooking everything but Niki's air.

Could that rolled-up blanket really pass for a baby? I got busy wheeling equipment into the bathroom, packing it in with as much care as a dockworker. I slammed the heart rate monitor down on the sink with so much force that I heard the mortar cracking. I nabbed the IV stand and battled it into a tilted position by the toilet.

Vlad was back. "They're getting close, maybe eight or nine doors down."

Maggie draped the extra blanket over the respirator and set the vase of flowers I'd sent to Niki on top. This *could* work. They'd be looking for tubes and blinking lights. When they looked in, they'd find the same scene they'd been seeing all along this ward, a woman sleeping with her baby.

Vlad went into the bathroom and stood on the toilet to make room for me to cram myself in. Maggie tilted Niki's head to the side, away from the door, making her look like she was asleep.

I could hear Niki whisper, "Let them kill m—me."

Maggie soothed with her voice. "Shh. It'll be okay."

Maggie was poised over Niki's air hose. I listened as the sound of opening doors came closer. Maggie stayed still, waiting as long as she could. Finally, she unhooked the plastic air hose from the stem that was planted in Niki's chest. Maggie dropped the hose, letting it fall to the floor. She pulled the plug on the suddenly noisier ventilator then tucked both the air hose and the power cord under the blanket and hustled for the bathroom.

"Her chest," I hissed.

Maggie skidded to a stop and pulled Niki's sheet up over the plastic valve poking out of her chest. I sucked my body in to make room for Maggie, who slammed into me. I started to tip over. Vlad steadied me with his hand. Maggie tried to yank the door closed, but my foot acted as a mashed-toe doorstop. I pulled my foot up and leaned into Vlad, while Maggie managed to make it latch on the second try.

I heard the door pop open next door. My heart was pounding. Any second now . . .

But then I heard another door open, this time closer and realized the first door I'd heard must've been two doors down.

"Damn," whispered Maggie. She'd pulled the hose too soon. Niki could suffocate before we got the hose reattached.

And then another door. A baby started crying and a muffled, "Sorry, ma'am," came through the bathroom wall.

Finally, Niki's door opened. The three of us were collectively holding our breath. I had my ear pressed up against the door. I had my piece in my left hand, and my right hand was on the doorknob, which was luckily a lever-style knob that I could easily open with my bad hand. Long seconds ticked by. I thought of my wife, lying there unable to breathe, thinking it had been too long already. Maggie had pulled the hose way too soon. She easily could've kept the air pumping for another twenty or thirty seconds and still would've had the time to hide.

The door closed. He was either inside or he'd moved on. I waited for the sound of the next door down, needing to breathe, but afraid of making any noise. I heard the latch pop next door, and let out the breath I was holding. We rushed to Niki's bed careful not to make any noise. Maggie snapped the air hose back in while I stuck the plug back into the outlet. The ventilator whooshed into life.

Niki's eyes were open. Her skin was red with enough blue underneath to border on purple, but her eyes were open, and I saw them move. Relief overwhelmed me as Niki began to lose a shade of red with every pump of the ventilator.

Vlad clapped his hand on Maggie's shoulder. "Nicely done."

Maggie nodded.

My legs felt weak. I took a seat on the end of Niki's bed. "Vlad, as soon as they're gone, get one of the doctors in here. We need to get her moved."

The flyer lifted off, then banked to the right. I looked through the rain-streaked window as we skimmed over a building that had tightly concentrated patches of exposed rebar poking up. Looking around, I noticed most of the buildings had that same unfinished look, so many of them topped by tarps instead of tile. It was rare that a Lagartan developer could afford to construct a building in its entirety. Instead, money permitting, they'd add a floor at a time, each time leaving the rebar exposed for the next layer to attach to.

We moved east, the flyer's hum drowning out Niki's respirator. Below, I could see the Koba River, a broad black stripe arcing through the expanse of city lights. The river was everything to this city, everything. I'd drunk its water my whole life. I was raised on its fish. It was our all-in-one transportation system, irrigation system, and sewer system, the one constant in this fucked-up world. Without it, nothing was possible. This city was fortunate to have such an unbreakable backbone to depend on. I looked at my wife, who was looking at me with despondent eyes, her backbone nowhere near as strong.

She'd given up arguing with me. We'd spent hours in that hospital room, fighting it out while Maggie made arrangements to transport Niki to the Orzo family's plantation. I'd been stupid to think things were going to get better after I confronted Niki with my knowledge of her secrets. It was never the secrets themselves that were killing her inside. It was the truth behind those secrets that had been torturing her for all these years. How could I have thought anything different?

She was still looking at me. She didn't look angry. She looked resigned and defeated. God, how could I do this to her? I didn't want to be the cause of her suffering. Right then, all I wanted to do was unhook her from the respirator. Anything to relieve her pain. Anything to keep her from looking at me like that. No, I told myself. Things will get better. I clung to those words like they were the only thing keeping me afloat even as the words sank into nothingness and took me with them.

I don't know how long I stayed like that, feeling like I was at the bottom of a well that had been filled back in with me still inside, the dirt pressing down on me, crushing me until I couldn't move or breathe. I was nothing. No, I was less than nothing, powerless and insignificant.

I had to stay busy. I snapped myself out of it and used the flyer's comm system to call up my financials. I stared at the numbers, but was unable to comprehend them. Balance statements looked out of focus. Medical bills looked like they were written in a foreign language. I gradually shook off the malaise and regretted it as the numbers began to come through in full high-debt clarity.

This flyer ride was already showing on my statement, although it showed as a generic medical expense. I'd insisted that the hospital list it that way. Ian would be monitoring my finances by now. It was unbelievable how much it cost. Maggie had tried to talk me into sharing the burden, but I refused. I don't take charity. First, she told me I was an idiot, then when I didn't respond, she came at me with a fresh argument, telling me that I was on her payroll, and I should think of relocating Niki as a business expense that she was responsible for. I told her not to argue. I'd had enough for one day.

We were skimming the jungle, or at least that was what the pilot said we were doing. When I looked out the window, all I could see was black.

It wasn't much longer before the flyer began losing altitude. Maggie said, "There it is."

I followed her gaze to a sprawling set of well-lit, interconnected buildings. I counted at least a dozen unique, brandy-era structures. They consisted of an open-air platform of polished wood raised on stilts with a pitched thatch roof on top. A series of raised walkways ran between the buildings, creating a network of giant jungle huts.

The flyer set down in a recently burned clearing, blackened vegetation all around. I unplugged the respirator from the flyer's outlet and plugged it into the portable generator I'd bought for the occasion. It was powered by kerosene, of all things. Lagarto was probably the only planet left that used crude oil products. The thing smelled awful, and it made a horrible racket, but the motor only had to kick in once every couple hours, and it only had to run for about ten minutes to charge the battery that could provide hours of power. I wedged the respirator under the gurney and folded Niki's legs to make room for the generator on the gurney's end. It took all three of us, Maggie, Vlad and me, to wheel Niki off the flyer's cargo loader. Then we made bumpy progress across the slashed-and-burned landing site, the still-smoldering foliage discharging puffs of choky black smoke.

The flyer took off behind us and made for Koba to pick up another high-priced charter. Maggie's aunt greeted us as we wheeled up the ramp. She was a stern-looking woman with a stiff smile. She gave Maggie a formal hug, and then the two Orzo women exchanged some starched niceties. Maggie introduced us all. Vlad and I received cold handshakes; she saved all her overly sugared warmth for Niki, who she talked to with a singsong voice most people reserved for the very young and the very old.

She ushered us from building to building, the gurney rattling over the horizontal wood slats, finally arriving in a private room with a curtain for a door. I was uneasy about the lack of doors and locks, but Maggie had assured me that the location was so remote there was nothing to worry about. The room was walled on three sides while the fourth was open to the jungle except for a railing. We moved Niki from the gurney to the bed and started puzzling over the best way to get Niki's tubes through the mosquito netting. The nurse I'd contracted thankfully arrived from a nearby jungle clinic soon after and, having a bit more experience on the matter, she was easily able to rig up a workable solution with the aid of some duct tape. With that settled, the nurse went looking for an extra bed. She wanted to sleep in Niki's room. Without any monitoring equipment, she said it was the best way to keep track.

Maggie went off to visit with her aunt, and then Vlad went searching for some food, which left Niki and me alone for the first time. After a generous dousing of bug spray, I sat next to Niki's bed.

"It's beautiful here," she said.

I nodded and allowed myself to relax enough that I could appreciate the chirps and squawks coming from the jungle outside. For the first time, I noticed the flickering iridescent light bugs fluttering about in delightful randomness. "We'll have to take a tour of the place."

"I'd like that."

"We should've taken more vacations."

"You're r—right. We should have."

Sorrow descended upon me like a sopping wet blanket. "I'll have to add that to the list."

"What list?" she wanted to know.

"The list of ways that I've failed you."

"Don't say that."

"I'm sorry, Niki."

"For w—what?"

"For being a bad husband."

"I told . . . you not to say . . . that."

"It's true. I was always too busy, too caught up in KOP. I thought what I was doing was important."

"You were trying . . . to make a d—difference."

"I did more bad than good. You know that. I should've spent more time with you. I should've been one of those collect-a-paycheck cops. If I'd just spent more time with you, you wouldn't have jumped off—"

"Don't you say . . . that!" she said with as much force as the respirator would allow. "It's not . . . your fault."

I shook my head, not believing her one bit.

"It's not," she repeated. "Don't you g—get it? I would've . . . done it that night . . . if it wasn't . . . for you. You're the o—only reason, I've . . . made it this . . . far."

I knew what night she was talking about. *That* night. "But if I had—"

She cut me off. "I don't . . . belong here, J—Juno. I never . . . have. That night, I th—thought that if I could convince . . . you that somebody else . . . had killed them, you'd want to p—protect

me. And I . . . thought that if I worked r—really hard at it, if
I . . . really tried, I could . . . make a normal . . . life with
you. . . . I tried, Juno . . . I really tried."

I lifted up the netting and wiped away the tear on her cheek
as I felt my own eyes beginning to tear up.

"All this time." She wheezed. "I've been trying . . . to be normal, but . . . it's too hard. I'm . . . so tired, Juno. I . . . can't do it
anym—more. I can't."

"Don't ask me to do this, Niki. I can't."

"I know you . . . can't. You still want . . . to protect me," she
said with a sad smile.

nineteen

"This is getting ridiculous."

"I agree."

"How long has it been?"

"Twenty hours."

Twenty hours holed up in an opium house and no Raj Gupta. Maggie and I wanted to have another brace session with the punk, see if we could learn a little about his movie career, like who funded the pictures and whom they were sold to. Find our snuff film buyer, and we likely find our barge murderer. Problem was the punk hadn't shown his pretty-boy face, and I was getting damn sick of this dump. "He must be in hiding," I said.

"What do you want to do?"

I had jungle on my mind. I wanted to fly back out to see Niki. I wanted to pick her up and carry her into the jungle with me. I wanted her to breathe normal so we could leave the respirator behind. I wanted to find a nice pile of leaves, maybe some soft moss under a tree and lay down with her, maybe sleeping, maybe not, the two of us just lying there until the jungle took us with its creeping vines and its sprawling root systems. That was what I wanted to do.

"What do you think, Juno?" Maggie was getting antsy. She was feeling the pressure of the clock. Adela's time was running out.

"Let's get the hell out of here," I said.

Maggie and I snuck out the back, careful not to step on any upturned nails poking out of the gnarled scrap wood that used to be the back porch.

"What now?" asked Maggie.

"Beats me."

"I can't keep calling in sick like this."

"Today's only the third day, isn't it?"

"Today's the second. Yesterday was already scheduled as a day off. But still . . ."

Since the three-hour boat ride back to Koba, we'd been striking out. We wanted to get the porn scheme fleshed out . . . so to speak. We tried tracking down Yuri Kiper, but according to his neighbors, the cameraman hadn't been home. We tried calling his work, but the people at Lagarto Libre said he was on vacation, and no, they didn't know where he'd gone. Ian was playing defense, and playing it well.

Maggie and I shuffled down the street, with no particular destination in mind, just walking to be walking. I was already sweating. I looked up and caught a rare view of blue sky. I was glad to see it, knowing full well that when the rains quit, it would be hot like this all the time, and it wouldn't take more than a couple sweat-soaked days for me to start wishing it was still raining.

Maggie said, "What do we know about Liz?"

We know how she sucks cock. We know what she looks like with a dick up her snatch. We know what she looks like with her throat cut. "Not much. I don't even know her real last name."

"Well, she's the only other person that we know who was involved in those movies."

"Yeah." I didn't want to talk to Liz. I didn't want to see her after watching those vids. Partly because she scared me, partly because she disgusted me, but mostly because she turned me on, and that was what scared and disgusted me more than anything else.

The clouds were back. It had only been a few hours, but the stars were all long gone. It felt good to be sitting outside and, at the same time, fully dry. I rubbed my good hand over my chest and didn't feel any chafing, unlike my legs, which stung where my thighs rubbed together from spending too much time in the rain. I'd have to put some salve down there—you leave a sore spot like that untreated long enough, and you were begging for the rot.

Maggie and I were sitting on the rooftop across the street from Liz's. There was a constant parade of people going in and out of the seafood place under her apartment. We kept an eye on her window, wishing we could see more than we could. The curtains were open and the lights were on, but all we could see was the living room, which was empty. We knew she was home. We saw her go in with Ian an hour ago, the lights coming on a few minutes after.

A door slammed nearby, and Maggie and I both jumped. We both felt edgy being this close to KOP station. The fear of running into one of Ian's cop friends around here had us looking over our shoulders like a couple of paranoids.

"There he is," said Maggie.

I looked at the window where a naked Ian was now standing, gazing down at the street with a drink in his hand. He had a classic 'roid-head physique—maxipecs up high and minipackage down low.

He turned around and gave us a view of his high-toned ass before stepping away and coming back a minute later, still naked but sans the drink. Liz appeared on his elbow in a lively red number that left no doubt that she was very much alive despite the lifeless state she was in the last time I'd seen her.

They talked for a few minutes, about what we couldn't tell. Then they exchanged a long, deep kiss that left Ian popping wood—or should I say twig? Ian left Liz standing by the window and came back shortly after with clothes on. Again they kissed, but this time it was just a peck that I figured for a goodbye kiss. They disappeared from the window. A couple minutes later, Ian exited the restaurant and strutted down the block.

"You sure about this, Juno?"

"Yeah. Call if you see Ian come back." I started walking away and then turned back. "I gave you the number, right?" We'd already made our new phones exchange numbers. I *remembered* syncing them up, yet I was driven to ask out of some nervous compulsion.

"Yeah. I got it."

"Good."

I took the elevator down to the main floor of the office building and crossed the lobby, stopping at the glass door to look out at the street. From my vantage, I scanned pedestrian faces, looking for cops and not seeing any. I swung the door wide and hustled across the street and into the restaurant. I ignored the maître d' and followed the same path across the restaurant floor that Ian had followed when we'd watched from the camera in his hair. I stepped into the kitchen and passed through, catching little notice from the kitchen staff. They must've been good and used to men heading upstairs.

I climbed the creaky steps and knocked on the door. Liz pulled the door open, and I thought I caught a twinkle in her eye upon recognizing me. "Come in," she said.

"Sorry to barge in on you," I mumbled.

"Who's barging in? I invited you, remember?"

I followed her into the living room. I went to the window where I'd be visible to Maggie, just in case. . . .

"Would you like a drink?"

"Brandy."

Liz stepped over to a freestanding liquor cabinet with a roll top and poured enough fingers to make a hand. She filled another glass for herself and came over to me. I took my glass, keenly aware of the brush she gave my hand in the exchange.

I hurried a long sip, feeling the need to dampen my jingling nerves.

"What brings you here, officer?"

"I'm not a cop."

"Indulge me."

"What is it with you and cops?"

She tasted her brandy instead of answering. I was glad to be catching a close-up of her red dress—slinky, silky, and oh so skimpy.

I took another deep swig. "How's your boyfriend?"

"Which one?"

"There's more than one?"

"Ian doesn't own me, officer."

"And he's okay with that?"

A playful smile flickered across her face. "You want me to call and ask him?"

"No. I think you're well aware of the fact that I don't want him knowing I'm here."

"He's very frustrated with you, you know. He doesn't like being suckered."

"It serves him right."

"For what?"

"For being an asshole."

She grinned despite herself. "He can be a real asshole, can't he?"

"I don't understand why you stay with him."

"He's a good man. Deep down he is." She added the "deep down" part when she realized how ridiculous her first statement sounded.

"No, he's not," I said. "He's a sadistic bastard."

"That's not true."

"Does he hurt you?"

"No. Never. He loves me. You don't know him like I do. Don't shake your head like that," she said a tad miffed. "I *know* he has a good heart."

"And how do you know that?"

"He used to be so sweet. He was always so gentle."

"That was before he turned into a pit bull. You see the soft side of him anymore?"

"Sometimes," she said shakily. I caught a flash of the real her again: an innocent, vulnerable little girl, confused about the ways of the world. And then it was gone. It had lasted for barely a second. She changed the subject. "How about you tell me about your enforcer days?"

"Actually, I'd prefer to learn a little more about you first."

"Like what?" She dipped her finger in her brandy and put it in her mouth, pulling it out seductively slow. I was amazed at how fast she could shift her moods.

"Let's start with your name," I said.

"My name's Liz."

"Liz Lagarto?" I studied her reaction and found it impossible to read.

"You've seen my movies?"

I nodded.

"My name is *Liz*."

"But that's just a stage name."

"It's my name."

"Why won't you just tell me your real name?"

"Why won't you tell me about your enforcer days?"

"Because I'm ashamed," I said with a sudden honesty that surprised me.

"Well, maybe I'm ashamed of my real name."

"Fair enough," I managed. "How about you tell me about your movies?"

"Which ones did you see?"

"Can't you just answer a question without asking another one?"

"Why? Does that bother you?"

She was trying to get under my skin, and that impish look on her face said she knew she was succeeding. I could feel my face flushing in frustration. "Cut the shit, Liz, and tell me about your movies."

"Ah, now there's the Juno Mozambe I've been hearing so much about. Is that how you used to talk when you were trying to get a confession out of some perp?"

This was suddenly going all wrong.

She laughed and shimmied up to me. "I'm sorry I upset you, Juno, really I am. I just wanted to see the angry side of you, that's all. Please don't be cross."

She was pressed up against me, her breasts pressed into my chest and her hair tickling my nose with a scent of jasmine. I was feeling hot, the kind of hot that makes you so uncomfortable that you want to step out of your skin. I stepped away from her, away from the window and out of Maggie's view.

"What was your favorite scene?" she asked as she vamped my way.

"I didn't have one," I said as my mind flashed through a salacious slide show.

"I don't believe you. Tell me what your favorite scene was, and we can watch it together."

"I have to go," I stammered. "I shouldn't have come."

"Please don't go," she said as she laughed. "I'll tell you about the movies. Really. I'll be good. C'mon, Juno, I was just teasing you, okay? I'll be good. I promise."

"Start talking."

"At least sit down for a minute. Jesus, you look like you're about to blow."

I took a seat on the sofa, and she sat across from me. I tried to get my scattering emotions under control, very wary of the fact that Maggie couldn't see me—I was swimming without a lifeline. "Talk. Start with Yuri Kiper."

"Yuri's the director. I know he doesn't look like much, but he's a genius. A true artist."

"He makes *porn*," I rebutted, making it clear with my tone of voice that porn and art didn't mix.

"He's an artist, Juno, probably the most talented filmmaker in the system."

"Film? You call that smut *film?*"

"Think whatever you want," she said curtly.

Now it was *me* who was getting under *her* skin. I resisted asking another question and stayed silent, knowing she wouldn't let it drop that easily.

"You don't know what you're talking about," she said. "If Yuri was an offworlder, he'd be directing major pictures. He has to make do with second-rate, no, third-rate equipment, and he doesn't have a whole staff of people working for him. He does it all by himself. He's a magician. He can make anything look real."

"What do you mean?"

"Lots of filmmakers can generate false footage with holos, but I can always tell the difference. Can't you?"

"I don't watch many movies."

She gave me a what's-wrong-with-you look. "What they do is they film live actors in order to generate high-quality holos, and then they use the holos for the stunt work and the action sequences. But when they're filming close-ups and emotional scenes they still use live actors most of the time. Holos are great in a lot of ways—you can make them jump, or fight, or fly, but they're no good for the dramatic work. Some low-budget filmmakers use them for everything, but they come off stiff. It's hard to capture nuanced emotion with holos. They're always superhappy or supersad. They *look* real, but they don't *act* real. They're always a little off, just enough that they don't seem human."

"Are you saying that all your movies were fakes?"

"Not the early ones we made. Yuri didn't have the money to buy computer time at the beginning. But once the movies started selling, he was able to start incorporating more holographic elements."

"How many movies do you sell?"

"I don't keep track."

"Who does?"

She didn't answer.

"Who funds the pictures?"

"Horst."

"Why is a travel agent making porn?"

"It helps business."

"How?"

She sipped her brandy. "Horst sells the vids offworld. He uses them as advertisements."

"Most tour companies show pictures of the hotel, maybe a pool."

She shrugged.

"Does Horst organize sex tours?"

She shrugged again and gave me a look that said next question.

"So tell me what was fake."

"Did you see *Liz Lagarto Gets Licked*?"

"Was that the one where you were wearing the tiger skin?"

"That's the one. I still have that costume, you know. Maybe I'll model it for you."

Again I was flushing, and again she was enjoying it. I took a sip of my brandy and wasn't surprised to see it was almost gone.

She pulled her legs up under her and reclined into the chair's cushions. "Do you remember the scene where the jungle girl has sex with the rich plantation owner?"

I said, "Yes," even though I didn't remember it specifically. In my mind the movies had all mingled together into an all-out orgy of pumping skin.

"That entire scene was holographic. That was Yuri's first all-holo work. It was the kind of thing any hack could do—there's not much need for nuanced human emotion in pornography—but it was still an achievement for somebody with no formal training."

"What else has he done?"

"He can't afford any serious computer time, so he mostly makes shorts. You know, little five-minute movies, but if you saw them, you'd swear they were real. He did one with a married couple in a restaurant, and it starts with the woman asking for a divorce. You can see the emotions running through her husband: surprise, anger, sadness . . . and it looks *real*. Live actors couldn't do any better."

I was beginning to understand how Ian had gotten a confession out of "Adela." Liz was right. Yuri had to be some kind of genius to pull that off. How did he know how to do her eyes? They were perfect. Perfect enough for me to believe she did it. Perfect enough for me to grill her. Damn it to hell. We had to get her out of there.

"But why not use actors in his movies?" I asked. "Wouldn't it be easier?"

"I told you at the beginning, Yuri's an artist, a filmmaker. If he uses holos, he can make a film that is one hundred per-cent *his* vision. When he makes his shorts, they're his movies and his alone. Regular directors have to collaborate with their actors and accept their actors' interpretations of the script. Us-ing holos, Yuri can truly implement his vision—from script, to set design, to acting, the whole thing. From beginning to end it's his."

"And you think he's the best in the system?"

"I don't know of anybody better."

"So if he wanted to film somebody getting murdered, he could?"

"Sure. I think he could do just about anything."

"Has he?"

Liz turned instantly wary. "Has he what?"

"Filmed a murder. Your murder."

"What are you talking about?"

"I watched you die, Liz. I watched some bastard use your back as an ashtray. I watched him slit your throat. What's the matter, Liz? You don't look too good."

"I'm just surprised, that's all."

"About what?"

"I'm surprised that you saw that one. It was distributed to a very exclusive clientele."

"And who would that be?"

"I don't know."

"Bullshit."

"Really, I don't know. And neither does Yuri. We just make the movies."

"Does Ian know?"

Liz looked away. "Maybe it's time for you to go."

I put my drink down and stood up with a little brandy-induced wobble. I wasn't about to leave. I stalked over to her and looked down on her with the authority of an enforcer. "Not until I get answers," I ordered. "I want to know who you made that movie for. I don't want to hear any more of this crap about Horst being a travel agent. I want to know what he's really into. I want to know who Horst's customers are. I want names, Liz. And you're going to tell me about Ian. I want to know where he fits in, and I'm not talking about between your legs."

"Ooh, is it interrogation time?" Liz turned on her "Liz Lagarto: Porn Star" persona. "I don't know anything about any of that, offither." She little-girl lisped the word *officer*.

I reeled from another sudden change. "Stop calling me officer."

"Yes, offither." She pouted.

What the fuck? Just a few seconds ago she was talking normal, like a regular person who had a passionate interest in film. But now she'd shifted into this naughty kitten with semipuckered lips. She was looking up at me from her seat. She had her arms squeezed tight against her sides to give her tits maximum lift. I was paralyzed. I had no idea what to do. How do you intimidate somebody who's *into* it? "Stop it, Liz."

She hiked her dress up over her knees. She pulled her shoulder straps off, baring her breasts. "Maybe you need to teach me a lethon, offither."

I felt weak as I took in her parted lips, her jasmine-smelling hair, her erect nipples. . . . "I said stop it." The words came out limp, as another part of me was becoming anything but.

"Make me." She said it like a five-year-old.

"Jesus Christ, Liz. Just tell me what I want to know, and I'll go."

"Make me," she repeated in a nanny-nanny-boo-boo way.

"Dammit, Liz!" I yelled as I shook her shoulders.

Her hands were on me. My zipper dropped, and her fingers

were inside. I sank the fingers of my good hand into her hair and grabbed hold. I yanked her head back hard, hard enough that I felt roots pulling free. She sucked in a sharp breath and a broad smile broke across her face. "Yeth, offither," she baby-talked as her fingers picked up the pace.

She was still looking up at me, her copper skin tinting red on her cheeks and down her neck to her chest, a flaming flag of desire. Her hands moved up to the snap on my pants. I stepped back, pulling free from her hair and her manipulating fingers. I kept my left fist closed and walked out, leaving her high, but not so dry.

I pounded my way down the stairs with heavy steps that echoed my throbbing heart. I hit the bottom of the stairs and stopped before entering the kitchen, waiting for another throbbing to subside so I could zip my fly.

I didn't want to loosen my left fist, so when the time came, I fumbled my zipper back up with my shaky splinted fingers. I paced through the kitchen, and then through the dining room, resisting a stop at the bar. Maggie entered the restaurant a few seconds before I reached the door.

"I was just coming to find you," she said. "You were supposed to stay by the window. I got worried."

"I'm okay," I said as we stepped out together.

She kept the rest of her unasked questions to herself as we double-timed away from the neighborhood of KOP station before Ian and crew came down on us. We had to assume that Liz called him even before I hit the stairs. We slowed our pace once we entered the warren of shop-lined alleys called the Phra Kaew market area.

Maggie and I took a serpentine path deep into the market, feeling safer and safer with every turn we made in the mazelike district.

"Come in with me," I said to Maggie as I ducked into a spice shop, nothing more than a walk-in closet with shelving all around packed tight with glass jars brimming with aromatic spice. I asked the woman behind the counter for a baggie.

I told Maggie to take the baggie. "Now help me bag this up," I said as I held up my closed left fist for her to see, long strands of black hair pinched between my fingers, white DNA-filled roots hanging on the ends.

twenty

Maggie and I found a Phra Kaew fish counter and took two of the four stools. I called Abdul, who was working late again, elbow deep in a fresh cadaver. I told him to come meet us when he was done—we had some DNA that needed analyzing. Maggie said she felt bad making him walk all the way down here, but we had little choice. We both knew there was no way we could set foot in KOP station, which was fine by me. I had no interest in going there ever again. The last time I was there was the day Diego Banks pulled off his coup. He had me arrested and kept me locked down while he and his coconspirators murdered Paul Chang and seized control. Then, once his takeover was complete, he took my badge and let me go. The SOB didn't even respect me enough to kill me.

Maggie and I ordered up a couple fish bowls and waited for Abdul. It didn't take long. Our fish was still frying when he came shuffling down the walk with a rickety gait that didn't seem to slow him down any. Abdul climbed up onto the stool next to mine and leaned heavily on the counter as he adjusted his shaky position until he found the right balance. I knew better than to offer any help. Abdul didn't need any, and he wasn't shy about letting you know.

"We already ordered," I said.

"I'll have whatever they're having," he said to the cook, who dropped another filet into the fryer.

Maggie reached around me to pass him the baggie of hair. "We need a rush job on this, Abdul."

"No problem," he said, and he took the baggy with his craggy hand and slid it into a shirt pocket. "I'll take care of it as soon as I get back to my office. I was glad to get your message, Juno. I've been trying to call you."

"I had to ditch my phone."

"They're looking for you," he said.

"I know. Ian's not too happy with me."

"It's not just Ian. He put out the word to all of KOP that you're wanted for questioning in a homicide."

"Great," I said, knowing full well that "questioning" was enforcer code for beating a confession out of somebody. "Whose homicide?"

"Gupta. Raj Gupta. That's the cadaver I was just working on."

Maggie swore under her breath. Just then, the cook set a bowl of steamy fish and noodles in front of me, my knotted stomach rebelling at the sight of it.

Maggie asked, "What's Ian's reason for questioning Juno?"

Abdul looked at me with his spectacled eyes. "He says he has a witness who saw Juno in the area at the time of the murder."

"How was Raj killed?"

"Knifed."

"Was the knife recovered from the scene?"

"No."

"Of course not."

We all knew what that meant. Ian would still have the knife, probably on his person. He'd be carrying it around so he could plant it on me once he found me. I wished I could say I was surprised to find myself wanted for murder, but I could hardly expect Ian to sit still while Maggie and I cranked up our investigation. What really had me going was the fact that I used to run KOP. All those cops had been in my control, mine and Paul's. All those years of running the show, and all it took to get the force turned against me was for Ian to say he wanted to question me. It was like I'd never been there.

Based on the way Maggie had started shoveling through her bowl, I assumed it was good fish, yet I couldn't stomach it. I picked around the fish, pulling noodles from underneath and twirling them onto my fork. I swallowed down a mouthful, not tasting anything.

"Oh, I have something else for you," said Abdul as he pulled out a data chip and passed it to Maggie. "Another barge murder. I though you might be interested."

"Thanks, Abdul."

"And I have something for you, too, Juno."

"What?"

I didn't like the way he paused before talking, a signal that he was about to lay something heavy on me. Finally, he said, "Niki called me."

"Christ." I dropped my fork into my bowl.

"Hear me out." He put his hand on my shoulder. "She's in a bad way, Juno."

"It's none of your business, Abdul."

"The hell it's not. She's my friend, and so are you."

I wanted to tell him to fuck off, but seeing him looking at me with his eyes magnified to giant size under his superthick lenses, I couldn't do it. "What did she tell you?"

"She asked me to pull the plug, Juno. She said you wouldn't do it, so she asked me."

I felt Maggie's hand on my other shoulder. I resisted the urge to yank my shoulder away. "What did you tell her?"

"I told her I'd think about it."

"Christ."

"I think it's the right thing, Juno."

I didn't know what to say. I picked up my fork and started pushing my noodles around.

Abdul ignored the bowl the cook set in front of him. "She wants to die."

"You think I don't know that?"

"I know you want to save her, but you can't. She'll just do it again. She'll never get over it."

"Get over what?" Maggie wanted to know.

Abdul asked me, "She doesn't know?"

I shook my head.

"Can I tell her?"

I kept pushing my noodles around as I mumbled a yes.

Abdul took off his glasses, and his eyes shrank to normal size. "Niki's father was abusive, Maggie. Sexually abusive. And one day Niki must've had enough, because she killed her parents. She killed them both in their sleep."

"I had no idea," Maggie whispered.

"Juno covered it up for her, and I helped him."

Now it was Maggie who had no idea what to say. In her head, she was probably replaying the conversation she and I had on the barge, when she'd referred to Adela saying, "What kind of girl kills her parents?"

The cook came in from the back and asked how our food was, clearly concerned that none of us were eating. I took a bite of fish and swallowed it down, again tasting nothing. Maggie and Abdul started picking through their bowls, and the cook went back to unpacking a crate of noodles.

Maggie asked, "Has she seen a psychiatrist?"

"Three." I admitted.

"What did they say?"

"What does it matter? What do some shrinks know about my wife?"

"What did they say, Juno?"

I dropped my fork again, letting it clang against the bowl. "They said she wanted to be taken off of life support. And they said she was of sound mind."

"How come they didn't do it? Don't they have to follow her wishes?"

"I talked them out of it."

"And how did you do that?"

"I was persuasive," I said.

"Isn't it illegal to keep her alive against her will?"

"That law doesn't make any sense," I snapped.

The shrinks had already tried to give me their little lecture on the law. They showed me old pictures of maimed freaks and brains in jars that had been kept alive for centuries before the Unified Worlds made it illegal to forcibly keep somebody alive against their will. They showed me bodies so atrophied that they looked like skeletons with shrink-wrap skin. All three of those asshole shrinks put me through the same shit, picture after picture of nothing but desperate, drooling, diapered shells of former humans. And then, when they thought I'd had enough, they came at me with their neutral speaking tones and their phony feel-my-pain faces, asking me, "Now is that what you really want for Niki?"

But those pics they showed me, they weren't Niki. She was fixable. I'd already replaced everything but the spine. They were wrong about me. I wasn't one of those selfish monsters they'd showed me, like the mother who rejuved her stillborn baby and kept dressing him in cute little ducky PJs even when the brain-dead sap was thirty years old. I wasn't so afraid to let go of Niki that I'd imprison her. I'd never hurt her. That wasn't me. They were wrong, all three of them, and I used my enforcer talents to make them see the goddamned light.

Abdul's put his hand on my shoulder again. "You shouldn't be so quick to dismiss the psychiatrists."

"She's not terminal, dammit. There won't be anything wrong with her when she gets her spine."

"There won't?"

"Listen, Abdul, I know she's depressed, but that'll change when she gets patched up."

"You sure about that?"

"You'd be depressed, too, if you couldn't move."

"C'mon, Juno, you know better than that. You know she was depressed before she broke her neck. She's always been depressed."

"Things will be different this time," I said defiantly.

Abdul shook his head. "I'm not getting through, am I? How about this? Once she's got her new spine, what's to keep her from doing it again? You'd have to lock her up."

"If that's what it takes."

"You're not being realistic."

I went back to pushing my noodles around.

Abdul took a few bites of his meal before talking again. "She begged me not to tell you, Juno. She just wanted me to come out and do it, but I thought you should know. I thought it was important for you to be onboard with this decision."

"Well, I'm not onboard."

"It's time for you to *get* onboard. Don't you want to say good-bye? Because one way or another, sooner or later, she's going to be gone."

"What are you saying, Abdul? Are you saying you're going to go behind my back and pull the plug?"

"No. I'm not saying that, but I am saying that if you don't promise me you'll think about it, and I mean think about it seriously, I'll do exactly that."

I pushed the noodles to the left then pushed them to the right, back and forth, back and forth.

"Promise me, Juno."

"Don't force me, Abdul."

"Promise."

I couldn't meet his gaze. I set the fork down. I rubbed my eyes to clear away my suddenly cloudy vision. *I don't want to lose her. I can't.*

Abdul leaned in. "I'm not leaving until I get an answer."

"I promise."

"You'll think about it?"

"Yes, damn you. I'll think about it, okay?"

My thoughts weren't coherent. I was in that semiasleep stage where half-assed ideas skip through the brain so fast as to create a constant stream of pure gibberish. Ian, Niki, Liz, Abdul, Maggie, they were all there, in my mind, talking nonsense.

The sound of the zipper snapped me fully awake. Maggie came through the tent flaps and zippered them up behind her.

"What was on the chip?" I asked, knowing she'd gone to sit by the canal as she read through the latest set of case files.

Maggie dropped into her hammock and positioned herself on a diagonal so she could lay a little flatter instead of being folded into a banana like I was. "It may be the worst one yet."

"Tell me."

"The crime scene was old, at least a month, but they can't pin it down for sure. Some kids were exploring the barge when they found it and called it in."

"Gene eaters?"

"Yeah. Same as the others. This guy is sick, Juno. He used vice grips this time."

"How?"

"There were nine of them, all attached to a human-shaped table. There were two for the ankles, another two for the knees, and two more pairs for wrists and elbows. The ninth was for the head. He put a man, or maybe a very tall woman, in them so he or she would be suspended from the table, held by the vices."

I didn't really want to hear any more, but Maggie continued. "He probably started with the ankles and worked his way up, tightening each vice until he crushed all the joints. Then he did the head."

Sick is right. I imagined myself in the victim's position, my head being squeezed. . . . I squirmed in my hammock. "Let's just hope Ian shoots me when he finds me instead of turning me over to that freak."

"It may not go down like that. . . ."

I waited for her to explain.

"What if another cop finds you first and hauls you in? Ian may not want to risk killing you while you're in custody. He'll just pin Raj Gupta's murder on you by planting the knife in your house. You could end up in the Zoo."

"Shit, Maggie, I thought you were going to try to make me feel *better*."

She laughed. "C'mon, Juno, the Zoo's not so bad. At least you'd be alive."

"Right. An ex-cop in the Zoo. I'd kill myself first." And I meant it.

Maggie's face turned serious in the lamplight.

"What is it?" I asked.

She started to say something but cut herself off and said, "Nothing."

"Spit it out, Maggie."

"I was just wondering what Niki would think if she heard you say that."

"Christ."

twenty-one

I'D changed my mind. It was as simple as that. I knew it was going to delay our investigation, but I couldn't let Niki suffer any longer. As soon as I'd made the decision, Maggie and I hustled from our tent down to the canal and woke up a half dozen boat captains until we found one who was willing to take the overnight charter.

The sun wouldn't be up for a few hours yet. I couldn't see the shoreline, but I could make out the dark black outline of treetops against the almost-as-black sky. The boat captain gave his young daughter a nudge. She woke up and crawled over Maggie's sleeping body, making her way to the bow. She rubbed sleep out of her eyes then snatched up a floodlight and lay facedown with her head hanging over the bow, aiming the floodlight out into the water where patches of reeds were beginning to form. We were navigating one of the Koba's many tributaries, putt-putting our way to the Orzo plantation.

The girl kept sweeping the floodlight from side to side and slapped the hull when she wanted to turn. One slap for left, two for right. We made slow progress snaking our way through the reeds, occasionally catching one with the prop and chopping it apart with a gurgling rumble.

I closed my eyes and tried to sleep. Couldn't. I tried putting my feet up. Didn't help. I pulled my flask out for the fifth time. Still empty. I was trapped, trapped on this boat with nothing to do but think of Niki.

I remembered the time we went to a banquet dinner and Niki followed my lead when I ate with the wrong fork. She knew better, but she didn't want me to look like the only ass at the table. I remembered the shoes she bought me when we were dating, custom-made and very expensive. I wore those things for years, even after the leather cracked through on the sides. I remembered her smile. I remembered the way she twirled her hair when she read her books.

I couldn't do it. I needed her. I'd already lost my job, which meant more to me than it should have. I'd lost the best friend I ever had in Paul. I couldn't lose her, too. I couldn't. If I lost her, what would be left for me? I should go with her, I thought. Together to the end. But I didn't have the guts to do myself in. I was a goddamn wuss that way. I'd be stuck here, sentenced to live with my fucked-up self, and she'd be gone.

But I didn't know what else to do. It had been over twenty-five years of battling against the inevitable. Antidepressants never did any good except in the short term. Therapy never worked, not the traditional verbal variety, nor the more modern mind-to-mind linkage offworlders favored. It always ended the same way, with me frantically racing an unconscious Niki to the hospital, calling ahead to tell them to get the stomach pump ready. We'd tried everything, absolutely everything short of implanting a false personality, which no matter how many times the docs tried to reassure her, she always said she wouldn't do. It was too extreme. She wouldn't be herself anymore. And she was right.

She was tired of trying to shake a past that the present could never outrun. This was what she wanted, and when I thought of it that way, it felt okay. It was when I thought of me that my stomach went cartwheeling.

I checked my watch. We were still an hour away. My phone rang. I picked up and Abdul's holo appeared in the seat next to mine. "Sorry it took so long, Juno, but I decided not to use the KOP system to do your DNA analysis."

I looked at Maggie curled up in the bottom of the boat and decided not to wake her. "Good. What did you find?"

"I got an ID. Liz has a record. She was picked up for prostitution six years ago. They picked her up on a raid of the Red Room."

No surprise there, I thought. I remembered that the Red Room was one of the snatch houses Idris mentioned as being frequented by the Jungle Expeditions customers. It was probably how she and Horst had met. "What's her real name?"

"Michelle Davies."

"Davies?"

"That's right. She's Ian's sister."

If I wasn't sitting, I would've fallen over. As it was, I found my good hand grabbing hold of my seat like I was about to fall into the drink.

The rain was drumming as Maggie and I stepped off the boat and down to the dock, now almost underwater. Another week of rain and it would have to be abandoned for a higher one. With the help of a rope handrail, we climbed the muddy riverbank steps up to the Orzo estate. I'd woken Maggie up and shared the news as soon as I'd hung up with Abdul. We talked about the incestuous Davies family the rest of the way. Ian and Liz, brother and sister. We remembered how he bought her shoes, how he caressed her feet, her calves, his *sister's* calves . . .

Or how about when they kissed in the window, Ian popping a brotherly boner? The whole discussion was beyond disturbing, but to me, it was a relief, a relief from thinking about what I was about to do.

We jogged over to the closest hut, and once under the cover of the thatch overhang, we stripped off our shoes and racked them upside down to keep them spider free. We followed the wood platforms from hut to hut, covering a kilometer or more, finally arriving at Niki's room. Vlad heard us coming and sat up straight in his chair. Maggie waited outside while I went in and woke up the nurse.

"What are . . . you doing here?" asked Niki.

I waited for the nurse to leave before saying, "I talked to Abdul."

"Dammit. I t—told him not to. . . ."

I interrupted her. "Stop. It's okay, Niki. We talked and . . ."

Her eyes took on a look of hope.

"He told me that . . . that . . ." I found myself unable to voice my feelings, which were shifting far too fast for me to even identify. "I know that you . . ." I pinched my lips shut, frustrated by my inability to express myself. Rather than launching into another false start, I decided to just cut to the chase. "Are you sure this is what you want?"

Her eyes melted with relief and gratitude. "Yes."

I pulled up the mosquito netting and kissed her cheek. She looked so different. Her body had withered down to her bones. Her skin had yellowed from the cinnamon color I remembered so well. Strands of what had always been raven-colored hair were growing in gray at the roots.

She smiled at me. Her smile still looked the same. She asked, "What do you s—say we take that tour . . . first?"

I pulled Niki out of her chair and set her into a hammock, and then I scrunched in next to her, cradling her head. The respirator was pumping its regular beat, but it was only a matter of time before it petered out. I'd already turned off the generator, leaving us about two hours of battery life.

We'd seen the entire place. Maggie pulled a pair of laborers off the bottling assembly line and told them to help me with

Niki's wheelchair and not-so-portable respirator. We started with the distillery and moved on to the cask cellar and then the tasting room. When the rain slowed to a drizzle, we carried more than wheeled Niki through the brandy tree orchards, where wet leaves sparkled whenever the morning sun peeked out from the clouds.

Lastly, we carried Niki up a series of scaffoldlike staircases that led up into the jungle canopy where there were a set of platforms interconnected by suspension bridges. We navigated from platform to platform until we settled on the largest. The platform looked like it was used for hosting parties. There was a bar, tables, a stage with a dance floor. When I'd asked her if she was ready to go back to her room, she said we should do it here.

We didn't talk. There was nothing to say. Now that the generator had been turned off, the sounds of the jungle were allowed to come through in peeping, buzzing, croaking, and warbling harmony.

What the hell was I doing? Just yesterday, I was dead set against this. Yet, here I was. I had no idea if this was the right thing, but it felt right, and that would have to be good enough. I held onto my wife. I held on tight, knowing our time was short, knowing how much of it I'd wasted with my working and my boozing. We were supposed to grow old together. There was always going to be plenty of time to make it up to her.

I lost all sense of time, lying there with Niki. Only the metronomic pumping of the respirator marked the passage of time, until even it finally stopped. Niki didn't stir when it happened. I couldn't say exactly when she passed, but I held on to her the whole time, wanting to stay with her forever. I took solace in the jungle, feeling a part of it and a little less alone. I still didn't want to leave, even as her skin began to cool.

twenty-two

"JUNO. We're almost there."

I opened my eyes. Maggie and I were still on the boat. I sat up and could see that we were back in Koba, riding alongside Floodbank. It was almost dark already. I'd slept the whole way. The first really good sleep I'd had in a long, long time. Then just when I was beginning to feel pretty good, the memories came crashing in. Was that even real? The jungle? The orchards? The sprawling tree house? It was real, I told myself. *She's gone.* But it all happened so fast. It couldn't be . . .

The young girl was already standing on the bow as we nudged closer and closer to Floodbank, the floating city within a city. The boat captain throttled the engine down to the point of almost idling, and then he swung the rudder ninety degrees, aiming the boat straight into Floodbank. We entered between a pair of floating restaurants and suddenly found ourselves in a knotted tangle of fishing boats and skiffs. The young girl used a splinter-ended pole to push off the other hulls while the motor plowed forward with a steady crawl until we eventually broke through the jam.

We angled into a narrow channel, barely wide enough for our boat, which was of the bulky fishing variety. We followed the meandering waterway around so many bends that I lost all sense of direction. We passed under arched bridges and weaved around dozens of fruit stands. The channel gradually tapered the deeper we penetrated into Floodbank. The young girl was now using her pole to keep us from bumping the channel walls, which were actually homes that we could see into. Hawkers came out from inside and leaned out over the water, tipping wood poles in close enough for us to reach, one with bags of nuts tied to the end, another with fruit, and yet another with cigarettes. Another hawker jumped onboard carrying a tray loaded down with "soda in a bag." The baggies were filled with cherry soda and then sealed up with rubber bands anchored around straws that poked out the tops. The boat captain bought one for himself and another for his daughter before the hawker jumped back off.

None of it felt real. It all felt dead to me, like the whole planet was dead, and I was the only person left. Or maybe it was me who was dead, and I was some kind of ghost that could move around and see the world but couldn't interact with it. Try to pick something up and my hand would just pass through. Try to talk and nobody would hear me. My theory proved false when I succeeded in buying up a bottle of supercheap hooch from a kid with a lazy eye.

When the channel became too narrow to proceed any farther, the pilot slapped the motor into reverse. Maggie and I would have to walk from here. I slipped a few bills to the captain, and remembering I didn't have a partially developed spine hanging over my head anymore, I passed another bill to the daughter.

Maggie stopped me once we'd stepped up onto the walkway. "Are you sure you're ready for this, Juno?"

"Yeah," I said. My voice sounded muffled, like my head was stuffed with cotton balls and my ears were filled with water.

Maggie and I hoofed along the floating walkway, which creaked with the river's gentle rocking. Floating buildings rubbed against one another with the sound of scraping wood. Ropes—all kinds of them—were all that held this place together.

Thin and thick, twines and tug ropes, they were all that kept Floodbank from pulling apart and floating downriver. There were ropes all around us, running every which way like the threads of a drunken spider's web.

We crossed a plank bridge that bowed under our weight and stepped in through the beaded curtain that substituted for a door. The one-room home was triangle shaped, custom-built for this particular gap in Floodbank. The man we'd come to see was eating a sandwich, looking at me with a surprised expression. "Juno?" he said.

"That's right, Ian. Long time no see."

Ian Davies, Sr., put his sandwich down. "What brings you here?"

Maggie and I took seats at his table. "This is Maggie," I said. "She's your kid's partner."

"So?"

"Have you talked to him recently?"

"No. I ain't seen him in a long time. He's an ungrateful punk." He pulled the top slice of bread off his half-eaten sandwich and tossed it through the back door where it skidded off the plank deck and down into the water. "I heard you retired, Juno."

"Something like that."

He picked the meat off what was left of his sandwich and tossed the other slice of bread. "You gonna tell me why you're here?"

"What? Can't a couple ol' retirees get together and have a chat about the old days?" I held up the bottle I'd bought.

He rolled up the lunch meat and took a bite. "Not today. I'm kind of busy."

I didn't let his sourpuss act dissuade me. I knew this guy—you get a couple drinks in him, and you can't shut him up. "Now you're being rude, Ian. You got any glasses?"

He took another bite of his lunch-meat cigar. "No."

Maggie reached behind her and pulled the cupboard open. She pulled out three dusty glasses and set them on the table. He had his arms crossed.

"Now don't be like that, Ian. We're just going to have some drinks, okay?" I took my time cleaning the glasses with my shirttail. Maggie poured the glasses half full, and I raised mine with my left. "To old times." I stayed in that pose, with my glass held high, for what must've been thirty seconds, waiting for a reluctant Ian to clink glasses.

Maggie stopped after one, but Ian and I were into our fourth when he started to loosen up. I smiled and laughed at all the right times while he yapped about the time he busted that pimp, how he had the pimp down, and he was about to cuff him when one of the guy's bitches came screaming in, buck naked, and started trying to pull Ian off her guy. He managed to snap the cuffs on the pimp, and then he wrestled her down, and since he didn't have another pair of cuffs, he had to restrain her until backup arrived. They came storming in, and there he was, lying on top of this bitch, and she's bucking like a fucking horse. . . .

He kept prattling on with that big mouth of his. Telling us about the time he stopped an armed robbery when he was off duty. He was just going to the store to pick up some booze, and there was this punk, you know the type, with the fresh tats and the hotshot attitude. And he could tell right away that the punk was up to no good. The punk was all jumpy and shit. Ian, Sr., played it cool; he acted all nonchalant and waited for the punk to make his move, and then he jumped the little bastard and took his lase-pistol. That was when the kid went after the owner with a blade, and Ian had to shoot him.

I remembered that incident. It was a long time ago, but the way I heard it, the kid was hopped up on stims when he tried to knock over the liquor store. Ian jumped out from one of the aisles and screamed at the kid to freeze, knocking over a whole rack of bottles in the process. The kid reflexively jumped away from the spray of shattering bottles, and Ian fried him in the back.

"You sure taught that punk a lesson," I said.

"Damn straight I did."

I kept tipping my glass to my mouth every so often, but I'd already stopped drinking. He kept rattling on, his tales getting taller and taller. He was talking mostly to Maggie now. Her face was a hell of a lot prettier than mine. I kept up the illusion that I was keeping up with him in the drinking department by emptying my glass through a hole in the floor, the cheap booze running down the side of an oil drum that served as a pontoon.

I kept the hooch flowing and soon enough Ian, Sr., was 180 proof. His exaggerated yarns were turning into paranoid rants. He was going off on some doctor now. "This bitch must think I'm stupid, trying to rip me off. She thinks I don't know how much a fucking pill costs? I ain't no damn pushover. She thinks those degrees on the wall give her a license to bend me over."

Blah, blah, blah . . . This was the way he'd always get at the bars. Always the victim of some imagined wrong, talking nonstop trash. I remembered how one night, he started off on some bullshit about a mechanic who jacked up the price on him and how he was going to go down there and teach him a lesson. "Let's go," I'd told him. I wanted to see him teach this mechanic a lesson. That's when he told me to butt the fuck out or he'd have to take me to school. Had we been alone, I might've blown the comment off, but I couldn't let him get away with it when there were other cops around, watching. What kind of enforcer would let something like that pass? I gave him a good ass-kicking that night, and if need be, I was ready to do it again. "Hey, whatever happened to your wife?"

"That whore? Who gives a shit?"

"When did she leave?"

"That was seventy-three. She ran off and never came back. She knew better than to come back. She knew she could beg all she wanted, but I wouldn't take her back. No way. She knew better."

"What a bitch, leaving you to raise two kids by yourself."

"Damn straight. I did right by my kids. Not that it did much good. They both got too much of their mother in them."

"What do you mean? Your son's a cop, and a good one."

"No thanks to her. I was the one that got him that job. You'd think he'd be thankful after all I did for him. He should be over here every night thanking me for getting him that job. Shit, Juno, you know how many favors I had to cash in to get him that job. They wouldn't even take him the first time. They thought he was too soft, so I got him that guard job at the Zoo. Remember that? A year as a zookeeper and there was no way they could call him soft anymore. He was such a momma's boy when he was little. He wanted to be a chef. You believe that? I had to drag his crying ass to the Zoo most every day. That toughened him up. You better believe it."

"What about your daughter? What's she up to?"

"How the fuck should I know? I disowned her."

"Why?"

"Because she's a whore, just like her mother. I tried to give those kids discipline. But how do they thank me? Michelle runs off with her loser boyfriend, and Ian Junior's too busy for his old man."

"How did you discipline them?" Maggie asked.

"I never laid a hand on either one of them, if that's what you're asking. I was a good father, dammit. I never touched them. I'd just talk to them, tell them how it was."

"Who was the boyfriend?"

"Sumari. Sumari Cho. Ian, Jr., caught him trying to rape his sister and beat his skull in."

Maggie was incredulous. "You're saying she ran off with the boy who tried to rape her?"

"I told you she was a whore. Just like her mother."

"Why didn't you arrest him?"

Ian turned venomous. "What makes you think I didn't, bitch? You whores are all alike."

My blood was rising. I got up and waited for Maggie to do the same. We walked out together before Ian, Sr., said something I couldn't let pass.

twenty-three

I LET Maggie lead the way. I didn't want to think. I didn't want to feel. I just kept following, looking down the whole way, hoping we'd get there fast. I needed to keep working. I didn't like this alone time one bit.

She found the fish market wedged between two other fish markets. A neon sign over the door read "Cho's." We crossed a wide wooden beam that bridged the gap between the walkway and the shop entrance. Fish hung in the window, lathered up in yellow antifly gel and hooked through the gills. Two men were behind the counter cutting and slicing. They wore bloody aprons dotted with flies that took off and landed with every filleting stroke.

The tall one took a long look at Maggie before saying, "Can I help you?"

"Yeah," I said. "We're looking for Sumari Cho."

"You got him."

His head looked normal. I didn't see any signs that this guy's skull had been beaten in by a young Ian. I figured it for one more of his Ian, Sr.'s, exaggerations. "This is Officer Orzo. I'm Officer Mozambe. We'd like to ask you some questions."

He looked Maggie up and down and up again, trying to be subtle, but not getting away with it. "What about?" he asked with fish slime smeared on his cheek.

"Is there someplace we can talk?"

"Yeah, sure." He wiped his hands on his apron and pulled off

the gloves. He brought a bucket of innards with him and took us
into the back room. He passed a sliding barn-style door that was
closed except for a small crack through which I could see the
river. Next to the door was a chute that Sumari made a show of
pouring the bucket through, trying to show off his muscles. Oily
fish pieces clung to the corners of the chute. The flies were having a heyday.

Sumari said, "You can ask me anything you want." His eyes
were on Maggie's chest, the outline of her bra showing
through her rain-dampened shirt.

I wasn't at all happy about an accused rapist looking at Maggie. "You can start by putting your eyes back in their sockets,
asshole. Tell us about Michelle Davies. We hear you tried to
rape her."

Sumari ran his fingers through his fish-oiled hair. He stopped
making eyes at Maggie and aimed them at the fish-scrap littered
floor. "That was a long time ago," he finally said. "I was cleared
of those charges."

"Listen," Maggie said in a serious voice, "we're not here to
air out your dirty laundry. We just want to know about the
Davies family."

He glanced at Maggie then looked away. All of the sudden
he was getting shy. "My lawyer told me not to talk about it."

"But you said yourself that that was a long time ago."

"Still . . . He said not to talk about it."

"Her father is still calling you a rapist," she said. "He told us
not ten minutes ago that you raped his daughter."

Sumari bit his lip. "He can't do that. I was cleared."

"Why don't you set us straight?"

"I can't. He's a cop."

"Not anymore. He retired. Don't you think it's time somebody heard your side of the story? Just tell us the truth."

He looked at her, in the eyes this time. "You won't tell anybody I talked to you?"

"Nope."

Sumari pulled three folding chairs from a stack leaning against the wall. He sat down with a grim expression. "Michelle and I met at school, and we started dating. We'd go to dances and parties, you know, kid stuff."

"Were you sexually active with her?"

"Yes. She was my first, but I'm pretty sure I wasn't hers."

"Why do you say that?"

"She knew what she was doing."

"And you didn't?" I asked.

He gave me a stare that said, "Grow up."

Maggie changed the subject. "How about her brother? Did you know him?"

"Yeah. I knew Ian. Couldn't get away from him. He was probably twelve or thirteen then."

"And how old was Michelle?"

"She was seventeen. He was like a little puppy always following her around. We'd go to a show, and he'd have to tag along. We'd hang out at her house, and he'd have to sit right next to her. He drove me crazy."

"Why didn't Michelle tell him to buzz off?"

"She said she felt bad for him since their mother ran off. I tried to tell her she wasn't doing the kid any favors. I mean, it had already been a couple years since their mom left. At some point, he needed to learn to take care of himself. She couldn't play mommy forever."

"Did she listen?"

"No. She broke up with me instead. She told me that she and her brother were a pair. I couldn't be with her unless I was willing to accept Ian."

"What did you do?"

Sumari laughed. "I apologized. I *begged* her to take me back."

"And she did?"

He nodded. "It was the dumbest thing I ever did in my life. That family was nuts, and I knew it, but I wanted to be with Michelle. I loved her. I didn't think I could live without her."

"How were they crazy?"

"Where do I start?" He paused like he really had to think about it. "I never met Michelle's mother, but if you ask me, she was the smart one to run away. Michelle's father was a real asshole. He couldn't open his mouth without putting you down. He'd pick at Michelle and Ian all the time, always telling them what they were doing wrong. I never heard him say anything nice, never. Michelle said dinnertime was the worst. He'd make them sit there for hours while he drank and told his bullshit stories. Michelle and Ian were kids, like they cared about his stupid stories. Some nights they'd still be sitting there past midnight. If one of them got up, or even if one of them looked like they weren't paying attention, he'd start yelling at them, telling them they were worthless. He used to call Michelle a whore all the time."

"Did he ever hit them?"

"No. Michelle used to say she wished he did. And she was serious. She said she'd rather take a beating and get it over with instead of having to listen to him rant hour after hour."

Maggie looked at me, nodding. The source of Liz's masochistic cop fetish had been laid at our feet. Years of being forced to listen to her father spewing his hate, sitting there at the dinner table, hearing him ramble on and on about how he was going to hurt this person or that person, always playing the victim. When she was little, she probably believed him, the way all kids do. She thought he was a real tough guy, the kind of guy everybody respected. But by the time she was a teenager, she would've known he was all talk, a blowhard with a badge, and she'd have to sit there, listening to him until she was ready to scream, wanting him to do it already, wanting him to punish her and get it over with. But instead he'd keep riding her, his constant toxic blather driving her insane.

I thought about Liz provoking me yesterday, trying to make me interrogate her. I was everything her father wasn't. Where he talked big, I talked small. Where he made empty threats, I was the real deal. She wanted me. She wanted what I could do to her. I was an expert in pain. She was into cops, especially those with a violent streak. She thought we were the antidote to her father's poison. She didn't get that we were really just poison of another kind.

Maggie asked, "Did she ever tell him to hit her?"

"More than once. It would just set him off into another tirade. She eventually learned the best thing was to just wait for him to run out of steam."

"What about Ian, Jr.? What would he do?"

"He'd just sit there and take it. When it was over, he'd crawl in bed with his sister and cry like a girl."

"Did you ever think there was more to Ian and Michelle's relationship than brother and sister?"

"What do you mean?"

Maggie didn't need to answer his question. She just waited for his mind to make the connection.

His face lit with understanding, "You mean . . . ?"

Maggie nodded.

"You think they were . . . intimate?"

"Were they?" I asked.

"Well, no. I don't think so. Or at least I didn't think so at the time."

"What do you think now?"

"Maybe," he said after a pause. "Ian was all hands with her. He was always snuggling up to her, slipping his hands inside her clothes, but I didn't think it was sexual. I thought he was just needy."

"Did Michelle respond?"

"Not that I saw. She'd just push his hands away when it bothered her. But remember how I told you that Ian would crawl in bed with her after their father's tirades? Sometimes I'd go over there in the mornings, and I'd find them in bed together. I never saw them doing anything, but they'd be naked."

"And you didn't think two naked teenagers sleeping in the same bed were doing anything with each other?"

"I thought they took their clothes off because it was hot. What do you want from me? I was a stupid teenager myself."

I leaned back in my chair. It made sense how it started—two distressed teenagers trying to comfort each other late at night, a little touching under the covers and then the flood of hormones would kick in and the touching would turn into something more. "Tell us about how you raped her," I said.

"I didn't rape her," he glared at me. "Michelle was into some strange shit, okay?" He ran his fingers through his hair again. "She liked . . ." He was having a hard time spitting it out.

"She liked it rough," I said.

"Yeah. I wasn't into it, you know. It didn't do anything for me, but she'd make me."

"And how did she do that?" asked a skeptical Maggie.

"She'd pinch me, or she'd bite me until I lashed out at her."

"You could have left."

"Eighteen-year-old boys don't turn down sex," he stated matter-of-fact.

"The rape. Get to the rape," I said.

"I'd go to Michelle's house in the early afternoon. That was the only time we could be alone. Ian would be at school, and her father would be working. Michelle would have me tie her up, and she had this whip."

"Whip?" My mind flashed to Hector and Margarita Juarez's lase-whipped corpses.

"Yeah. It was one of those cheap souvenirs. You know the ones they make out of braided monitor hide?"

I nodded.

"Well, she'd make me use it on her. I'd give her a few whacks, the kind that'd sting, but wouldn't break the skin. And then we'd . . . you know . . . do it. We did it that way at least five or six times. It wasn't rape. It was all her idea."

"We believe you," I said reassuringly. "Then what happened?"

"Her brother came home early one day. We didn't even hear him come in. He must've peeked in on us, and there I was whipping his naked sister who was all tied up."

"What did he do?"

"He brained me with a frying pan, one of those cast-iron ones. I never saw it coming."

"How bad?"

"I didn't wake up for seven months. That's how bad."

Sumari leaned forward and turned his head around. He took Maggie's hand and ran her fingers under his hair. "Feel that?"

"Yeah," she said.

He took my good hand and ran it into the greasy hair at the base of his skull. From the corner of my eye, I saw Maggie wipe her fingers on her pant leg. My fingers ran up from his neck and into a dent, a big dent, a dent that made me want to yank my hand away. Ian, Sr., had been telling the truth—for once.

"Feel it?" he asked.

"Yeah."

"I still get headaches. Bad ones."

"I can imagine."

"They should've locked that kid up, but her father came up with this rape bullshit to save his kid. You want to know the worst part? Michelle showed up at my home a few weeks after they let me out of the hospital. She'd run away, and she begged my parents to let her stay with us."

"What did they say?"

"No."

"Where did she go?"

"Last I heard, she was living on the street."

I let Maggie cross first and then I stepped across the wood-beam bridge, the black water of the Koba running underneath.

"Do you think Ian really thought she was being raped?" I asked when my feet hit the walkway.

"I don't know. Could be he was just jealous. But if Liz is right that he was once a sweet kid, he could've been just trying to protect her. What does a young kid know about kinky sex? Her all tied up and getting whipped, it could easily look like a rape to a kid, even to an adult.

I nodded. Bastard of a father. Runaway mother. A too-early introduction to sex and violence. Almost made me fell bad for him. Almost.

"Ian killed Adela's parents, Juno. The fact that they were whipped to death is too big a coincidence. He's probably had thing for whips ever since he walked in on her and her boyfriend. And Liz figured it out. She's always known what we just learned. When it was revealed during Adela's trial that the murder weapon was a whip, she knew it was Ian. She knows her brother *way* better than most sisters do."

"You can say that again," I said with a shiver. Ian and Liz's incestuous relationship was giving me a case of the heebie-jeebies.

"Liz was my anonymous caller. She's the one who called me at the beginning of all this and told me Adela didn't do it."

I nodded. Maggie's reasoning was flawless. It tracked.

She said, "She told me she knew who the real killer was. I wish she'd called sooner, before the conviction."

"I'm sure she didn't want to call at all. She didn't want her brother to go to jail. She was probably just hoping they'd find Adela innocent."

"I always knew Ian was an asshole," she said, "but I had no idea he was so . . ."

"Fucked up."

"Yeah."

We turned onto a wider walkway that led back toward the shore. *Every time you come to an intersection, take the wider walkway, and you'll be on the shore in no time.* That was what they'd always tell the offworld tourists who were afraid of getting lost in Floodbank's never-ending maze of convoluted walkways. It didn't always work, but it was as good a system as any.

"So the question is why. Why did Ian kill them?"

Maggie stopped short. I picked up an alarmed vibe from her. I felt it reverb right through me. I looked straight ahead, and there was Hoshi, already reaching for his piece. *Shit!*

Maggie spun around and bolted a half step ahead of my own panicked footfalls. Standing and fighting was the wrong move. He was already reaching. He'd fry us both before we could draw a bead on him, and with my left hand, I doubted I could hit him with all the time in the world. We sped back the way we came, our arms spread wide for balance. The slatted walkways pitched and lurched as we slammed one foot down after another. Water splashed up as our feet made contact with the platforms and drove them down into the water. Entire homes began to rock from the disturbance. We wound left and right through the haphazard warren of strung-together homes, the lack of any kind of straightaway our only saving grace. Hoshi would have to get close, very close in order to get off a clear burn.

Maggie was gaining distance ahead of me, which was a bad sign. It meant Hoshi was likely gaining ground behind me. People were clearing out of our way; our rope-stretching, wood-scraping, water-slapping approach had the locals grabbing ropes and leaning out over the edge, some of them pulling their feet up off the walkway until we safely passed underneath. We hit an intersection, and Maggie wisely took the wider path. We were near the outer edge of Floodbank, and a narrow walkway was likely to dead end.

She took another turn, and I went the opposite way, knowing Hoshi would stay with me. Maggie would get away clean. I was losing sight of her anyway. My guess was Hoshi's eyes were glimpsing my fleeing back on and off, and at this point, likely more on than off. He'd be opening fire soon.

I cranked up my speed for one final lung-burning push. I could hear him behind me. He sounded so close. I kept my eyes scanning the edges, looking for a gap that was big enough. . . .

There! I dove. The platform under my feet gave way, and I lost my balance, my dive turning into more of a slide. I skidded across the walkway, splinters digging into my stomach. I scrabbled forward, my head already underwater. I lunged down, my feet the last to feel the cool water. I kicked straight down, knowing lase-fire couldn't penetrate deep into the water. I swam deeper, my feet tingling with the anticipation of being fried off. Flashes of diffused light went off all around me as Hoshi took potshots into the water. I needed air, and I needed it bad. I spun my body around and swam in the opposite direction of my dive. I stroked, once, twice, wanting to put distance between me and my entry point. *Shit! I need air!* I kicked straight up. My head cracked into an oil drum. River slime oozed across my face. My legs kept driving me up as I slid around to the side and found a pocket of air under somebody's floor.

I sucked air, my lungs struggling to keep up with demand. I could hear somebody's feet dancing across the floor above me. I couldn't control my breathing. I was being too loud.

"Officer! Officer! I can hear him! He's under there!"

The house rocked as Hoshi jumped onboard. I sucked a last breath and went back under. I swam down until my ears hurt, then aimed my body in the same direction as the current. I propelled myself with long strokes, my clothes dragging my pace down to one that just barely outran the current.

I needed to surface. I looked up and targeted a patch of light. My right hand smacked a rope that stung my broken fingers. My foot kicked that same rope a second later as I slipped past and approached the light. I broke the surface and launched into a gulping, choking, and panting fit. Again, I was being too loud, but I couldn't stop my painful wheezing.

I listened intently, but I didn't hear anything outside of the Floodbank norm. I looked up at the source of the light, a round hole maybe a meter over my head. Recognizing the oval shape, I noticed the flies and the smell for the first time. *Son of a bitch.* I decided to move on before the light was eclipsed by some wide-mouthed brown bomber.

I let myself float with the current, leaving the shitter behind. I ducked and dipped under ropes and oil drums, moving from home to home, neighborhood to neighborhood, glad that the filth and garbage I was passing through was obscured by the darkness. Progress was slow as I kept hitting impassible thickets of crisscrossed rope that forced me to backtrack and choose another path.

It took me an hour to reach the end of Floodbank, my head finally coming up with open river ahead. I swam to a dock ladder and climbed up.

I checked my phone. Dead. They built them to be rain-resistant, but holding them underwater for so long must've been a different story.

I started on the long, soggy walk to Tenttown.

twenty-four

I TRUDGED through the Tenttown mud. My head was itching. I hadn't realized I'd cut myself when I torpedoed that oil drum, but I clearly had, because my skin was crawling up there, crawling with maggots. Leave an open wound exposed for even a couple minutes and you were likely to get infested. *Fucking flies.* Lots of planets have flies of one sort or another, but Darwin sure whipped up a special batch for us.

So Ian and his pop weren't entirely estranged. Pop must've called when we left, told him we were snooping around. He told him we were asking about Michelle. From there, Ian must've suspected that we'd made the Michelle-Liz connection and therefore, the fish market might be a likely destination for us. Likely enough to send Hoshi over to check it out, but, in his mind, not likely enough to warrant more attention than that.

It itches so bad. My scalp was driving me insane. I resisted the urge to scratch, knowing I'd just make it worse. I hoped Maggie had made it back to the tent so she could play nursemaid like Niki used to do. *Niki.* It still didn't seem real—the jungle, the orchards, any of it. It had happened so fast. It couldn't be real. The drizzling rain was real. The maggots eating my scalp were real. But that scene in the jungle, it couldn't be. Niki was still alive. Her spine was coming along nicely. I told myself she'd be her old self soon, but the empty feeling in my gut persisted. I noticed that the knot in my stomach had uncoiled. Gone was the cramping, a hollow left in its place. I thought about having a drink but nixed the idea. I didn't want to dull the emptiness. It felt wrong to dull it. Like I'd be dulling the memory of her. It felt right to suffer.

Besides, I had a job to do. Adela Juarez was going to get gassed in two days. I was going to get arrested for Raj's murder. And Maggie? Ian was going to kill her. Bringing down that kind of heat on himself was the last thing he wanted, but we were leaving him no choice. And it wasn't just Ian. There were other forces in play, the offworld travel agent, and the offworld serial with fourteen murders to his name.

I found Maggie sitting on a rock outside our tent.

"What took you so long?" she wanted to know.

Maggie did a horrible job patching me up. She started by dumping enough fly gel on my head to kill a damn swarm. Then she nicked me twice when she shaved the hair around the wound. And then she got all squeamish about cleaning out the dead maggots. When she was finally done with my head, she practically tweezed her way into my intestines as she pulled out the handful of splinters in my stomach.

"Good as new?" she asked.

"Good as new," I repeated.

"Sorry it took so long."

"You did great, Maggie. Thanks."

She called Customs again to see if the woman she'd been dealing with had finally gotten approval to share their records on Jungle Expeditions. The woman had indeed gotten approval, but in typical government fashion, she hadn't bothered to pull the records yet. When Maggie complained, the woman got all pissy, and Maggie ripped into her with an uncharacteristic loss of temper. She kept poking the woman's holo with her finger while she made her demands clear. "You will get me my data, and you will do it now." When the woman put Maggie on hold, her holo turned into a logo for the Office of Customs. I could see that Maggie was preparing for another fight as she waited for the woman to come back on the line. Luckily for the woman, she never did. She served up one of her underlings instead, who came on the line and streamed the names and numbers into Maggie's digital paper pad.

Maggie immediately dove into the data like she'd never lost her cool. Her eyes swiveled from side to side as she skimmed the records, making sure she'd gotten what she asked for.

Maggie handed me the pad. I strained to read the names in the tent's lamplight. "Can you make this thing brighter?"

"Sure." Maggie took it back for a few seconds then handed the digital paper back to me.

I looked through the first few names, not recognizing any. These were the 342 Jungle Expeditions clients from the past year, or at least the 342 who had taken the time to list Jungle Expeditions on their customs forms. No telling how many just left it blank. I groaned, overwhelmed by the hopeless prospect of narrowing this list down to one serial killer. I didn't have the energy for it. "There's no way we can get through this list before it's too late."

"Got any better ideas?"

I strained my Niki-hazed brain. There had to be a better way. Going though this list was solid police procedure, but it would take too damn long. And even if we managed to find our off-world serial, we'd still have to flip him to get to Horst, and then flip Horst to get to Ian, and then, as if that wasn't enough, we'd have to hope that somewhere along the way we got the evidence we needed to free Adela.

It was hopeless. I didn't want to upset Maggie by saying it, but Adela was as good as dead. There just wasn't enough time. I wished we could visit her at the Zoo, let her know that we believed her. It could make a big difference to her to know, before she died, that somebody believed her. If nothing else, I could at least apologize for making her cry. But Adela was off-limits. We couldn't get into the Zoo without one of Ian's old guard buddies calling him. We'd never get out alive.

"Well?" Maggie asked, waiting for my answer.

I didn't have any better ideas. Not as long as Yuri Kiper stayed underground.

Maggie said, "We either go through this list or we risk approaching Liz. You ready to charm her again?"

God, I didn't want to see her. Just the thought of her made my stomach tumble. I couldn't believe I'd flirted with her. How could I have done that to Niki? Betray her like that when she'd been in the state she was in. I doubted Niki would've cared. She wasn't a prude. But I cared. I cared plenty.

But Liz could help us. She knew things she hadn't told us. And she was Maggie's anonymous caller. If we asked, she might just tell us what she knew. Then again, I'd already turned down Liz/Michelle's little S&M fantasy once, and she wasn't the kind of woman who was used to rejection. She'd been after me to be her ultimate S. But if I approached her again, she might think I'd make a better M. I pictured myself going in there and trying to play her un-father, trying to get her to open up to me. I could see Liz turning the tables on me, trapping me with one of her bondage toys and then bringing her little brother in, the two of them using me as the Davies family's perv pet.

Maggie was still waiting.

"I don't want to see Liz," I said. I scanned down to the bottom of Maggie's list of offworlders. Not a single name jumped out at me. "Do you recognize any of them?" I asked.

"No. But I starred the ones who are onplanet right now."

I sorted so the starred names topped the list, nine of them. I looked at their dates of entry. Seven of the nine had just arrived over the last couple days. It probably meant that they were all on the same tour. We'd have to check them out one by one, hoping that one of them was our serial. It was the only safe play. Half the damn city was on the lookout for us, but we knew for a fact that these offworlders would be in the dark. Can you imagine tour operator Horst Jeffers telling his customers to let him know if they saw a couple cops snooping around? Not the kind of thing customers on a sex-tour wanted to hear. These people were unsuspecting. These were people we could watch.

"Can I have that back?" Maggie asked. "I want to compare their entry and exit dates to the barge murder dates."

I passed the sheet of digital paper back to her and lay back in my hammock, thinking it would be tough to get any kind of definitive date matches. Most of the barge murder scenes were found long after the actual murders occurred. Some of the time-of-death estimates had a margin of error of a month or more.

My head hurt. I closed my eyes and tried to close it all out, leaving myself alone with my hollowness.

Maggie whispered, "Are you asleep?"

"No," I said without opening my eyes.

"Are you okay?"

"No."

"Is there anything I can do?"

"No."

"I'm sorry I got you into this."

"I know."

"We'll get him, Juno. It'll be over soon."

I wasn't so confident, but I still said, "Yeah."

"It'll be over soon," she repeated.

She was right about that. It was only a matter of time before

Ian's crew started asking around Tenttown. *Seen an old dog with a shaking splint of a right hand walking around with a long-haired beauty wearing high-priced duds?* Shit, they could be surrounding this tent right now. Ian could come barging through those flaps any second with his biceps-by-'roid and his boy-o charm. The possibility that we might survive was growing more remote by the minute. And if we did manage to pull through? That almost scared me more than Ian. What the hell would I do then?

Maggie interrupted my self-administered career counseling. "Pick a name: Peter Wynn or Jacque Benoit."

"Benoit. What do I win?"

"A stakeout with a lovely lady."

twenty-five

I TOOK a seat next to Maggie at the bar. We were both tech-naked. No phones, no weapons, no digital notepads, nothing. You want to surveil an offworlder, you have to go low tech, and there was nothing more low tech than our eyeballs.

We'd been following Jacque Benoit all day. We watched him eat breakfast. We watched him drink coffee on the square. We watched him spend his afternoon meandering through the Phra Kaew market. We watched him hurry to the bank, just barely beating closing time.

He was a regular on Lagarto. He knew where he was going when he walked. The shop owners all knew him, nothing but hugs and smiles when he walked in. Maggie and I would hang across the street while the shop owners would serve him tea and snap their fingers at houseboys who would carry in one high-priced item after another. He made a fair number of purchases: handmade pottery, a set of monitor hide chairs, a wool rug.

We tailed him back to the hotel restaurant, where he was sitting in a group of four men, all offworlders. His hair was more white than blond, and his teeth were whiter still. I looked over the other three, sitting there with their unblemished skin and their whiskerless faces. When they smiled, their faces beamed cool attitudes, and when they talked, they were all debonair charm. They were drinking imported coffee. Just like offworlders to come all the way down to the surface only to drink their orbital-grown coffee.

Maggie and I sat at the bar and tried to blend in. Maggie was wearing a set of whites that we had picked up in Tenttown. Loose-fitting cotton pants, with a matching V-neck top that had embroidered flowers bordering the V. She'd donated her jewelry to a panhandler and dumped her shoes for a pair of jellies. Lastly, she'd pulled her salon 'do back into a pony, and her conversion from blue blood to blue collar was complete. Me, I was dressed like usual, in whites of my own, except I had purchased a cheap panama to cover up the bandaged bald patch on my head.

Maggie held up two fingers for the bartender then turned to me. "I think that's Peter Wynn sitting on his left."

"Who?"

"The other guy from the list. The other one that matched six murder dates."

"Was that the largest number of matches?"

"Of the group that's currently onplanet, yes. But of the entire three hundred and forty-two there were three who matched eight of the barge murder dates."

"You realize how low the odds are that one of these guy's is our serial?"

"Yeah. Maybe we should give up on these guys and go see Liz. This time tomorrow, it'll be too late for Adela."

"Let's give it another hour before we move on and see if he exhibits any serial killer behavior."

"And what exactly is serial killer behavior?"

"You know, putting on a necklace made of human ears or masturbating over a dead animal."

Maggie smiled. I didn't, didn't feel up to it. Making a joke was one thing, but laughing at it was another entirely.

"Ooh, that looks good." The second Maggie said it, I realized how hungry I was. I looked across the room at the clay oven that served as the restaurant's centerpiece. The cook had just pulled out an earthenware dish. Looked like fish in a brown sauce, spiced with cinnamon and cumin by the smell of it. The cook turned his attention back to the oven and re-arranged a series of dishes to get at a round of bread.

Maggie sipped her drink. I saw her studying my untouched glass. "You know my offer's still open, Juno."

"What offer?"

"You know what offer."

I did know. She'd been after me almost since we first met. "They'll never take a woman," I said.

"Why not? Women occupy all kinds of government posts."

"Not on Lagarto, Maggie. You know how it is. Us Lagartans can't afford to raise our babies in tanks. It's women's bellies here. Women have a different role, a more traditional role. It's what people expect."

"It doesn't matter what they expect. It's not like people vote for chief of police. It's an appointed post. And stop trying to talk me out of it."

"Don't get me wrong, Maggie. I'm behind you. I know you'd make a great chief, better than Paul. I just don't see it happening."

"That's why I need your help. You took over KOP once before."

"That was Paul."

"Bullshit. Chief Chang couldn't have done it without you."

"Sure he could have. There's no shortage of muscle in the force."

"Can't you see it, Juno? You weren't just muscle, you ran the whole operation. When Chief Chang was giving face time to the public, you were the one who was running the show. The sergeants, the lieutenants, they all reported to you."

I started thinking that drink was looking pretty good. No. Leave it alone. Don't dull the hollowness. Don't dull her memory. I turned my focus back on the offworld quartet. They were all sitting on one side of the table while one of them held a digital pad out so they could all see.

Maggie kept at me. "Listen, Juno, I know you're resistant because you think things went badly the first time, but you did a lot of good, too. And it can be different this time. When I'm chief, we're going to clean up this city. Just imagine what a clean KOP can do for this place. It will change everything."

I acted like I wasn't listening, but I was. What else would I do? "What makes you think we'll even survive the next few days?"

"I don't see much point in thinking any other way."

Our golden boy offworlder took the pad from his Don Juan pal to get a closer look. He handed it back after taking a long look and put his hands up like they were the paws of a begging dog. He panted, his tongue flopping out like a dog's. In fact, it *was* a dog's tongue; long, wide, and flat. The others laughed lasciviously at his doggie imitation, one of them fake-licking the pad's display, bringing out more laughs.

"What the hell are they looking at?" I asked.

"And why are they using a digital pad?"

Maggie's question was rhetorical. The answer was obvious to both of us. They didn't want anybody to see what they were looking at, otherwise they would be popping up 3-D holos over their table instead of sharing a single 2-D pad.

Maggie said, "I'm going to find out." And before I could stop her, she was up and heading for their table. My heart rate sped up like a revving outboard. Maggie walked by the oven and then around to the back side of the table. She slowed down to an agonizing pace as she approached the group from behind. She came right up to their backs and took a long look at their pad. They stayed oblivious, the whole group enraptured by their digital display. The maître d' didn't stay so unaware. He was already crossing the floor, approaching Maggie and giving her the evil eye. Maggie saw him coming and set a brisk pace in the opposite direction. She joined me at the bar just in time to see the bartender take away our drinks with a scolding look. We skulked our way to the exit while the maître d' dirty-looked us all the way out.

We went through the revolving doors and stepped into the rain, the maître d' following us a half block to emphasize his point. He probably thought we were a couple thieves looking to make away with some high-tech swag, and he wanted to make it clear that we weren't welcome within half a block of his restaurant.

Maggie and I stepped under the awning of a café. Rain sheeted off the canvas, closing us in behind a curtain of water. Maggie's face was screwed up in thought.

"Well?" I asked.

"They were looking at stills. Nude photos."

"And?"

"It was Adela Juarez. They were looking at nude shots of Adela Juarez."

"It was that punk Raj. He probably talked her into letting him take some keepsakes then turned around and sold—"

"No," she said. "There were bars."

"Bars?"

"She was behind bars. Those pics were taken at the Zoo."

My face must've screwed up just like hers as I tried to reason it out. How did these offworld tourists wind up with nude photos of Adela Juarez? Something was tickling the back of my brain. There was a memory back there if I could only pull it out of my head. "Pictures," I finally said. "When I visited Adela, she asked me if I was there to take pictures."

"Did you ask her why?"

"Yeah, but she didn't answer. I didn't think it was important, so I didn't push it."

"We have to go to the Zoo."

"Yeah."

Maggie and I glided into the dock. I climbed out of the rented skiff and walked the short distance to land, the Zoo lights barely visible through the downpour. I looked back at Maggie, who was staying nice and dry under the skiff's tin roof, and then approached the newsstand, the same one I'd visited both just before and just after my finger-breaking episode with Ian. I took up a stool under the overhang and ordered up a cup of stale coffee.

I watched as boats pulled into the dock and discharged night shift zookeepers who filed up the riverbank steps to report to work. Soon thereafter, other guards started coming down the steps as the shift change progressed. I kept my panama angled over my face and kept my eyes zeroed on the wide-waisted.

I thought I saw him struggling his mass down the stairs, walking like a two-year-old, dropping one foot down to the next stair and bringing his other foot down to that same step before trying the next one. Coworkers passed him by as he kept up his slow descent. It was him. I could see his crumbcatcher beard. He was the supervisor, the one who had called Ian. I sipped my coffee, my broken fingers tingling with the memory of Ian and Hoshi holding me down snap after snap.

The plan was a quick snatch and grab, but watching this guy labor down the stairs, I thought it might be more of a hook and tow. I downed the last sip of overcooked coffee and fell in step behind him as he passed. I followed him onto the dock. I had my piece out, letting it hang in my left hand as I walked. I kept cool, letting him make his way down the creaking dock.

I looked at Maggie. She was already pulling the tether from the cleat.

I surveyed the dock. There was a group at the dock's end, pooling their money for a shared ride on a double-long skiff. I looked over my shoulder. There were three more zookeepers coming down the stairs, none of them close enough to create any trouble. I closed the gap, pulling right in behind him. I drove my piece into his back flab. "Get in that boat," I said.

He stopped short. "What?"

"Now!" I said, as I drove my piece in deep.

He stammered out some curses but complied. Maggie started the motor while he stepped over to the dock's edge.

I scanned in every direction. Nobody close yet. "Move it," I told him. He picked one foot up and held it tentatively in the air as he tried to decide the best way to step down into the boat. I gave him a shove and sent him tumbling down. He smashed into the seats, his impact sending the shallow-bottomed craft into such a wobble that it took on water over the sides.

Maggie lost her balance and fell down. "Dammit, Juno!"

"Go!" I told her as I hopped down.

She gunned the motor. It took a second for the prop to bite before we started edging free of the dock. I stood on the side rail, steadying my balance by hooking my bad hand over one of the bars that held up the tin roof. The zookeeper was on the floor, struggling to get up, trying to get his knees under his mass. I tucked my piece back in my waistband. I grabbed hold of one of the roof supports with my good hand and swung over the zookeeper, monkey-style. I stomped down with both feet, driving him back down to the boat's bottom, stuffing his mass between the seats. He tried to extricate himself, but he was wedged in good and tight. He squirmed and wriggled, but one arm was pinned under his body, and the other wasn't strong enough to pull himself free. He was throwing an immobilized fit, yelling so loud that he was almost overpowering the sound of the outboard.

I looked back at the dock to see if there was anybody making chase, but we'd gotten away clean. Maggie aimed us for deeper water. I stayed silent, letting him sweat it out, and by the looks of it, he was sweating plenty. We rode out into the gray water, the dimness of sunset draining the color out of everything. Maggie navigated us away from the shore, away from all the other riverboats, finding a nice, private expanse of river for us to carry out our interrogation. Maggie gave the motor one last throttle and shut it off. All was silence except for the rain rattling on the tin roof.

I watched him in the light of the single bulb that hung naked from the roof, waiting for him to quit his struggles. His body jerked a couple more times, but he couldn't pry loose. He was stuck between the seats like a giant lump of bread dough that had been left to rise far too long.

When he finally quit, I said, "Remember me?"

"I know who you are," he responded more calmly than I'd expected.

"How about Detective Orzo? You know her?"

"Heard of her."

"From who?"

"Screw you. I'm not talking to you."

"You'll talk. You have no choice."

"The hell I don't," he said as defiantly as a man in his position could.

I was still standing on the side, and I leaned back, pulling the roof with me, tipping the skiff to one side. I stood straight up, letting the boat return to normal, then leaned back again, this time tipping back a little further. "You know what the problem is with these skiffs?" I said as I kept rocking the boat from side to side. "They're so shallow. Catch a little wave and you take on water." I leaned back again, pulling hard enough that the boat's rail dipped below the waterline. Cool water ran in and soaked the zookeeper's clothes.

He was scared. I could see it on his face, in his eyes. But he was keeping a lid on it, probably telling himself I wouldn't really do it. I rocked back again, this time taking on twice as much water as before. Water sloshed over his face and pooled around his shoulders.

I kept the boat rocking like we were in heavy surf. "Ready to talk yet?"

"No," he said.

Another dip.

And another.

And another.

The boat was already hanging heavy in the water. All I had to do now was tilt my body, and I could run water over the edge in a steady stream. "You know how to swim, right, Maggie?"

"Sure do," she said. She had her feet pulled up onto the seat to keep them out of the water. She was playing along this time, not trying to calm me down like she did when I braced Raj. Those pictures of Adela had her worked up. An innocent girl, framed for her parents' murder, and now forced to demean herself by posing naked. Maggie knew that if we had any chance of saving her, we couldn't be worried about procedure. There was no more time. Adela's execution was scheduled for tomorrow.

I kept tipping back, letting the water trickle over the lip, watching him watch the water. "This is it," I said, and I meant it. "I'm not going to ask you again."

He looked me in the eye, searching for any sign that I'd stop. I kept up my cold-blooded stare. If this dumbass had any idea whom he was playing chicken with . . .

The water kept trickling in. It wouldn't be long before the river grabbed permanent hold and sucked this skiff down for good. He was really beginning to piss me off. This guy was going to make me swim back to shore. He was still looking at me, wrongly thinking I'd flinch first. I wished he was a cop. Then he'd know my rep. I was the undefeated champ of chicken.

Nothing to do but wait him out. If the boat went under, it would be his own fault for doubting me. The water was gathering around his head. He looked at Maggie, who was standing upright, getting ready to dive. His desperate eyes turned back on me. I met them with my own. I wasn't afraid to look him in the eye. He wouldn't be the first man I'd killed.

The water was creeping up his face diagonally. He turned his head away from me, toward the high side of the tilted boat, keeping his mouth and nose out of the rising water. Maybe we wouldn't have to swim after all, I thought. He might just drown before the boat went under.

He turned his head to look at me again, but his face went under when he did. He sputtered as water ran up his nose. He went into a choking fit and turned away again, straining to hold his head up out of the water. He let out such a violent cough that his head jerked back into the water, and he caught another gagging mouthful.

Maggie turned away, and she covered her ears. I kept the water coming, no longer caring much if he talked or not.

"Okay!" he choked. "Okay!"

I kept the water trickling in, punishing him for making it take so long.

"I'll talk," he spluttered. "Stop! Make him stop!"

I leveled the boat, and the water went from diagonal to horizontal, his head now fully under. I reached into the water and pulled it up by the hair.

His body wracked as he fought to clear his lungs. "Crazy motherfucker!"

Maggie tossed him a cup. "Start bailing or we still might go under."

He took hold of the cup with his free hand and dunked it full of water then tossed the contents toward the river, half the water hitting the side and rolling back down into the boat.

I gave him a minute to get his breathing under control. "What's your name?"

"Wozniak. George Wozniak."

"Okay, George, tell me about Adela Juarez. Somebody's been making her do smut pics."

"My arm hurts. You gonna pull me up?"

"No."

"C'mon, man, just pull me up."

I let go of his hair. His head dropped under like a stone. His free hand swiped at me but caught nothing but air. He tried to lift his head over the waterline, but all that surfaced was his forehead. He kicked with his legs, found some wiggle room, and managed to get his eyes up out of the water, but his nose and his mouth, they were still under. His face looked like it was about to blow from the pressure. I waited as his head fell back all the way under. I grabbed hold of his hair again and pulled him up.

His mouth sprayed water like it was a blowhole, then he went into another round of choking and coughing.

I used my foot to push the bailing cup back into his reach. "You were telling us about Adela Juarez."

"Yeah, Adela Juarez," he said, defeated. "That was Ian who took those pics. He brought some photographer with him."

"Who?"

"I don't know the guy's name."

"What did he look like?"

"He was fat, a real porker, if you know what I mean."

Looking at George, seeing his thigh-sized arm working the bailing cup, I said, "Yeah, I know what you mean. Was his name Yuri?"

"Could be. I told you I don't know his name. Ian said I didn't need to know his name."

"What else can you tell me about him?"

"He was all nervous and shit. When we brought him onto death row, he was always looking over his shoulder like he was afraid one of those cages would pop open any second."

It was Yuri all right. "And he took the pics?"

"Yeah. You should've seen the RIPs in the cages."

Maggie interrupted. "Rips?"

"Yeah, you know, Rest in Peace. These assholes, they're already dead. That's what we call them. Anyway, these RIPs were all jerking off and shit. Last time any of them were going to see some titty. And that girl had a nice pair on her, too."

"You didn't think of bringing her someplace private?"

"Ian didn't want to. He wanted to shoot her in her cage."

"How did he get her to pose?"

"He told her we'd pass her around the cages if she didn't. He said he'd move her from cage to cage, an hour in each one. He said it loud enough for the RIPs to hear. They went apeshit thinking they were going to get some."

Maggie put her face in her hands. Her voice came out muffled. "You told her she'd get raped if she didn't strip."

"Don't get all righteous now. That girl is a damn murderer. Making her strip is nothing compared to what she did to her parents. Beside, it's not like she was a virgin or something."

Maggie pulled her hands away, revealing a face I'd never seen before. "Dunk him," she said.

George stopped bailing. "Shit, lady, calm down. We weren't really going to do it. Ian didn't want anybody screwing her, not even us guards. Nobody touched that girl."

She was pointing at me. "Dammit, Juno, I told you to dunk him."

I shook my head at her, saying no and shaming her at the same time. This wasn't her. "Why did Ian give the hands-off order?" I asked.

"Ian wanted to keep her fresh. He had plans for her."

"What kind of plans?"

"You gonna let me go if I tell?"

I nodded.

"How about you?" he said to Maggie. "You gonna let me go?"

Maggie made a disgusted face but nodded.

"What about Ian?" he asked. "What am I gonna do if he finds out I talked?"

"We'll take care of Ian," I said.

"But what if you don't?"

"Would you rather die now?"

That finally did it. "Ian came to me almost a year ago," he said. "I hardly recognized him. When he started at the Zoo, he was this little stick boy. I took him with me on rounds his first day. I was showin' him around, and he looked like he was about to cry, his eyes were all misty, and his nose kept running. The kid was scared, seeing all those faces looking out at him from the cages. I thought, this kid's never gonna last, but he hung in there. Gotta hand it to him, he hung in there, long enough to get a posting at KOP. Anyway, he came up to me about a year ago, and I couldn't believe I was looking at the same guy. He had all these muscles and shit, and he had this new attitude, actin' like he was the man, you know what I'm sayin'?"

"What did he want?"

"RIPs."

"I don't get it."

"He buys RIPs, man."

I still wasn't getting it. "Take it from the beginning," I told him.

He took a deep breath. "Ian told me he had a partner, right? An offworlder. I never met him. Like I said, Ian tried to keep everything on a need-to-know basis, so I don't even know his name, but Ian told me the guy's story. This offworlder opened a business doing sex tours for offworlders. But he found out real quick that that shit's a competitive business. He had to take any business he could get. So when he'd get these crazy-ass requests from people, he'd try to accommodate them when the competition wouldn't. No matter how freaky the fantasy, he'd try to set it up. He did that for a long time, long enough that he eventually got known as the go-to guy for anything outside the norm. At least that's what Ian told me."

"Go on."

"Well, from time to time he'd get these S&Mers who were into snuff. They'd never come out and say it, but they'd hint around, see? They'd ask questions like, 'You ever wonder what it would be like to kill a person?' So Ian's offworld partner took the hint. He saw a big money opportunity and started checking into how to go about it. He scoped out the barges and found some good isolated sites. Then he hit the streets and started befriending some opium heads and orphans, looking for good candidates. You know, the kind that don't have any friends or family that would miss them. He got it all together, but when it actually came time for his clients to pay up, none of them came through."

"Why not?"

"At first he thought they were just trying to get him to cut the price. So he made it clear that price was negotiable, but he still didn't get any takers. None of them had the guts to go through with it. He almost let the whole idea go, thinking they were all talk."

"Were they scared of getting caught?"

"That's what I thought, but Ian's partner was smart. It occurred to him that the problem might be that these people actually had a conscience, you know what I'm saying? These offworlders aren't used to seeing O addicts and orphans where they're from, and they feel sorry for them."

It was beginning to make sense to me. "So he figures that if he can find victims who deserve to die, it might help sales."

"Right. He dropped all that snuff talk and started marketing it as your chance to be an executioner. Shit, that's when it took off. He had enough customers lining up that he was able to auction off the first RIP. We're talking serious money."

"How many did he do?"

"I don't know. I didn't count. At least twenty."

"And he auctioned every one of them off."

"Like I said, big money."

Maggie was disbelieving. "So you're trying to tell us that instead of putting the death row inmates into the gas chamber, you sell them off so the highest bidder can execute them?"

"Right."

"But that's impossible," she said. "All the gassings are authenticated by witnesses."

"Those witnesses aren't in the same room, though," he said. "We bring in the judge and the families, and they watch it from the visitor's center, on a vid screen. That photographer guy, the one that took pics of the Juarez girl, I let him come in one time to film the gas chamber. That guy can work some magic, I tell you. He just puts holos overtop the gas chamber background, and it looks real. He does the whole thing, the executioner doing the strap down, the cloud of gas that keeps getting thicker. Hell, I couldn't tell the vids weren't real, and I *knew* they weren't real. All I have to do is run the vids on the vid screen in the visitors center."

I let go of his head, the constant bailing having finally lowered the water level enough that his face could stay above the surface without my help. My brain blossomed with understanding. So many things suddenly made sense, starting with why nobody ever missed the barge murder victims. They were all going to die anyway. And then there were the offworlders who were checking out the nudie pics of Adela Juarez, the whole lot of them preparing to outbid each other for the right to execute her. Or how about the realization that there was no serial killer, just a string of rich offworlders playing dress-up, which explained why it was so hard for Maggie to match up murder dates to a single offworlder.

"How do you get them out?" Maggie asked.

"They get moved into solitary two days before they get gassed. I just go back there and walk them out through the kitchen. I bring their bodies back in the same way."

"Then what do you do with the bodies?"

"We bake 'em until they're nothing but ashes."

"You handle this whole operation by yourself?"

"No. The executioner who runs the gas chamber is in on it. And so are two other guards."

Maggie pulled out her digital pad. "Names."

"Jay Reedy, Karim Fahd, Hideki Saito."

"And that's it?"

"That's it. Pretty sweet deal, huh?"

Maggie was staring at him. She looked like she wanted to spit in his face.

"I don't know why you two are getting so worked up," he said. "You guys are cops, right? You know that getting gassed is way too humane for these animals. They don't deserve that kind of respect. They never showed that kind of respect to their victims, you can be sure of that."

"What about Adela? Has she been moved into solitary yet?"

"Yes. And I led her out and gave her to Ian a couple hours ago."

Maggie's voice took on an alarmed tone. "But she's not scheduled until tomorrow."

He tried to shrug his shoulders.

twenty-six

MAGGIE and I raced from block to block, our splashing feet splattering angry pedestrians. We'd dropped off the skiff back at the dock we'd rented it from. When the owner saw the giant upended bug jammed between the seats, I paid him a little extra and told him he might want to get some butter. I wasn't worried about the guard calling Ian. He wouldn't want anybody knowing he was a rat.

Unfortunately, George didn't know where Ian had taken Adela. Ian had no reason to tell him. We'd have to find her ourselves, and fast.

Maggie entered the restaurant a step ahead of me. Dinnertime was at its peak. We crossed the main floor, pausing multiple times to let the hustling wait staff through. We sped through the kitchen, the steam clinging to my lungs. We took the steps up, the duffel bag bouncing on my shoulder. I banged on the door, then when there was no immediate answer, banged again.

The door opened to an alarmed Liz, who, upon seeing Maggie and me, soured her face into a pucker. "What do you want?"

My heart was racing, and not just because we'd run up the stairs. I shoved my emotions down and tried to lock them up, "We need to talk, Liz."

She didn't hold the door for us. Instead, she just let it hang open and stepped away, letting us in but making sure we felt unwelcome.

She took a seat on the sofa. She was wearing a black robe that was tied short of snug. Half her hair was up in curlers while the other half rolled down the left side of her face. She was somehow prettier in this disheveled state, yet her sex appeal was now completely lost on me. Knowing her history, the emotional wounds she'd suffered at the hands of her father, she was no longer the stuff of erotic fantasy. Instead of wanting that robe to fall the rest of the way open, I wanted to find a blanket to cover her up. Where I'd once had flashes of holding her down under my bucking, sweating body, all I wanted to do now was hold her like a bird with a broken wing. It was like Niki all over again.

"What do you want?" she said as she pulled a curler free.

Maggie said, "Do you know who I am?"

"Yes."

"We need your help. We need you to tell us where Ian is."

"Why would I do that?" She winced as the second curler got hung up on a knot.

"Because an innocent girl is going to die if you don't."

"That's not my problem."

"Yes, it is," I said.

"I'm not responsible for Ian."

"Yes, you are. You're his big sister, aren't you?" I could have punched her in the face, and she still would've looked less stunned than she did now. "We know who you are, Michelle."

She looked away and pulled out another curler, dropping it into a growing pile on her lap. She pulled at the coil of hair she'd unleashed, stretching it down past her chin before letting it spring back up. She met my eyes as she spoke, somehow mustering up some fragile dignity. "So the two of you are better detectives than my brother gave you credit for."

"You called me," Maggie said. "You knew Ian was responsible

for the deaths of Hector and Margarita Juarez. When you saw
that their daughter was convicted, you called me and told me
you knew who the real killer was."

"That wasn't me," she said.

"You called because you knew your brother did it."

"No. That doesn't make sense. Why would Ian kill them?"

Maggie laid it out as simply as she could. "He and Horst are in
the snuff trade. They sell the executions of death row inmates to
offworlders. Ian killed the girl's parents and framed her so she'd
get the death penalty. He wanted to sell her."

"Ian wouldn't do that."

"You know that's not true, Liz," I said. "As soon as you heard
that they were whipped to death, you knew. You *knew*. Just like
we knew when we talked to Sumari. He told us about the
whipping games you liked to play. He showed us the dent in his
head, the dent he got when your brother brained him."

She stayed silent for a long minute, her eyes taking on a far-
away look. When she finally spoke, her tone was less than convincing. "That wasn't Ian's fault. He didn't understand," she said.
"He was too young. He thought he needed to save me. He felt
bad afterward. He was a good kid. Really, he was. It's not his fault
he turned out this way."

"How can you be so sure he was trying to save you? Maybe
he was just jealous."

She ignored me. She kept working the curlers, her eyes staring off into nothingness. Maggie reached across and took her
hand, forcing her to snap out of her trance. "You called me because you wanted to save Adela. Help us, and there's still a
chance we can."

"But what will happen to Ian?"

"It's too late for him," Maggie said. "He's beyond saving."

Michelle's eyes began to cloud over. "I don't know where
he is."

"You can call him. We'll run a trace."

"He won't answer. You can't track him if he doesn't answer."

"That's why we need you to call. He'll answer for you."

"No. I can't do it."

"They're going to kill Adela," Maggie insisted. "Ian and Horst. They sold her execution to the highest bidder. That's what they do. Don't you understand? They smuggle death row inmates out of the Zoo, and they *sell* them."

"So? Those people deserve to die."

"Not Adela. Adela's innocent. Your brother framed her. He killed her parents and set her up to take the fall. Some rich offworlder is going to torture her, and then he's going to kill her. He could be torturing her right now, Liz. She's already lost her parents. She's been through enough."

Liz stopped with the curlers, although she'd missed two. They were both on the same side of her head, making her hair look as unbalanced as her mental state. She was staring off again with blank, vacant eyes that said nobody was home. "You can't make me betray my brother," she stated unconvincingly.

"You already have," I said. "You called Maggie. You knew then that it might come to this, and you still made the call."

She kept her eyes aimed up and out, like she was talking to somebody floating in the air. "I knew Hector Juarez," she whispered. "He was a pervert. Yuri and Horst used the Libre studios to film my . . . my movies. Hector would let us in late at night, when nobody else was there. He liked to watch. He'd always be there during filming. I had a hard time performing when he was there, always staring at me with these hungry eyes. I asked Horst to make him leave, but he was afraid he'd lose the studio space. There aren't any other quality studios on Lagarto. I eventually learned to pretend he wasn't there. I'd come in for my scene, and I wouldn't look at him. When he'd stand by the camera to get the best view, I would keep my eyes on my partner, or sometimes I'd just close them. If I didn't look at him, I could tell myself he wasn't there."

"Tell us about that night, the night he and his wife were killed."

"Ian came to me that night. He had bloody clothes, and he had burns on his wrists. I wanted to clean him up, but he wanted to . . . to . . ." Her mouth was still open, but the words just stopped coming out of her, like she was a windup toy that had run out.

I gave the turnkey a twist. "He wanted to have sex, didn't he?"

She nodded—just barely. "He was passionate. He told me he had just broken up a robbery. He said they had lase-blades, and the burns he'd gotten were defensive. He said he could've died. That's what I thought it was about. I thought he'd just had a near death experience and he wanted to, you know, celebrate. I didn't know about Hector then. I heard about it the next day, but I didn't make the connection. All they said on the news was that Hector and Margarita were murdered in their own home. To be honest, I didn't really care that much at the time. When the news said the daughter confessed, I believed it. I had no reason not to. I figured that with a father like that, it was no wonder the daughter was so screwed up.

"But then I saw a news report about the trial. It had to be a month later, maybe more. And they mentioned the lase-whip. They'd never said that before. Up 'til then, they'd just say 'brutally murdered' or 'senselessly slaughtered.' They never said anything about a lase-whip until it came up in that trial. That's when I knew he did it. He did it, and then he came to be with me right after."

Liz looked like a ghost. Maggie looked like she was about to shiver.

"And then you called Maggie," I said.

"I don't care about Hector. He was a pervert. But why did Ian have to kill his wife, too? And the girl, she never did anything wrong. How come he has to be so cruel?"

"He's not that little boy you used to take care of, anymore," I said. "He's changed. The brother you knew is already dead."

"But that can't be. He's still in there somewhere. He has to be."

I shook my head. "You really think Ian could do the things he does if the brother you knew was still in there?"

"Horst did this to him, you know. Ian was a good boy until he met Horst."

I said, "We don't have much time, Liz."

She looked at me, her eyes begging for mercy, begging me to tell her she didn't need to do this, that there was some other way.

"Call him," I said.

twenty-seven

"TRY it again," I said.

"He's not going to answer."

"One more time," I said for the third time.

She did it, and a second later, Ian's holo blinked into existence. *Gotcha, asshole.* Maggie was already up, holding out her digital pad, showing me the map with the blinking red dot.

"What's wrong?" said Holo-Ian with a hint of panic in his voice. "Are you okay?"

"I-I'm okay," Liz responded with a stammer. "I just needed to talk to you."

"Don't scare me like that. You called me six times."

"I'm sorry. I didn't mean to scare you. It's just that your partner was here. She came with Juno, and they started asking all kinds of questions. I thought you'd want to know."

"Did you tell them anything?"

"No."

"Good. Listen, when I'm done here, I'll come by. Okay?"

"When?"

"Soon."

Liz didn't say anything.

"I'll be by soon, okay?"

Again she didn't speak, her eyes getting glassy.

"Okay?" he repeated.

"Okay," she said.

Holo-Ian vanished. Liz kept looking at the place where he'd

stood. I opened my mouth to say something, but didn't. Maggie was at the door. She had it opened, with one foot standing in the hall. I followed her out.

I hustled down the steps to the pier, almost slipping twice but not slowing down. Maggie was already at the bottom, waiting for me. We split the cache of weapons. Maggie took two lase-pistols in addition to her standard issue. She had one in hand, one in holster and one strapped to her ankle.

I kept the broad-beam. It had a limited range, but it didn't require much accuracy. I checked my three blades, waistband, ass pocket, and ankle. I slung the lase-rifle over my shoulder and carried the broad-beam lefty.

We jogged across the quay, sticking to the shadows and keeping our bodies hunched over, making ourselves smaller targets. A fence separated us from the gangway, which ran diagonally up from bow to stern of the *Jungle Pride*. The gate was hitched but not locked, and in an attempt to make as little noise as possible, Maggie opened it in super slo-mo.

We stepped onto the gangway. I took the lead and crept slowly up the steep slope. I kept my eyes peeled on the top of the gangway, ready to fry the whole fucking area with my broad-beam. I let my hip rub against the railing, using it as a guide so I wouldn't have to look where I was stepping. It wasn't raining, but the air was soggy, and the railings were sweating giant-sized drops that soaked through my pants and ran down my leg. The gangway creaked under our weight and bowed down under each step, getting maddeningly bouncier and squeakier as we approached the middle.

We were halfway up. There was only one way on or off this boat, and this was it. If they'd posted a guard, he'd be at the top of the gangway. It was dark, but not so dark that he couldn't have seen us cross the quay if he was looking. He could be watching us right now, waiting in the shadows, letting us get nice and close. . . .

I kept moving. What was the worst thing that could happen? I could die? That didn't scare me. I felt dead already. Shit, dying would be a damn relief. Niki had been right about that.

I made it to the top and leaned my back against the ship's hull, its sweat soaking into my shirt. Cold metal chilled my spine. I looked back at Maggie. She rubbed her free hand across the hull, then ran her fingers through a couple stray locks of hair, wetting them down to keep them out of her face. She looked at me with determined eyes—nothing but confidence in that woman.

We gave each other a nod, and I ran onto the deck. I went down a second later with a pain so sharp shooting through my shin that I thought I'd been shot, but the sound didn't match. It wasn't a crackle that I'd heard; it was more of a clang. I couldn't see shit, it was so dark.

"You okay, Juno?" Maggie whispered.

I put my piece down and rubbed my hand over my shin. I didn't feel anything sticky. I didn't smell burnt meat. My shin was screaming just the same. "Yeah, I just smacked into something." I could just barely see the outline of one poorly placed pipe.

Somebody was coming. Not running, just walking. He was coming to check on the noise, alone. I picked my piece back up. I looked in the direction of the footsteps. I strained to pick up some movement in the black shadows. He was close, but I couldn't see. I suddenly realized he was above us, on the upper deck. His footsteps passed directly overhead. They went a ways farther, and then I could tell by the sound that he was coming down a set of stairs. I still couldn't see him, but he was *so close*.

I aimed my broad-beam in the direction of the footsteps, ready to squeeze off a burst the instant I made eye contact. He wouldn't see us until it was too late, and I wasn't going to wait to find out who it was. Whoever he was, he was going to burn.

Then Maggie called, "Freeze."

A beam of light blinded me as it fried over my head. My hair curled and crinkled from the heat as the beam scorched across the deck. I went flat while another beam sizzled out of Maggie's piece, targeting the source of the light. Her beam went long, stretching out into the night. She swept it to the right and it shortened down as she made contact, a flash of steam kicking up. And then there was nothing.

I got up and hobbled over to the site. Maggie had my back. She stayed a couple paces behind me and approached with her piece leveled. The BBQ odor would've smelled good if you didn't know what it was. I tucked my piece under my arm and pulled my penlight. I flicked it into life and waved it over the corpse, casting enough light to ID him. Detective Hoshi Reyes. The dumbass had panicked, firing in the direction of Maggie's voice, giving away his position. It's a lot easier to target with your eyes than your ears.

His chest was split open, smoke drifting up out of the wound. His right arm was almost severed. I tried to pull his weapon out of his right hand, but his finger got caught in the trigger guard, and I almost pulled his arm the rest of the way off. I twisted the lase-pistol free and tossed it over the rail.

We startled at a sound, a clank of metal on metal echoing across the deck. Maggie and I froze, our ears tuned to coming footsteps, but there were none to be heard. The clank sounded far away, near the bow. I whispered, "I think we surprised Hoshi. I don't think he had time to call the others."

"Alerted or not, they'll miss him soon."

With that we moved on. We found the staircase that Hoshi had used and climbed it to the upper deck. It was easier to see up here, city lights illuminating the low-hanging clouds. We made for the bow, toward the clank. I scanned left to right as I walked. Debris crunched under my feet, broken glass and lizard eggshells. Then the deck turned soft as we crossed a mat of moss near the bow.

We found a staircase that led down into the ship's interior. I took the stairs slow, wondering why my heart was pounding so loudly in my ears. I was okay with dying, wasn't I?

The hatch was closed partway. I swung the heavy metal to the side, careful not to let it clang into the wall. We slinked through, and then Maggie let the hatch swing back to its partly open state. The corridor was lit with neon green lightsticks that had been dropped on the floor. We followed the lights, weapons raised. Sweat stung my eyes. I walked softly, like I was on a sheet of thin ice that could break any second. My right hand was shaking out of control, and my left hand wasn't doing much better. There were geckos all over the walls. I could picture them eating through my stomach, with their miniteeth, their lizard lips smeared with my blood, their stomachs full of my flesh. . . . Visions of being flayed alive—some offworlder leaning over me, beaming the most perfect smile while he peels me, pulling the skin off in long sheets—sent shivers up and down my body.

We took another set of steps down. The air was stale and rotten. I was only a second away from running away screaming, but I kept moving, the two of us stepping through bulkhead after bulkhead. Peeled paint flakes littered the rusty floor like confetti. Water dripped from the pipes over our heads. We could see the end to the lightsticks. There were three of them on the floor outside a hatch on the right. Yellow light poured through the hatchway, out into the corridor.

There were voices, more than two, but I couldn't tell how many. They were men's voices. If they were offworlders, they'd be detecting us by now, our weapons kicking off an electromagnetic field. I was primed for a firefight, but nobody came storming out. Maybe the metal walls were interfering. Or maybe they thought it was just Ian and Hoshi coming. Maggie and I kept approaching, the voices getting louder. They were enjoying themselves. There was joking. There was laughter.

We reached the last bulkhead, Maggie and I on either side. Our eyes met. Hers were grim. "Just because we don't hear her doesn't mean she's not in there," she said under her breath.

I nodded and switched weapons, taking one of her lase-pistols. Going in with a broad-beam wouldn't allow much selectivity in targets. I looked at Maggie and nodded my readiness. We didn't stand much chance, but one way or the other, at least it would be quick. She held up three fingers, ready for a countdown, but lowered her hand when somebody came out. He saw us straightaway and froze in front of the hatchway. Maggie already had a bead on him, and he knew it, his eyes popping. I grinned at him and waved my piece, telling him to come closer.

Yuri Kiper took one last look in through the hatchway, checking to see if anybody would come to his rescue, but they hadn't noticed, their rolling laughter ricocheting down the corridor. Yuri came with his head hung low, like a dog getting in trouble for making a mess on the floor. He was carrying a tripod and three separate bags of equipment.

Maggie kept her piece steady on his chest. She made the shush sign with her free index finger as she whispered, "Who's in there?"

"Offworlders," he whispered back.

"How many?"

"Six."

"Anybody else?"

"Hoshi's around here somewhere. Ian and Horst already left."

"The girl?"

"She's dead."

Maggie twitched. It was almost imperceptible, but it was there, a little wrinkling of the eyes, a little ripple through her body as her worst fear came true. Me, I don't know if my face changed or not, but I felt what little hope I'd had of saving her blow out of me like I was a popped balloon. We were too god-damned late.

Maggie kept to the task at hand—no time to mourn. "What are they doing in there?" she asked.

"They're having a toast before it's time to clear out."

I turned my eyes back on the hatchway. I didn't want to know what they did to her, but I couldn't keep myself from imagining it. I remembered the way I'd grilled her. I was so harsh, a real brute, a total son of a bitch. Damn it to hell! She was *innocent*.

I was ready to do some damage.

I turned to Yuri. "Where are the gene eaters?"

Yuri used his double chin to point at his shirt pocket.

I tucked my weapon away and pulled the little cannister from his pocket. It was no bigger than an inhaler. I pulled the safety seal off the aerosol head. "What's the delay?"

"Sixty seconds."

I checked my watch and pushed the head down, then twisted it into a locked position. Maggie gave me a disapproving look.

"Close me in if you have to," I told her as I stepped through the bulkhead. She knew better than to try and stop me.

I moved up on the hatchway, my left hand clutching the gene eaters in a cramp-inducing grip. I was tempted to throw it blind, but decided it was worth a peek first so I wouldn't end up tossing it within any of their reaches. I didn't want one of them disarming it before it let loose on the fuckers. I checked my watch again. Maggie had Yuri on the floor, one wrist cuffed to a pipe running along the floor. She was ready to slam her hatch shut at the first sign of gene eaters in the corridor.

I checked my watch. They were having a grand time in there, sounding like a bunch of businessmen three drinks into an office party, or maybe a group of old school buddies yukking it up over a string of remember-whens. I watched the seconds tick by. It was time. I wheeled into the hatchway. I was only there for a second, but I saw a lot in that second. It was a large cabin, maybe a mess hall. Whatever it was, it was large enough to justify a hatch instead of a flimsy wooden door. They were seated at one end of a long table, tall glasses of brandy all around. They were wearing hooded robes, the hoods folded down onto their backs. I recognized the four from the hotel restaurant. They wore puzzled smiles, not sure who I was and whether or not I was a threat.

I threw a grounder into the farthest corner. I swung the hatch shut just as I saw the fogger begin to kick up a cloudy mist. The hatch slammed shut with such force that my hand stung from the vibration. I flipped the latch, but there was no lock. I shoved my back against the hatch, using my legs to push against the opposite wall. I was barely into position when the latch popped back open. They were screaming now, pushing on the hatch. I pushed back with all the strength in my legs, pressing myself into the hatch so hard that I couldn't breathe. The latch snapped back into place, but I didn't let up. I pushed with everything I had. My legs burned, and so did my lungs, and so did my eyes, which were filling up with sweat. They had the strength to overpower me. They were offworlders, for chrissakes. They were all genetically enhanced athletes with glands-on-demand that could serve up superhuman cocktails of adrenaline and endorphins in an instant. . . .

But I had position. I had a wall to push against while they didn't have anything but a damp floor to anchor their feet on. That, and the hatch wasn't very large, too small for all six of them to find a purchase. And then there was the fact that I didn't have gene eaters gnawing at my flesh, digging into my lungs, converting my eyes into jelly.

The latch popped, and there was a sustained push. My legs felt ready to buckle. It wouldn't take much, just the slightest opening would be enough to let the gene eaters out. Maggie showed up next to me. If I'd had any energy to spare, I would've yelled at her to go away. She quickly got into position, pushing with her arms, using the opposite wall to brace her feet.

I thought that I could hear them wheezing as their lungs lost their form. I thought I could hear them scratching at the walls, digging with fingernails that peeled off on the bare metal. I thought I heard a lot of things that I couldn't have possibly heard.

I thought I heard silence. I let up just a tad, just as a test, but as soon as I did, I knew I was done. I slumped over onto the floor, my lungs bursting. Maggie held firm for a few extra seconds, and then she gave in, too.

The corridor began to dim as some of the lightsticks began to peter out. I felt the weight of six more bodies being added to my name. Screw it. I wasn't going to let myself worry about those sadistic bastards. They weren't human. They were trash. Trash with wives who loved them, trash with kids . . . *Stop it.* I quashed that train of thought before it went off the tracks. They killed Adela. Fuck 'em.

My heaving lungs gradually synced with the soft rocking of the ship. Maggie was standing next to me, waiting on me, the old man. I stood up, a little too quickly. I had to brace myself by leaning on the wall. I followed Maggie back to Yuri on rubber legs.

He was a weeping mess, his cheeks streaked with running tears. He was on the floor, his wrist cuffs looped around a water pipe. He pulled his hands up as far as they could go, tilting the cuffs' keypads up as if Maggie was going to let him go. "Thank you for rescuing me," he said.

Maggie frowned at him. "Save it."

"They s-said they'd k-kill me if I didn't do what they s-said."

"I said save it. I'm not in the mood for bullshit."

"I'm s-sorry," he sobbed like a nasal two-year-old.

Maggie's lips were pinched tight. They parted just wide enough for her speak through her teeth. "Why today, dammit?" she asked. "Her execution wasn't supposed to be until tomorrow."

"I'm so s-sorry. Please believe m-me," he said, his voice trailing into wracking sobs.

"Answer me."

"It was o-one of the offworlders. S-something came up at his work, and he h-had to leave planet early, so Horst m-moved it up a day."

"We were supposed to have one more day." Maggie's stony face began to fracture. Her anger crumbled away, and her eyes misted over. "We were supposed to have one more day."

I looked at Yuri, and I looked at Maggie, both of them crying, and I suddenly realized that it should've been me who was crying. I was the one who'd just lost his wife. I felt emotions beginning to gush up from my gut. I stomped them back down with an enforcer's cruel efficiency. "Where did Ian and Horst go?"

"Horst h-had a dinner to go to, and Ian c-carried the body out. Ian had to bring it b-back to the Z-zoo."

Already, Adela was an "it." "How long ago?"
"I don't know. M-maybe fifteen minutes."
"What about the rest of Ian's crew? Where are they?"
"Looking for you two."
"Let's go," I said to Maggie.

twenty-eight

I STOPPED Maggie when we made it back down to the pier. "I'm going after Ian alone," I told her.

"The hell you are."

"C'mon, Maggie, you know what has to be done."

"We're going to arrest him, Juno. We'll get the cameraman's testimony. We'll organize a raid of the Zoo, pick up the guards. They'll talk, and we'll find Adela's body."

No. We weren't going to do that at all. If that was what we were going to do, Maggie would be on the phone already, briefing her superiors and securing warrants. She knew as well as I did what I was going to do, what I *had* to do.

I was going to kill him. I was going to hustle down to the Zoo and catch him on his way back out from dropping off Adela's body. I was going to hide in the weeds and gun him down. I was going to murder Detective Ian Davies.

"There has to be another way," she said.

There wasn't. She couldn't arrest him. Not if she wanted to be chief. She'd be the cop who arrested another cop. It didn't matter that Ian was dirty. The whole force was corrupt. KOP was rotten to the core. Just about all of them were on the take in one form or another. She'd be a threat to the brass. They'd never bring her into their inner circle. They'd be afraid that she might start arresting them once she became privy to their secrets. Her career would be over. But, they wouldn't fire her. She had too high a profile for anything that overt. Instead, they'd neuter her by banishing her to the records department, or maybe they'd put her on river patrol, or they might even give her a position in PR, make her go out to the schools and put on little skits for the juvies. Or if they felt really threatened, they'd arrange for her to die, probably in a "bust gone wrong."

Killing him was the only way to make him pay, and she knew it. Her conscience was just making its last stand.

I wrapped my arms around her. I didn't know why. I just did. She succumbed to the hug, squeezing me back, our bond growing as tight as any true father-daughter bond. With Maggie, there was a chance. A chance that she could actually change things. Chief Paul Chang was a great man, and I'd loved him like a brother. He'd had ideals once, too. He wanted to change things. You couldn't live on this backwater planet and not want to change things. But he'd had to put those ideals on hold in order to get ahead. We both did. First we had to seize control. Only then would we have the power to go about instituting change. It took us fifteen years to get there. Fifteen years of bribes and frame jobs. Fifteen years of beatdowns and executions. We were the most ruthless sons of bitches you ever saw. You got a nasty habit? We cut off your supply. You got a pretty face? We knock out your teeth. You got a gambling problem? We buy out your debt and become your new loan sharks. You're a fag? We out you. You're having an affair? We film you. You're a fucking saint? Well, then we just plant shit on you.

Fifteen years.

By the time we got there, right and wrong had become far-away concepts, nothing more than unproven theories. Such things were only good for academic discussion. They had no place in the real world.

But with Maggie, it wasn't too late. She still had a heart. I had to protect her from the ugliness—the backstabbing, the violence, the perversion, the greed, all of it. I remembered the look on her face when she'd told me to dunk the zookeeper. That face wasn't her. She'd seen and done enough. I couldn't let her get corrupted any further. My soul was already damned. I could take the burden for her. She was *family*.

I'd be her guardian angel.

Or guardian devil.

She broke the hug. "I'm going with you," she insisted.

"No. You can't be involved in this, not if you're going to be chief one day. From now on the dirty work is my job," I said. "Let me handle it. I'll make the whole thing go away."

She studied me from out of the shadows. "You're going to help me take over KOP?"

"I won't stop until you're chief."

"It could take years, Juno."

"I know. I'm in it for the long haul, okay? But right now, I need you to go back home. I'll call you."

"No way, Juno. After all this, how can I just go home? I have to see this through."

"Listen, Maggie, from this point on, it's all about protecting your plausible deniability. You have to take the long view. You can't clean up KOP until you get to the top, and you won't get to the top going out on assassination runs with me. You can't take the risk. Just let me do what I do."

She stayed silent for long seconds. "I wanted to do this clean," she finally said.

"I know you did. But there's no other way. Please, Maggie, just let me do what I do."

I fought through the scrub, vines snatching at my ankles. I kicked through, ripping up clumpy root systems that dragged along behind me. I was on the south side of the Zoo, crossing through an open field that was overdue for a slash and burn.

George told us that they'd snuck the inmates out through

the kitchen. There were three separate cargo bays on the south side. Which one was closest to the kitchen I had no idea, but I was certain that the Zoo's mess hall was on the south side.

I stopped short of the road that ran alongside the south walls, and far short of the reach of the tower lights. From here, I had a good view of the three bays, all of which had their doors sealed shut. I took the lase-rifle off my shoulder. I had no intention of getting into a duel with Ian. I'd take him out at long range.

I kneeled on the ground, a blanket of weeds bending under my knees. Targeting could be a problem with my shaky karate-chop hand. I experimented a bit, trying different ways of holding the rifle before settling on lying face down in the weeds with the rifle jammed against my left shoulder, the barrel resting on a rock. I kept my right hand in the weeds where it could shake all it wanted without affecting my aim. This could work.

I kept my eyes on the cargo bays, waiting for him to come out. Something was biting me, down on my ankles. I tried to make it stop my rubbing my ankles together like a cricket. *Where is he?* Was I too late? No, I thought. Ian had gotten a head start on me, but he wouldn't have raced the river the way I did. He had a dead body with him. He wouldn't have wanted to attract any attention to himself. He would've taken the trip slow and casual. Then he would've needed help carrying Adela's body up the riverbank. No, he couldn't have come and gone already. He was still inside. He had to be.

Maybe not. I might've spent too much time talking to Maggie on the pier. I caught some movement in the corner of my eye. *There he is.* Damn. He was coming from the wrong direction. I was expecting him to come out of the Zoo, but he was coming from the river. I was wrong about him needing help carrying the body up the riverbank. He had the body bag draped over his right shoulder and seemed to be doing just fine without any help other than the 'roids raging through his body. I was surprised I'd beaten him here. He must've made a couple stops on the way. Or maybe he'd been waiting all this time for his zookeeper accomplices to give him the green light to bring the body in.

He was crossing the same field I'd crossed, but from a different angle. I was facing the wrong way. I rolled over once, twice, reorienting my body in the process. Without a rock to rest the rifle on, I used my right forearm as the fulcrum on which I could pivot my aim. The balance was all off, but it would have to do.

My heart was fucking pounding. I told myself to calm down; I had plenty of time, so just calm down and do it right. I slowly swiveled the rifle until I had him in the scope. I could see him clearly with the night vision, his smug face, his arrogant stride. I couldn't keep the crosshairs level, but it didn't matter. I didn't need them to line up perfectly. I fired the targeting device, a bug-sized heat seeker that only required an accuracy of ten meters. It squealed out across the weeds, honing in on his body heat. He heard it and knew what it was. He dropped the body bag and sprinted back the way he had come. He yelped when the heat seeker hit him, not from the pain but from what he knew would be coming next. The heat seeker itself didn't carry a deadly payload. It was built for speed and maneuverability. It dug into his flesh, deep like a tick, and then it began broadcasting a signal back to the lase-rifle. All I had to do was hold the trigger down and swing the rifle in his general direction, or better yet, aim way out ahead of him and just hold the weapon steady, waiting for him to cross the rifle's path. When the rifle locked onto the heat seeker's signal, it would fire a single pulse at the speed of light.

He stopped running. He was a dead man, and he knew it. "Juno!" he yelled. "Is that you?"

Damn straight it is.

"Juno! Where are you?" His voice came rolling across the jungle brush, desperate, pleading. I pulled my finger off the trigger and watched him through the scope. He had his shirt pulled up, and he was digging into his side with his fingernails, trying to get to the heat seeker. "Juno!" he cried. "JUNO! Don't do this, Juno. Please! Please!" He gave up on the heat seeker and dropped to his knees. "P-please!" he wailed. His face was all wrinkled up, a giant, bawling baby's face.

Looks like Ian hasn't changed so much after all. In the end, the guy is still a pussy.

I held down the trigger and swept the barrel from one side to the other until the automated firing system let loose. People always imagined the burst barreling across the open space like one of the spokes of an exploding Roman candle. But the pulse moved faster than the eye could track. One instant Ian was groveling on his knees and the next, he was blown back in a burst of bright energy.

I stood up and swung the rifle over my shoulder. I reached down to scratch my ankles, and then I crossed the fifty meters, stopping when I reached Ian's body. I bent over the corpse and pulled up the pant legs. Nothing. I rolled him face up. He was crisped beyond recognition. Twisted metal poked out from his biceps, his freakish strength enhanced by mechanical implants. Evidently, the steroids hadn't been enough for him to erase his inner weakling.

I looked over at the Zoo. I heard no sirens, saw no searchlights. The guards in the towers hadn't seen anything. They'd been facing the other way, looking toward the inside just like they were supposed to.

I pulled Ian's smoldering shirt open. There, inside a charred leather sheath, was the blade. It was hot, too hot to touch. I used my left hand and tried to snatch it out fast without ever really grabbing hold. It took three tries before I managed to pull it free and fling it into the weeds.

I pulled the penlight from my pocket and shined it on the knife. It was stained with blood, Raj Gupta's blood. True to form, Ian was carrying it on his person, ready to plant it on me as soon as the cops nabbed me. I picked it up and dropped it two more times before it had finally cooled enough to hold.

twenty-nine

I PUTTERED up to the *Jungle Pride*, me and my two-cadaver cargo, one still in the wrapper, the other cooked medium well. I wondered how Yuri was doing in the dark. A check of my watch told me it had been more than two hours since we'd left him cuffed to that pipe. It was already half past midnight.

I'd stayed in that field with Ian's body for at least an hour, hashing it all out in my head. The plan was solid. All I had to do was get Maggie to sell it to her lieutenant. The rest was up to me.

I killed the motor and stood up, my legs telling me they weren't ready for more exertion. Hauling those two bodies out of that field had wasted what was left of my strength. And after having used these same legs to hold off a group of panicked off-worlders, I hadn't had much to begin with. I suddenly remembered the knife, the one used to kill Raj. I picked it up from the boat's floor and heaved it into the river. That was a murder that would remain unsolved. I tied off and hauled myself up to the rippled pier. I made my way along the decrepit docking, choosing my path carefully, trying to stay away from the collapsed portions.

Yuri was going to have a hell of a time carrying those bodies across. I'd have to check the skiff for life vests. He'd need one if he fell through.

My knees creaked as I climbed the gangway. At the top, I could hear the drone of a thousand buzzing flies. I turned on the penlight. Hoshi's body was crawling with lizards, all of them chattering and clicking. Some fled when I passed, others hissed, and the rest just kept feeding.

I found Yuri where I'd left him. He looked relieved to see me. Two hours was plenty of time for him to start thinking I wasn't coming back for him.

I sat down on the floor. I caught a whiff of urine, and saw the stains running down the wall a short ways down. "Couldn't you hold it?" I said.

"Not for two hours," he said petulantly.

He was already ticking me off with his big-baby routine. I told myself to let it go. At least he wasn't crying anymore. "Do you know who I am?"

"No. But Ian told me to look out for a guy with his hand in a cast."

"What did he say about me?"

"Nothing. He just said to call him if I saw you."

He had no idea who I was. As I'd hoped, I could be anybody I wanted. Ian's little need-to-know policy was about to bite Yuri in the ass. I kept my face straight. "I'm a cop, Yuri."

"I figured that."

"I'm a captain. I'm Ian's boss's boss. Consider yourself caught. We have you on so many counts, I haven't had time to add them all up."

He nodded, his jowls puffing in and out under his chin. I could tell he was ready to talk. The guy was caught so red-handed that he could pass for somebody who sliced beets for a living. When you caught a guy dead to rights like that, he'd usually just come out with it, no lies, no arguments. Could be a guilty conscience that would make them confess, or maybe it was just the fact that they'd spent so much time looking over their shoulders that it was a relief to finally look straight ahead. Either way, Yuri was ready, and I made it a little easier on him by telling him the code to his cuffs so he could free his wrists.

"I think we can help each other," I said.

He perked up a little. "How's that?"

"Why don't you tell me what you know first, and we'll see."

"What do you want to know?"

"I want to know how you got into the business of selling executions. Start with Horst Jeffers. Tell me how you met him."

Yuri didn't look me in the eye as he talked. Instead, he picked at a fold in his pants. "He hired me for a job. He had a tour group going on a tiger hunt, and he wanted somebody to film it so he could sell the vids to them."

"I thought tiger hunts were just a cover."

"They were, but sometimes people would sign up anyway. Horst doesn't like to turn money away."

I nodded. "Go on."

"Well, like I said, he hired me. He saw one of my ads on a lamppost. I used to freelance a lot, you know, weddings, parties, that kind of thing. The tiger hunt was a three-day job, so I took some sick days to do it."

"The pay was good?"

"The pay was great. I told Horst that whenever he needed me, I'd be available."

"Is that when he told you about the fuck flicks he wanted to make?"

"That wasn't until later, but yeah, he approached me about the movies. He knew I worked for Lagarto Libre, and he thought I might be able to let him in late at night so we could use the studio space."

"And you approached your boss about it?"

"No. I thought I'd get fired if Hector found out what we were doing. I was really careful, but he found out anyway. I think one of the cleaning crew tipped him off."

"Was he angry?"

"He acted angry, but he wasn't really. He just wanted a cut of the profits."

"I heard he liked to be there during the shoots."

"Yeah," he said. "He'd say he had to be there to make sure nothing went wrong. He had the reputation of the Libre as a news organization to think about. But that was all a bunch of bull. He really just liked to watch Liz. He drove me crazy. He was always in the way. I don't know if he had bad eyes or what, but he was always trying to get way too close. I'd be looking through my viewfinder and all the sudden, there's Hector's shoulder in my shot, or there's his head, coming in from the side. What really sent me over the edge was that whenever I'd move in for a close-up, he'd follow me in so I'd end up bumping into him when I tried to pull back out. But what could I do? He was my boss."

"What did Liz think of him?"

"He creeped Liz out. He'd have his hands in his pockets all the time. Confront him on it, and he'd actually say his hands were cold, like that was going to fool anybody. I mean you could see his hands moving around in there. He was a damn nuisance, and I told Horst that, but Horst said we had to humor him. One time, Hector even asked Horst how much it would cost to be with Liz himself. Horst gave him a flat no. Liz wasn't into him at all. Like I said, he creeped her out."

"Why did Ian kill him and his wife?"

Yuri gave me a puzzled face, trying to figure out how I knew so much. "Hector paid him to do it."

"Hector wanted to die?"

"No. He paid Ian to kill his wife. She wanted a divorce. She was going to take him for all he was worth. He used to complain about it all the time. He'd tell anybody who would listen that she was a whore. He'd go on and on about how she cheated on him, and how now she thought she was entitled to his money. The guy was bitter."

"I'd imagine so," I said, finally picturing it in its entirety. I could imagine what it was like for Hector, your typical middle-aged guy with your typical once-a-week humdrum sex life, waking up from his suburban slumber the moment he found out one of his cameramen was shooting late-night porn in his news studios. Instead of being outraged like any respectable business-man, his dick took control and started tickling his brain with these funny feelings. He decided that there would be no harm in doing a little spectating, just to see what it was all about. And then there he was, in a dark studio, watching "Liz Lagarto" go to work on Raj Gupta, watching their bodies writhing and grinding, bumping and bouncing. He was hooked. It was all he could think about. I could see him sitting in his office, trying to get his work done but suddenly finding his hand in his pants, reaching though the holes in his pockets and wishing he was wearing a loincloth. He tried to get with Liz, but when he was rebuffed, he did the next best thing by talking his wife into doing little reen-actments with jungle-boy Raj. And that got him off, got him off big time, until it all fell apart when she dumped the schmuck for the jungle boy and decided to take all his money. It was fucking beautiful the way it worked out for him.

"Why didn't Hector do his wife in himself?" I asked

"I don't know. I guess he was a coward. He went to Ian to see if Ian could put him in touch with somebody who did that kind of work."

"And Ian volunteered to do himself."

"Right. Hector paid Ian to do it. Ian just about cleaned him out, he charged so much. Hector was so stupid. I mean, what's the point of killing her to keep her from getting your money when you have to break the bank to do it?"

"I guess it wasn't about the money."

Yuri fingered the fold in his pants with averted eyes.

"You still haven't told me why Ian killed Hector" I said.

Yuri took a deep breath. "It was the family photo that did it."

"What family photo?"

"Hector gave Ian a copy of the holo-pic he kept on his desk so Ian would know what his wife looked like. Hector was very specific about how he wanted it done. He wanted Ian to do it at the hotel where she'd go to meet her boyfriend. He wanted him to walk in on them together and do them both in. But when Ian saw that picture of the Juarez family, he decided to take Hector out along with his wife."

"Why?"

"The prices Horst was getting on the executions were dropping. The first five or six paydays were huge, but the auctions were getting smaller and so were the bids. Horst was good at getting first timers hooked into bidding wars, but when the repeat customers started outnumbering the first timers, the price started to fall. The repeat customers were looking for bargains, you see what I mean? They'd bid up to their limit, and if that wasn't enough, it wasn't enough. No big deal, there'd be another auction coming up soon enough. So when Ian saw Hector's daughter in that picture, he saw an opportunity. You know what she looks like, right?"

"Yeah."

"Then you know how gorgeous she is, or was. Ian took one look at her and thought she could bring some excitement back into the bidding. He said her execution could bring in a record price, and he was right. There aren't many women on death row, and none of them look like her. Ian juiced it up by selling her to the press as a spoiled brat who killed her parents because she couldn't get her way. The rags played right into it. Did you see their headlines? They ran that one that said, 'Kitten Turned Killer.' And then there was the one that went, 'Prep School

Princess Pares Parents.' The bidding went crazy. Those offworlders were all dying to be the one to teach the little bitch a
lesson."

"So he decided to kill both parents and let her take the fall."

"Right. Had he just killed the wife and tried to frame Adela,
Hector might've confessed in order to save his daughter. If it
was going to work, he had to kill both the parents. Ian ran the
idea by Horst, and Horst signed off on it. Hector was a pain in
the ass anyway. And besides, by that time, I was doing almost
all holo work, so we didn't really need the studios anymore."

That was some cold shit Ian pulled off—killing Hector and
his wife *and* getting Hector to pay for it. And all that spoiled-
brat crap was nothing more than a sales ploy. And I fell for it.
I'd made her cry. I closed my eyes and rubbed my face with my
good hand in an effort to keep from screaming. I wanted to
smash something, like Yuri's face. I wanted to drive my fist into
it until it went pulpy. I forced out a calm tone. "Did they frame
any of the others?"

"No. Adela Juarez was the first. The others all came from
death row. That was the only way Horst could sell it. His slogan
was, 'The thrill of the kill without the pain or the shame.' They
were all going to die anyway. He'd tell his customers they didn't
have to worry about feeling guilty. You can't kill what's already
dead. Besides, these people all deserved it. These were the worst
of the worst. Rapists. Murderers. Horst's customers were just
meting out justice. They were performing a public service."

I hadn't opened Adela's body bag. I was afraid of what I
might find, but I still had to know. "How did they kill her?"

"The high bidder plagued her while the others watched."

"He used a needle?"

"No." He doubled up his fidgeting.

"What did he use, Yuri?"

"His semen was infected."

Just when I thought it couldn't get any worse . . . I looked down the corridor, taking some satisfaction in the hideous deaths of the six offworlders, their bodies reduced to nothing more than jelly, bubonic balls and all.

It was hard to fathom what that poor girl went through. First, finding her slaughtered parents. Then, getting convicted for their murders and sentenced to death. And as if that wasn't enough, she died a day early, raped in front of spectators, infected with accelerated plague, her skin breaking out in red blotches that quickly turned black, her lymph nodes swelling to the point of bursting—and innocent all the while. I didn't want to face it. I just sent her down into that same hollow in my gut with Niki and tried to ignore her.

I was looking at Yuri, running it through my head one more time, getting a feel for how to play it. I was hardly in a position to take the moral high ground with anybody, but I wasn't about to let that stop me from doing what I had to do. "How could you go along with all this, Yuri?"

"I had no choice."

"Don't lie to me, Yuri. You made Adela's fake confession. You made the fake execution vids they use at the Zoo. And you filmed all the real executions so those sick bastards would have little keepsakes."

"It wasn't my fault," he whined. "They made me do it."

"They didn't make you do anything. You went along because you wanted to. Tell me why."

He stared at the floor.

"Tell me, Yuri. You'll feel better."

"You said we could help each other?"

"I think we can. But not until I know why you did it. You have to convince me you're worth saving."

"I just wanted to make movies," he whimpered.

"That's it?"

He looked me in the eyes again, searching for understanding, searching for forgiveness. "I never wanted to hurt anybody. It started with the pornography. I know people frown on it, but nobody was being forced into doing anything they didn't want to do. It was all consensual."

I met his eyes, trying to keep my anger bottled up. "How did you get from there to filming executions?"

His eyes began to water. "It was the way Horst described it. It didn't sound so wrong when he explained it. The first one was just a beheading. Dying that way is supposed to be painless. It happens so fast. That guy was going to get gassed anyway, so what did it matter? And I got to make the vid they showed at the Zoo. I wanted to see if I could make them believe it was real using nothing but holos. And I did it," he said proudly. "They thought it was real. Nobody knew the difference. After that, the executions got worse, a lot worse, but it was too late, don't you see? I was already a part of it."

"You just wanted to make movies," I said with far more understanding in my voice than I actually felt.

"Yes," he whined. "I just wanted to express my art."

"You couldn't have made movies on your own?"

He shook his head. He counted the reasons on his fingers. "No equipment. No funding. No distribution outlets. There aren't any drama schools on this hellhole planet, which means no acting talent. You have to pay a fortune in bribes for filming permits."

I put up my hand, telling him to stop before he started counting on his other hand. This was something I understood. This planet held everybody below their potential. The harder you tried to succeed, the harder Lagarto slapped you down.

He looked at me, all weepy. "What's going to happen to me, Captain?"

I tried to make myself believe my lies. I was a captain, third-generation KOP. I stole from Maggie's anticorruption personality, incorporating it into my speech. "I'm going to clean up KOP, Yuri. My father was a cop and so was my grandfather. It hurts me to see KOP go to hell, you understand me?"

Eager to please, he said that he did.

"The Koba Office of Police was once a symbol of pride. That's the way it was in my grandfather's day, but now it's turned rotten. Everybody knows it. Cops are out for their own personal gain. They have no respect for the institution, you get me? Ian Davies was rotten, and I killed him."

Yuri's eyelid twitched.

"Hoshi was rotten, too. He's dead, Yuri. I killed him, too. They disgraced their badges. They put everybody's reputation on the line when they put those badges on. They were a disgrace. Conspiring with offworlders against their own kind. I can't think of a higher form of treason."

"You're absolutely right. They were bad seeds," Yuri said, already in full suck-up mode.

This was going to be easier than I thought. "I know you're just a pawn in all this, Yuri. I'm going to offer you a deal."

He was leaning forward now, hanging on my every word.

"I'm going to restore KOP back to its glory days, and you're going to help me. First you're going to bring Adela's body down here and put her in one of these cabins. Then you're going to drag Ian and Hoshi's bodies down here and set them in front of that door. When you're done with that, I'm going to take your statement."

"What should I say?" he wanted to know.

"You're the only survivor, the only witness. You're going to explain how the offworlders killed the girl, and they forced you to film it or they would've killed you, too."

"Yep, no problem," he said. "I can do that."

"You're going to mention the names of four guards at the

Zoo, the ones who smuggled Adela out. You have to mention them. They must be punished."

"Got it," he said.

"Then you're going to say that Ian and Hoshi tried to save Adela. The offworlders shot them, Yuri, but not before Ian managed to throw the gene eaters in. You're going to explain how Ian and Hoshi held that door shut. They were wounded and dying, but all they could think about was doing their duty. They didn't try to run away and save themselves. Instead they stayed and made sure the offworlders couldn't get away. They're going to become heroes for the next generation of cops to aspire to. You understand me?"

"Nobody's going to believe that part," he said. "The forensics won't match."

"They'll believe you, Yuri. The coroner is in my pocket. He's going to write reports that match your story. Okay?"

He nodded. "Okay. I can do it."

"That's not all. After I take your statement, you're going to call Ian's crew. You're going to tell them you want to meet. You're going to get them to implicate themselves, and I'm going to film it. They need to be purged out of KOP, Yuri. Every one of them. I'll use it to make them resign. If they contradict the official story in any way, I'll go to the DA."

"I understand."

"Because if you do all I ask, I'll give you your freedom. But if you don't, I'll see to it that you'll pay for your crimes. The Zoo is an unpleasant place, Yuri."

He nodded.

"Do you think you can do everything I ask?"

"Yes." He was smiling, relieved.

I had him. "Good," I said.

thirty

THE rain was coming down again, this time as glass needles that stung when they struck my back. I was on the roof of an old warehouse, hunched over a viewscreen, trying to keep it dry. It was receiving a vid stream from the camera Yuri placed inside the warehouse. On screen was Yuri, who was waiting inside for Ian's crew to arrive. He paced the floor, passing in front of broken-out windows through which the rain came slanting through and pelted the crumbled concrete floor.

Yuri had done everything I'd told him to. He'd sweated over each of the dead bodies, carrying them a few hurried steps at a time before inevitably losing his grip and dropping them on the decking with sickening thuds. He would swat at the flies dogfighting around his face and then go back to wrestling the bodies along until he managed to get Ian and Hoshi in position, their backs leaning up against the sealed hatchway. He'd brought up Adela's body last, dragging her by one of the body bag's handles.

We'd rehearsed his statement three times before going live. I didn't appear in the recording in any way. When I wanted to say something to Yuri, I'd stop the recording first. I coached him along and, using his statement, I'd created a movie of my own, starring Ian as the hero and Hoshi as his sidekick, with Adela Juarez playing the role of the death-row damsel in distress, and the dastardly offworlders starring as the mustachioed villains.

I'd beamed the completed statement to Maggie and Abdul,

who were already writing evidence reports to match. There'd be no mention of the gap between Ian and Hoshi's times of death or the fact that Ian had burned vegetation embedded in his wounds. The reports wouldn't mention that the bodies had been moved. They'd died trying to hold that hatchway closed. Just like Yuri said.

Maggie's lieutenant would keep it hush-hush. He'd keep everybody off that boat except for Maggie and Abdul. Nobody would see the repeated bloody splotches on the deck created by Yuri's corpse-carrying fumbles. Nobody would ask about the scorch marks from a brief firefight near the gangway. My fingerprints would go completely unnoticed. Lieutenant Rusedski would play along. It was an easy choice for him. He could either take the credit for his detectives solving the barge murders and dying heroically in the process, or he could admit he had two dirty detectives working on his staff, one of whom he'd already publicly supported for the squad leader post.

Maggie would arrest the four zookeepers. She'd shave off time in exchange for them fingering one of the dead offworlders as the ringleader of the operation. The whole thing would be cinched up. Nobody would look any closer. There'd be no reason to. Yuri wasn't the only one who knew how to make a pile of bullshit look real.

I checked the uplink one more time. Yuri had set up all the equipment. I didn't want to leave room for somebody to call the vid a fake, especially anybody who knew about Yuri's holo work. Yuri had told me he could arrange for the feed to be beamed up to the Orbital so it could be digitally signed by a security authority. I grilled him about it, asking all kinds of questions he patiently answered. "No, the digital signature can't be faked." "No, you couldn't feed them false footage for them to sign. We were using one of their own cams." "No, you can't tamper with their cams. You can't even open up the case. Exposure to oxygen melts half the components."

Yuri had no idea how completely I'd set him up. He was a damn fool to believe I'd ever set him free. I'd sentenced him to death. He just didn't know it yet.

There was a knock at the warehouse door. Yuri walked over to the cockeyed door and scraped it open. The crew came through, all five of them. Wu looked like the new de facto leader of the group. He took head-of-the-pack position, face to face with Yuri while Froelich, Lumbela, Kripsen, and Deluski fanned out behind.

Yuri greeted them. "Am I g-glad to see you," he said nervously.

Wu's face was unreadable.

"I'm sorry I called you," Yuri said. "I didn't know what else to do. Ian's dead. So is Hoshi. Those two cops you've been looking for raided the barge, and they killed them. I barely g-got away."

"We know."

Yuri's face screwed up. This wasn't going the way he thought. As far as he knew, the plan was that he would break the news to them that Ian was dead. They'd be shocked and panicked. The five of them would start arguing about what to do, and he'd just sit by and let them work it out. He'd let them bring up the barge murders. He'd listen while they talked about Horst and his off-world customers. He'd play along with them until I had enough evidence.

And, if he felt like he was in danger at any time, all he had to do was say, "I'm thirsty." Say that, and I'd be there in a flash, ready to rescue him. So he thought.

Yuri had no idea that I'd already had Maggie call the barge scene in. He didn't know that the five cops he was facing had already been down to the barge. He didn't know that once they got there, Lieutenant Rusedski called them out, telling them he wanted to see them all in his office tomorrow morning. Yuri didn't know that Maggie put out an APB on him, stating he was a witness in a cop killing.

And here he was, trying to chat them up, unsuspecting of the fact that they'd already been searching for him when he called. He had no idea how desperate they were to save themselves. Ian was already dead, and so was Hoshi. And Maggie was closing in on them. Why else would Rusedski call them into a meeting? Just them and nobody else. They were under suspicion, and they knew it. But they hadn't been arrested yet. There was still time to cover their tracks. They had to find Yuri before Maggie did. If she found him first, he'd talk. She'd have all she needed to send them to the Zoo for life. . . .

Wu pulled his piece.

Yuri choked on the words, "I'm thirsty. I'm thirsty!"

Wu bunched up his eyebrows, thinking that was a strange thing for Yuri to say at a time like this, and then he sizzled off the top of Yuri's head.

I checked the feed again and verified that it was still working.

Lumbela, Kripsen, and Deluski picked up the body and carried it to the door. So Wu was definitely the new leader, and those three were the grunts. That made sense. Wu and Froehlich were both homicide, while the others were just beat cops. I watched them finish the cleanup and move off, the camera rolling all the while.

Amateurs.

The grin on my face took a long time to evaporate in the rainy weather.

Then I called Liz. I still had to deal with Horst.

thirty-one

I WALKED through the kitchen and climbed the stairs that were becoming too familiar. I rapped on the door.

Liz opened it. She was dressed like a normal person, in a set of whites with her hair pulled up off her shoulders, very domestic. She gave me a curt nod and ushered me in.

Horst was there. He'd come to the door to greet me. He shook my hand, his pale skin contrasting sharply with my own. "Mr. Mozambe," he said, velvet-voiced. He gave me a bottomless gaze that made the hair on my arms stand up. He'd already scanned me. He knew I was unarmed. No weapons. No cameras. Nothing but me. Totally vulnerable.

I erased the nervousness from my voice before responding. "Mr. Jeffers."

Liz led us into her kitchen and sat us at the table. They already had a bottle of brandy going, and Horst poured a glass for me. I took the seat opposite him.

Liz had something going on the stove. "Dinner will be ready in just a few minutes," she said.

"It smells wonderful," Horst said with a captivating, fangless smile. I still expected fangs every time I saw his teeth. It didn't make him any less dangerous. Fangs or no fangs, he was hardly toothless. He was an offworlder, and that meant his body was loaded with high-tech self-defense systems. He could kill me before I knew what happened.

"Thanks for meeting with me," I said before taking a sip of brandy.

"I was surprised to hear from you, Mr. Mozambe. When Liz called and said you wanted to meet, I could hardly wait to hear what you had to say."

Liz set a bowl of nuts on the table. Horst snatched up a couple and popped them in his mouth. "I love these nuts," he said. "They grow them downriver, you know."

"I know."

"But do you know why they grow them downriver?"

"No."

"It's the trees. They can't survive without regular sunlight, so they only grow down south. They can't survive the depths of Koba's winter, when it's nothing but darkness, twenty-two seven. Of course, the downside is that they don't get much rainwater down there because it's so much hotter and drier. That's why you only find them growing around lakes and on riverbanks. Even then, they don't get much water, so they generally have a small yield. A bowl like this is probably two tree's worth of nuts."

"Spoken like a true tour guide."

His smile was pure silk. "Have you ever been down to the deserts, Mr. Mozambe?"

"No."

"You really should some time. It's harsh territory, but it is stunningly beautiful. Do you have any salt, Liz?"

She fished in a cupboard and pulled out a shaker.

Horst took the shaker and sprinkled the bowl. "Have some," he said.

I thought it would look funny if I didn't, so I took two. I cupped them in my hand and shook them around like a pair of dice, stalling long enough for Horst to eat a salted nut before I tossed them in my mouth.

"Thanks for offering to host dinner," Horst said to Liz.

"I didn't offer," she responded.

"Dinner was my idea," I said. "I thought this might be a nice neutral place for us to chat."

"And a grand idea it was," he said. "Liz is really quite the cook, so any excuse that gets her in the kitchen is fine by me. What do you say we get down to business?"

I nodded.

"Tell me what it is that you want to talk to me about."

My heart kicked into a new gear. I could feel it pounding in my chest and pulsing through my temples. I'd rehearsed everything in my head, but I suddenly couldn't remember my damn lines. It was stupid to get so nervous. It didn't matter much what I said. All that mattered was that we kept talking until Liz served dinner. *Just say something already!*

"I thought you might want to hire me," I said.

He laughed a warm laugh that I knew not to trust. "And why would I want to do that?" he asked as he dipped into the bowl of nuts.

"Because I hear you've got some openings."

"Thanks to you."

"Couldn't be helped."

Liz was staring at us with pained eyes as the two of us talked about her dead brother like he was nothing more than a minor point of negotiation in a business dispute.

Horst didn't even notice. "I can't believe your nerve, Mr. Mozambe. You think that killing my employees is the best way to create an opportunity for yourself?"

I put down the glass I was drinking from and looked him square in that pasty face. "Listen to me, and listen to me good. Ian pinched my wife's air hose until she turned blue. That's why he's dead. Nobody pulls that kind of shit on me and lives. I don't care if he was your damn son. Got it?"

Liz was looking at me with wide-open eyes. Ian must not have told her about that particular air-hose-cinching sin of his.

"Is that how the law of the jungle works?" Horst said with a wisecrack grin.

"He threatened my wife, and now he's dead. Call it whatever the hell you want."

"Okay, Mr. Mozambe," he said. "So let's say that I accept the fact that you're a vindictive son of a bitch. Surely, you can't think that absolves you of all your behavior. I've lost my in with Koba's police force and—"

I interrupted him. "You haven't lost anything. You have me."

"What standing do you have with KOP? You're retired."

"Have the police come to talk to you? They haven't because I have plenty of standing. I say leave you alone, they leave you alone. Ian was just a detective. He was nothing compared to me. I used to run that place. I have friends all the way up and down the ranks."

He closed his eyes for a second and sighed before speaking again, making it very obvious to me that he was running short on patience. "My police contacts are hardly all I've lost due to you. Yuri Kiper has gone missing. Do you know how valuable he was? His kind of talent was rare."

"That wasn't me," I said. "I don't know what happened to him."

"And I lost six customers on that barge. Do you know what kind of dampening effect that's going to have on my business? It's only been a day, and I'm already suffering almost fifty percent cancellations."

"That's temporary. Business will bounce back."

Horst was shaking his head. He wasn't buying it.

Liz set plates in front of us. Fish over rice.

"Ah, this looks wonderful, Liz," he said.

That it did. She'd made some kind of an herbal sauce that

had been drizzled over top. "Ian taught me how to make it," she said. "It was one of his favorite dishes."

Horst cut into his with his fork. "The fish looks perfect." It was a whitefish, light and flaky near the edges and translucent in the middle. He scooped up a piece and lifted it to his nose. He took a deep whiff, the pallor of his cheeks matching the color of the fish's rare center. He slid the bite through his thin lips. "Delicious," he said.

I cut into mine, pulling a piece free with my fork. I took one last glance at Liz, who was looking at me blankly. It would look strange if I didn't eat. I had to trust her. I lifted it to my lips, putting my trust in the conversation we'd had that morning. . . .

I'd taken a seat in Liz's armchair. She'd tried to close the door on me, but I insisted that she let me in. Her apartment was a disaster. Brandy empties littered the floor. Three distinct piles of crumpled tissues on the sofa. Next to the door was a short stack of plates from the downstairs restaurant with crusty-looking food scraps squeezing out from between the layered ceramics.

She was wearing nothing but her robe. Her hair looked unwashed and was pillow-pressed on one side. She was watching me, waiting for me to say something.

"I'm sorry about your brother." I opened.

"No, you're not. You're glad he's dead."

I rolled with the punch. "You're right," I confessed. "But I *am* sorry to see you hurting like this. I know how you must feel."

"Bullshit. You have no idea how I feel."

"I just lost my wife," I stated matter of fact.

"I didn't know you had a wife."

"I do. I did."

"When?"

"Three days ago."

"How did it happen?"

"She jumped off a bridge a few months ago. She was paralyzed and wanted me to take her off her respirator."

"Was she terminal?"

"No."

"She wanted to die?"

I nodded.

"Why?"

"Her father abused her, and she never got over it."

Liz teared up. And watching her, the emptiness inside me took hold. I felt tears in my own eyes. I wanted to let it out. I ached to let loose. Liz and I could help each other. We could share our pain, and maybe together we could find a way to make it bearable. I opened my mouth, not knowing what I'd say. I made a false start, the first part of an unknown syllable hanging in the air. I didn't know what to say. I didn't know how. . . .

And then it passed. The moment was gone, vanished as mysteriously as it had come. And I was glad it was gone. I could never let myself get involved with Liz. She was broken in a way that couldn't ever be fixed. It would be like Niki all over again. I wiped my cheeks and sniffled my nose clear.

Liz had the tissues out, and she offered me one.

I declined.

She blew her nose. "Tell me how Ian died and don't give me any of that hero bullshit they said on the news."

I was in a haze, thoughts of Niki clouding my mind. Still, I managed to answer her question. "I shot him."

"Was it in self-defense?"

"No. He didn't even know I was there until it was too late."

"I hate you."

"I know."

"You made me help you find him."

"You did what was right, Liz. He and Horst killed that girl. He'd become a monster. There was no saving him."

"He wasn't always like that, you know."

I was still in a haze. Her words were coming at me through layers of fog. I forced myself to think of Adela, the way she died. I summoned the anger, letting it fill the empty hole in my soul. I let the anger burn off the fog and sharpen my mind. I came here for a reason, and it was time I stopped letting things like sappy feelings get in the way. Horst was going to pay, and Liz was going to help me.

"What was Ian like before?" I asked, humoring her.

"He was shy and sweet."

Shy? Maybe. Sweet? Never. The way I saw it, Ian was a sadistic bastard with a hard-on for his sister, a weak, disturbed girl who couldn't set any boundaries—mothering him, protecting him, fucking him. To her, it was all the same thing. But I didn't contradict her. I let her remember her brother however she wanted.

"He wasn't cut out for police work," she said. "He was going to quit."

"When was that?"

"Right before he met Horst. That was about a year ago. Horst took him under his wing when he found out he was a cop. Ian was really taken with him. You've seen how charming Horst can be. Ian would've done absolutely anything for Horst."

"Did Horst know the two of you were related?"

"No. He just thought we were childhood lovers who would still see each other now and again. I should've never introduced Ian to him. Ian was confused and vulnerable. He had no confidence in himself, you know what I mean?"

"I do. I remember what Ian was like when he first joined KOP."

"Then you know," she insisted. "He wasn't always the person he was at the end."

"I know," I said, consoling.

She cried again. I hugged her. I patted her shoulder. I wiped her tears away. I held her and waited, my mind drifting to Horst. . . . Arresting him was out of the question. He could contradict my version of events on the barge. He could say that Ian was alive and heading for the Zoo the last time he saw him. Maggie couldn't be known to have anything to do with Ian's death. She needed to be kept clear. Just the implication that she was somehow investigating Ian was enough to stain her as a rat for the rest of her career. I couldn't let that happen. Maggie's image was and would always remain true blue.

Liz pulled away when the tears stopped, and I moved back to the armchair, giving her a minute to just be.

"I'm sorry about your wife." She said it so sincerely that I was taken aback. The hollowness inside me was suddenly all-consuming. Tears were about to overflow the dam I'd propped up. I wanted to tell her about Niki, about how I tried to save her and how I wasn't any good at it. I wanted to tell her about what a good a person Niki was and about all the times she'd tried to save me from my drinking and my enforcing. I wanted to tell her how much I loved Niki, the way she'd cut the buttons off my shirts and replace them with snaps, the way she would smile at my jokes, even when they weren't funny.

This was my opportunity. . . .

Fuck it. I didn't deserve her consolation, or anybody else's.

For a long while, we didn't talk, each of us alone with our own thoughts. I worked hard at corralling my emotions. When I felt like I'd finally managed to pen them up, I broke the silence. "I want to talk about Horst."

"I don't," she stated.

"All right," I said. "Then just listen. You tell me if I get any of it wrong. Okay?"

She didn't say anything, but she looked like she was listening. The trick was to get her thinking about Horst, about how he corrupted her brother. I wanted her to blame Horst for Ian's death. Not me, not herself, but Horst.

"Ian was a good guy," I said as if I meant it. "Sure, he was screwed up, but he didn't hurt anybody. That incident with your old boyfriend was just a mistake. He thought he needed to protect you. His heart was in the right place. Since you were children, his heart was always in the right place. He wanted to be a chef, right? He didn't want to get mixed up in any of this. It was Horst that did it to him. It was Horst that got him hooked on steroids, wasn't it?"

She nodded absently.

"He turned Ian into what he was. Horst is a user. He uses people when they can be helpful to him and throws them away when they're used up. He didn't care about Ian. He only wanted what Ian could give him as a cop. He convinced Ian to stay with KOP when everybody knew it wasn't right for him."

Again, she nodded.

"You used to hook at the Red Room, right?" I paused briefly, and she nodded. "You had no choice. Your father kicked you out on the street. How else were going to support yourself? You hated it. All prostitutes do. Sometimes you could rationalize it away, but deep down you hated it. All those needy johns and their hang-ups. That's how you met Horst, isn't it? He used to bring his kinky clients to the Red Room."

I got yet another nod.

"He told you he wanted you to star in his movies. You jumped at the chance. You thought he was saving you from prostitution. But now you know that wasn't true. If he'd really wanted to save you, he would have given you a job in his tour company. You'd be living a normal life, answering phones or doing paperwork in his office. But that's not what he did with you. He made you degrade yourself on camera. It's nothing you hadn't done before, but if he really cared, he wouldn't let you be seen like that. He wouldn't be making money off it."

She didn't respond, but I could see she was still listening.

"He latched onto your brother," I said. "Not because he cared about him. Not because he cared about you. He saw how vulnerable Ian was, and he took advantage of him. Horst doesn't like getting his hands dirty. He told your brother how important he was, but Ian meant nothing to him. Ian was just his fucking janitor. He just needed somebody to clean up all his shit. If it wasn't for Horst, your brother would be alive right now. He'd be taking chef classes."

Her eyes were locked on mine.

"Am I right?" I asked.

"Yes," she said, clear and concise.

"Horst killed your brother, Liz. He didn't actually pull the trigger, but the brother you knew was already dead. Horst took the soul of a good kid and corrupted it. He killed your brother when he turned him into a murderer."

She was staring into my eyes, her expression cold and sober. I had her convinced. I could see it on her face. Not that it took that much convincing. She'd probably already come to the same conclusion. It was Horst's fault. Everything she was feeling, all that pain, all that anguish, all Horst's fault.

She wanted to believe it. Horst was an easy scapegoat, a way for her to avoid having to look at her own role in Ian's stunted development. She still wanted to think the best of her brother, and telling herself that Horst made Ian do the things he did made it easier to think that way.

I leaned forward. "Horst killed your brother, Liz. He needs to pay. Help me make him pay."

Her eyes took on a feral quality. "I'll help on one condition."

"Name it."

"I get to do the bastard in myself."

I felt the fish on my tongue, its flavor seeping down into my taste buds. I didn't want to chew, but I did. I bit down and released a burst of flavor. I chewed slowly, not wanting to swallow even though I knew that if she'd decided to kill me instead, it was already too late.

The fish was good, and I concentrated on eating instead of talking. It could take a couple minutes yet.

Half of Horst's fish was already gone. "What do you think of the fish?" he asked.

"I think it's fantastic."

"So how do you think this job interview is going so far?"

"I think it's going well," I said.

"I hate to correct you, Mr. Mozambe, but I have to tell you that you're failing miserably. What I see in front of me is a man who has lost me a great deal of money. You haven't convinced me you can make it up to me yet, and I sincerely doubt you'll be able to at all. But I'm feeling generous. This marvelous fish has me in a good mood, so I won't cut off our talk just yet. I'll give you at least until d-dessert."

He grinned menacingly. He was doing his best to ignore the little stutter at the end, but I heard it. The poison was already attacking his nervous system. He'd be completely paralyzed within a minute of the onset of symptoms.

I tried to make my case again, my voice taking on a rambling quality. There was sweat beading on his brow. He hadn't figured it out yet. He thought he was just having some odd reaction to the food. Maybe the fish was bad. Liz crept out of the kitchen to the safety of the living room. I kept prattling on, not making much sense. He dropped his fork. I saw the terror in his eyes when he realized. I tossed the table. Plates and glasses shattered. He brought his hands up but they spasmed out of control. I threw a shoulder into his chest and knocked him over backward in his chair. He tried to bring his right hand up, laser claws emerging where fingernails used to be. I booted his hand, my shoe kicking up smoke when it made contact. I stepped on his other wrist, pinning it to the floor as needles came firing out his pinky. His legs wheeled around helplessly. He came at me with his laser-claw hand, but it swung so slowly that I easily managed to pin it down with my free foot.

I stayed in position, standing on his wrists, waiting for the paralysis to take full control. He tried to shock me, but I was wearing the thickest rubber soles I could find. The electricity found the refrigerator instead and arced across the floor, a blue lightning bolt that blew the compressor and popped the refrigerator door open with a puff of acrid smoke.

A more natural color came to his cheeks as his control over the tech that bleached his skin began to fail. It was disconcerting to see his skin looking healthier. His mouth hung open and drool began to run down his cheek. I got off his wrists, and they stayed where I left them. The only things that were still moving were his eyes, which were darting left and right. I had no idea if he was still aware of what was happening to him. The poison had taken hold and would stop his heart soon. "Ten minutes tops," I'd been assured by the apothecary. "Even if he has blood scrubbers. You give him a big enough dose and there's no way he'll be able to purge the toxin fast enough. Those little salamanders don't look like much, but their venom can fell the biggest monitor you've ever seen in under ten."

The only way to beat an offworlder was to go low tech.

"Bring him in here." I heard Liz call from the living room.

I grabbed him by his shirt collar and dragged him across the linoleum out into the middle of the living room floor.

Liz was waiting there in her dominatrix getup. She was holding a monitor-hide whip, and she was finishing off a knot, tying a barb to the end. She used her teeth to pull the leather tight. I took one last look at the offworlder, his limbs wrenched up into unnatural angles, his face locked into a horrified rictus.

Even then, he looked more human than I'd ever seen him.

I went to the door and stepped out an instant before I heard the first crack.

thirty-two

I was at Roby's. I'd decided to meet them on their own turf. It was morning, and the place was empty except for the six of us. I took my time looking them over. Their faces were marked with a mixture of anger and worry. There was lip biting. There were clenched jaws. There was plenty of leg tapping. I remembered Yuri's face when they killed him, when I let them kill him. I remembered the way he looked when he realized that nobody was going to save him. I was glad Maggie hadn't seen it. She didn't need that image in her head.

This planet was a damn garbage dump, and Maggie was the lone flower growing in the middle of it. I'd make sure she had a nice patch of clean earth to grow in. I'd keep the trash from getting too close. I'd scorch the weeds that tried to take her sunlight. I'd squash the bugs that wanted to nibble on her leaves. She'd be allowed to do what was natural for her, which was to rise up and inspire an entire garden to take root.

The five faces were looking at me, waiting. I'd already sent them all copies of the vid with instructions to meet me here today. For two days now, they'd been sweating it out, knowing that I had incontrovertible footage of them killing Yuri but not knowing my intentions. They were more than ready to listen to what I had to say.

I was set on seizing back the power I'd lost. I had to start somewhere, and co-opting my own squad was a good place to start. I was quite certain Maggie wouldn't like it, but like it or not, KOP wouldn't just fall into her hands. It had to be *taken*.

Looking at this crew, *my* crew, my gut raged like a stoked furnace.

I was back.

I broke out in a vicious grin. I leaned forward in my chair and pointed with my shaky splinted fingers. "I *own* you motherfuckers."

TOR